COVERT ACTION

NEW YORK TIMES #1 BESTSELLER **TONY LEE** WRITING AS

JACK GATLAND

This is a work of fiction. Names, characters, places and incidents are either the product of the author's imagination or are used fictitiously, and any resemblance to actual persons, living or dead, business establishments, places of learning, events or locales is entirely coincidental.

Published by Hooded Man Media.

Cover design by L1graphics

First Edition: May 2023

PRAISE FOR JACK GATLAND

'This is one of those books that will keep you up past your bedtime, as each chapter lures you into reading just one more.'

'This book was excellent! A great plot which kept you guessing until the end.'

'Couldn't put it down, fast paced with twists and turns.'

'The story was captivating, good plot, twists you never saw and really likeable characters. Can't wait for the next one!'

'I got sucked into this book from the very first page, thoroughly enjoyed it, can't wait for the next one.'

'Totally addictive. Thoroughly recommend.'

'Moves at a fast pace and carries you along with it.'

'Just couldn't put this book down, from the first page to the last one it kept you wondering what would happen next.'

There's a new Detective Inspector in town...

Before Tom Marlowe had his own series, he was a recurring character in the DI Declan Walsh books!

An EXCLUSIVE PREQUEL, completely free to anyone who joins the Jack Gatland Reader's Club!

Join at www.subscribepage.com/jackgatland

Also by Jack Gatland

DI DECLAN WALSH BOOKS

LETTER FROM THE DEAD

MURDER OF ANGELS

HUNTER HUNTED

WHISPER FOR THE REAPER

TO HUNT A MAGPIE

A RITUAL FOR THE DYING

KILLING THE MUSIC

A DINNER TO DIE FOR

BEHIND THE WIRE

HEAVY IS THE CROWN

STALKING THE RIPPER

A QUIVER OF SORROWS

MURDER BY MISTLETOE

BENEATH THE BODIES

KILL YOUR DARLINGS

KISSING A KILLER

ELLIE RECKLESS BOOKS

PAINT THE DEAD

STEAL THE GOLD

HUNT THE PREY

FIND THE LADY

TOM MARLOWE BOOKS

SLEEPING SOLDIERS

TARGET LOCKED

COVERT ACTION

COUNTER ATTACK

DAMIAN LUCAS BOOKS

THE LIONHEART CURSE

STANDALONE BOOKS

THE BOARDROOM

AS TONY LEE

DODGE & TWIST

For Mum, who inspired me to write.

For Tracy, who inspires me to write.

CONTENTS

PROLOGUE

It was supposed to have been a simple job.

Rexxon Industries was a multi-national corporation, with each sub-department based in an unfamiliar area of the country. For example, the oil and gas departments were still based in Texas, but the renewable energy buildings were in California. And, as Marlowe had recently arrived in California with a few days to kill, he thought it was a good idea to take the job on.

The contact had been a man named Karl. Marlowe had worked with him a couple of times over the years, mainly when Karl was running small, inter-agency gigs that MI5, or, rather Emilia Wintergreen's Section D – the department in Whitehall Marlowe was a part of until recently – had a vested interest in. Karl didn't have a surname, at least he didn't have one Marlowe had ever heard spoken, and Marlowe didn't even know where Karl's loyalties lay; all he knew was there was a very strong chance Karl wasn't even *named* Karl, and was someone high in the NSA.

Either way, Karl and Marlowe had worked together

several times over the years, and now Marlowe had been burnt by MI5, cast out into the wild and allowed to sink or swim, Karl had been one of the first people to contact him, which in itself was an impressive feat, offering Marlowe gigs if he was ever in a part of the world Karl had a vested interest in.

Places like Los Angeles, for example – in particular, a high-rise office block off the Sunset Strip.

It wasn't the usual kind of location for such a business, but then at the same time, Marlowe didn't need to enter the offices of the actual business. His job, given to him by Karl, was to pass on a message, nothing more. Or, more accurately, pass on a message in the most terrifying way possible. Really hammer the message home and make sure the person getting it didn't think for one second there was any kind of confusion about it.

The message was simple.

We know who you are
We see you always
You need to back down – or suffer the consequences

It was a little stalkerish, but from someone who worked for the NSA and had terrifying powers at his disposal, to have such a message from Karl was a whole different level of worrying. Marlowe didn't know what the message meant, or even why the target was receiving it, but that didn't matter, as Marlowe was being paid handsomely for the gig.

And, more importantly, in this situation, he was doing something for a man who could, down the line, help him get his life back on track. He wasn't naive; he knew the chances of MI5 allowing him back into the Security Service were small, but at the same time he was currently a nomad, a man with no protection. Anyone with a grudge, from tin-pot dictators and Somali pirates up to rogue nations, could off him at a moment's notice, and nobody would retaliate.

Working for Karl meant down the line he might have at least some protection. Even the most minimal coverage was better than nothing.

And so Marlowe now sat in his hired car, parked down a side road that faced the building's frontage, watching the employees as they entered and exited the building.

His target was a director, a VP of something – Karl had been quite vague with the details, but Marlowe didn't need to watch for him to make the entrance attempt. He'd spent the last two days parked here, in fact, working on his laptop, leeching the Wi-Fi from the coffee shop beside him. Well, he *said* coffee shop, but it was more a small cafe within a medical centre, one he'd only been in once. He'd made the mistake of ordering a breakfast bun served in a croissant, which he'd expected as being some kind of sausage placed into a standard-sized croissant, but in the end turned into a monstrosity of cheese, egg, sausage and crispy bacon, which was cut in half and so large it covered his lunch as well.

He could have had one every day, but his waistline would have hated him. As it was, the time away from the service was lessening his daily exercise resolve, and in the last week he'd only gone for his daily run two or three times.

That said, the run itself, from Venice Beach to Santa Monica and back, was *glorious*.

And now he sat in the car, forcing himself not to enter the cafe next door and buy more fattening, artery-hardening foods, instead snacking on some trail mix while he watched the main entrance as the evening shift began and the nine-to-five workers were slowly leaving the building.

There were dozens, if not hundreds, of people working for Rexxon – Marlowe hadn't done the maths here. He didn't need to know for the mission; all he needed were four or five main targets to work on, all of which he'd found in the space of a couple of hours trawling through the website, and then working through Facebook pages, looking for images that matched the people and places he wanted, gaining information on what he needed.

He knew that Clarence the night-shift guard was recently back from India, a "bucket list" vacation, but had suffered what he called "Delhi Belly", a mild gastro infection, which made him constantly run to the toilet. It didn't help he was lactose intolerant, and these runs always seemed to be shortly after his ten pm coffee. His subordinate, Winston, knew now to not expect Clarence back for at least fifteen minutes, and so took this opportunity for a crafty cigarette break. Marlowe was actually convinced Winston was deliberately upping the lactose in the coffees, just to ensure such a run.

There were others Marlowe had mapped out, following their lives online. Cheryl was depressed at being ghosted by the love of her life. Michael was concerned about a mole growing on his shoulder. And Brett was undergoing a new midlife crisis, and had recently started going daily to a new gym after work.

It was Brett that Marlowe was looking for.

After about fifteen minutes of people leaving, Marlowe spied Brett: short, dumpy, balding and wearing a suit that wasn't shaped to fit him, leave the building, a gym bag over his shoulder. Marlowe reached across to the passenger seat and grabbed his own duffel, climbing out of the car and, keeping an assured distance between them, followed Brett to his gym of choice.

Marlowe knew that "Crossfitters" was Brett's gym by the branding in some of his photos, and had taken a visit, under an assumed name and ID the previous day, signing up for a seven-day trial, and gaining a tour of the premises. He knew from Brett's social over-sharing that once changed into his branded and probably over-expensive gym kit, he spent twenty minutes on the treadmill before moving to the weights; or, rather, the weight machines, having not yet gained the confidence to go into either the weights room or the CrossFit tower area. Which meant Marlowe had plenty of time to do what he needed to do.

Once he arrived at the gym, allowing Brett to sign in and leave the counter before him, Marlowe swiped his guest pass – upgraded after a week if he wanted to stay on – and followed through, heading into the back, and the men's changing rooms. These were a basic locker-room style, with padlocked lockers along one wall, benches in the middle, and mirrors and hairdryers on the other side, the toilets and showers in cubicles at the end. He'd timed it right, and saw Brett, now in his running gear, click his padlock before leaving, so Marlowe chose the locker two down from Brett's, changing into his own gear. After all, he was getting a free workout here, so he might as well get some use from it.

He allowed the room to empty as he changed, and once alone, he hastened to the padlock on Brett's locker. The gym suggested you brought your own locker padlocks, and Brett had done what Marlowe had expected; he'd reused a padlock he'd bought for something else, in this case a "TSA Friendly" combination padlock used to lock flight check-in luggage, with a little symbol showing any TSA agents examining this, that they could open it with the TSA "Master" key. Unfortunately, although Brett had probably used this thinking the TSA logo meant the lock was better than most others, this was sadly not the case, and, using a small lock pick to rake the lock quickly, Marlowe pulled it free and opened the locker in one motion. He knew the ID card he needed was in Brett's jacket pocket, so grabbed it and closed the door again, spinning the combination to lock the padlock once more. Then, ID in his own bag, he locked his own locker and moved outside for a workout.

When he returned forty minutes later, he saw Brett dressing in his work clothes once more, not even checking his jacket as he gathered his items together into the bag and left. Marlowe knew he probably wouldn't even realise the ID was gone until the following morning, at which point Marlowe would have finished, leaving the ID on Brett's desk. After taking a shower – after all, the last thing Marlowe wanted to do tonight was drip sweat anywhere – he sauntered back to his car, pulling on a blue polo shirt and cap as he placed his duffel in the car's boot.

Or, as the Americans liked to say, the trunk.

Marlowe hadn't shaved for a while, and his beard was now full. His hair was a little longer than he was used to, and he knew if he walked to the door in a suit, his facial appearance would set him apart – everyone else was clean-shaven and short-haired. However, with a cap and shirt on, holding a box, he looked just the type of person a security guard would expect a delivery man to be.

Now with an A4 box in hand, he walked up to the doors of the building, waving at the guard to help him through.

Walking to the main reception desk, he smiled as he placed the box on the top.

'Delivery for Brett Radcliffe,' he said. 'Needs to be signed for.'

'He's gone for the day,' the receptionist, a burly, suited Hispanic man replied.

'You can sign for it then,' Marlowe shrugged, passing a clipboard with a sheet of paper pinned to the top. 'I only get paid when it's taken, not when the right person takes it.'

The guard took the sheet, signing and printing his name in the relevant spots on the sheet. Nodding thanks, Marlowe took the clipboard.

'Are your bathrooms still open?' he nodded down the corridor to where the visitor bathrooms were.

Already returning to his paper, the guard nodded.

'You know the way?'

'Yeah, I've been here before. Thanks,' Marlowe tipped his cap.

Now, walking to the toilets, Marlowe knew he had a few minutes before the receptionist would alert security – there was only one entrance and exit, based on the floorplans he'd found earlier in a local planning office, and if Marlowe didn't walk out through it, he had to still be in the building. But he wasn't worried, as he wasn't intending to race to finish this job.

He'd spent time checking the building's layout based on the plans, and if they'd stayed true, he knew there was an emergency exit up the stairs, leading out onto a ground-floor roof. Quickly, he walked to the door, pulling a sheet of A4 paper out of his clipboard and slapping it onto the inside of the door, the printed message visible to everyone.

PLEASE DO NOT CLOSE THIS DOOR – LOCK KEEPS CATCHING

This done, Marlowe ran back down the stairs and walked back out of the main entrance, making sure to be seen doing his fly back up as he nodded to the receptionist guard.

Now outside, he walked across the plaza and back to his car. Once inside it, he pulled the cap off and settled down to grab a couple of hours' sleep; it was three and a half hours before Clarence's inevitable toilet trip, and he had nothing to do but wait until then.

AROUND NINE-FIFTY, MARLOWE CLIMBED OUT OF THE CAR ONCE more, pulling on a black fleece jumper and baseball cap. This one didn't have a logo on, and was there purely to hide his face from any cameras that could see him. Making sure he had Brett's pass in his pocket, Marlowe hurried across the street and then down one of the small side alleys that spaced the Rexxon building from the one next to it. It was dark now, the car lights throwing shadows against the buildings, and Marlowe knew this would help him as he performed his task for the night. He'd been down here the previous evening and left some boxes and pipes around, hoping they wouldn't get picked up by the garbage vans until later in the week. He was in luck, as the boxes were still there. And, using a waste bin as a base, he created a makeshift staircase and ladder to get him onto the first floor roof.

As he expected, there was nobody there; and to his delight, the door at the end, the one he'd placed a sign on, was slightly ajar.

Someone walking down the stairs and seeing the message had complied.

Marlowe smiled. Human nature meant that when given a rule, you followed it. And a sign saying "please do not do this" would usually force people to unconsciously comply, as people were trained from an early age to follow rules. In addition, the sheet was on the inside of the door, so obviously from someone within the building, and on Rexxon headed paper.

It had to be legit.

Of course, the "headed paper" was just the website banner placed at the top of a sheet and printed out, but nobody would spend too much time checking. All that mattered was that the rule was followed. And the door was open.

Marlowe leant over the edge of the roof and looked down. From here, he had a perfect view of reception, and could see Clarence already talking to Winston before walking off. And then, the moment he was alone, Winston grabbed his cigarettes from the counter and walked towards the main doors for his crafty smoke.

The way now clear, Marlowe slipped into the building, moving quickly up the stairs, gaining access to the main floor with Brett's key card. Then, slipping into the stairwell, he almost sprinted up the four flights of stairs to the executive level, for the first time that day regretting his gym visit as his calves burned.

Now on the floor he needed, he moved swiftly to the last door on the left, opening it and slipping inside. This was the office of Gene Dawson, the man Karl wanted to give a message to. Sitting at the desk, Marlowe grabbed a pen and paper, writing the message quickly but clearly, before rising once more to leave.

Something on the shelf to his side stopped him.

An image, a wedding photo of Dawson and a blonde woman, laughing at the camera. There was something about this image that didn't sit right with Marlowe, and so he pulled out his phone, moving closer and snapping a shot of it, placing the phone back in his pocket as he made his way back out of the building, taking the sheet of paper off the door as he passed through, noting as he hurried along the rooftop that Clarence had arrived back at his post earlier than usual, and was now arguing with Winston, caught having a smoke when he should have been on duty.

It was only when Marlowe reached the car that he realised he still had Brett's ID in his pocket.

Shit.

He didn't want the poor bastard to be blamed for this, so he quickly hurried back to the gym, saying he'd left his phone in his locker earlier that day and asking whether it had been handed in. When they said it hadn't, he went to the changing room to check, coming back with it in his hand and with a relieved expression on his face, but also passing over Brett's ID, saying he'd also found this on the floor beside the lockers, and thought it was probably important. As the receptionist called Brett's mobile phone to let him know they had his ID, Marlowe escaped the gym quietly, returning to his car and, once he sat inside it, he finally relaxed.

This hadn't been a high-level infiltration, but at the same time, he hadn't been doing many of these lately. And to be brutally honest, he'd struggled a little here. He ought to ask Karl for some easier missions, maybe a wedding or a dinner party—

Karl.

Marlowe didn't have a photographic memory as such, but he'd spent years using various tricks and mentalism tropes to gain one that could keep more than the usual person. And one thing he was good at was faces.

The woman in the picture, the blonde with Dawson, likely on their wedding day – Marlowe had seen her almost a year earlier, on one of the few face-to-face meetings he'd had with Karl, during a Washington ball. He'd introduced her as his date for the evening, and it had been obvious they were close. Marlowe remembered this because Marshall Kirk, the man he'd been there with that night, had commented that Karl usually liked his hookers to be Asian. It was a throwaway comment, but one that turned Marlowe's attention away from the woman.

But now, it seemed there was more to it.

Picking up his phone, he dialled a number.

'Is it done?' Karl asked as he answered, not even introducing himself.

'Message passed on,' Marlowe replied. 'This Dawson guy. He one of the bad ones?'

'You never usually ask,' Karl's voice was cautious now. 'You're usually a point-and-click kind of guy.'

'I'm asking this time,' Marlowe replied. 'I want to know I spent days infiltrating a company and leaving a threat on a man's desk because he's a threat himself, and to the nation.'

'Well rest assured, Brit, it's true. He's a threat.'

'To the nation?'

There was a pause.

'Just say what you want to,' Karl replied. 'Not like you to mince words.'

'I just wanted to know whether he's a threat to America, or to the affair you're having with his wife.'

This time, the pause down the line felt more ominous.

'Goddamned spooks,' Karl muttered. 'Always going beyond what you ask for.'

'I did this job as a favour—'

'You did it because no other mug's gonna hire you,' Karl snapped as an interruption. 'Yeah, I'm seeing his wife, and yeah, he's asking questions. This was to stop him. And if you have a problem with it, just say so.'

'I have a problem with it,' Marlowe replied. 'And you can lose my number.'

'Now you listen here, you jumped up little—' Karl didn't continue his rant, mainly because Marlowe disconnected the call, leaning back on the seat of his car and blowing out a long breath.

That's the NSA now throwing you on their shit list, he thought to himself, damning his morals. They *always* got him into more trouble than his actual spying.

He knew now that he'd have to find a way to smooth that over down the line, either by making good with Karl, or finding someone higher up the chain who could shut him down.

Luckily, he was on his way right now to meet the exact person to do that.

1

SHOVELLING THE DIRT

MARLOWE WAS STILL MULLING OVER THE MISSION WHEN HE arrived back at the hotel he was staying at.

He'd tried to move past it, ignore the problem he had, but, he knew how he'd feel if he was Dawson, and it irked him that someone like Karl could do such a thing.

And, because of this, he'd written a note while it was too early to stop himself, typed on a computer in a late-night computer cafe, printed out the same time and now folded into an envelope addressed to Dawson, care of the Rexxon building.

It was a simple message, just telling Dawson his wife was cheating on him, giving Karl's name, number and Pentagon extension, as well as warning him to be careful.

This done, he placed the envelope into another, larger one, writing a completely different address on it, one in Illinois, rather than California.

This done, he stared at the envelope for a good hour, deciding whether to simply burn the damned thing, or go ahead.

Eventually, deciding the latter, he made a phone call. He reckoned there was a two-hour difference between the person he was calling and Pacific Time, so it wouldn't be past nine-thirty, and they would still be up.

'Hello?' the woman's voice answered.

'It's Marlowe,' he said, smiling as he heard the voice of Tessa Kirk down the line. 'How's Chicago?'

'Cold,' Tessa replied. 'Are you supposed to be calling me? Last I heard you were burnt.'

'Yeah,' Marlowe didn't mention the unspoken elephant in the room, that he'd been burnt while making sure she had a quiet and uneventful life. 'I need a favour.'

'Anything,' Tessa replied. 'I owe you – we owe you everything.'

'You're going to get a letter from California in a couple of days,' Marlowe looked down at the envelope. 'Inside it is another letter, back to California. Stick some stamps on it, and send it from the centre of the city, please.'

'You don't want someone knowing you sent the letter?'

'Let's just say I need some plausible deniability,' Marlowe smiled down the line. 'It's not important, but it'd mean a lot to me.'

'I can do that,' Tessa replied. 'So, you're in California? Trix said you were East Coast.'

Marlowe had guessed Trix Preston was probably still in touch with Tessa Kirk; what he hadn't figured on was Trix being Tessa's point woman for all things Marlowe.

'Still trying to find a way back,' he said. 'How's your dad?'

'Bored,' Tessa laughed. 'Sitting back in the UK and moaning constantly. So, if you have anything going that needs an out-of-shape, grumbling bastard, then Dad's completely your man.'

Marlowe laughed at this. Marshall Kirk was his mentor in the Secret Service, and the last thing he thought about him was that he was ever going to be out-of-shape.

The grumbling and moaning, however, was right on point.

'I'll consider it,' he said. 'And thanks, Tessa.'

'Will I ever see you again?' Tessa blurted before the end of the call. 'It was a little ... sudden.'

'I was thrown into an MI5 black site,' Marlowe mused. 'They don't really allow sweet farewells.'

'You saved the US President,' Tessa's voice had an edge to it now. 'That's not on.'

'I know, but it is what it is,' Marlowe replied, sighing. 'Stay safe, Tessa. Speak soon.'

He disconnected before Tessa started asking how he knew what address to write to – her secondment in Chicago was only known to a few people, while she was shadowing someone in the British Embassy, learning the ropes.

She wanted to be a politician, if Marlowe remembered correctly, and there was every chance that, if he did this, sent the envelope to her to send back, Karl in the NSA would learn its origin and work the route back to her.

No. This was a mistake.

'Sorry, Tessa, but I don't think you *can* help me, actually,' he muttered to himself, pulling the smaller envelope out of the larger one and, after staring at it for a long moment, he tore it into pieces.

He was annoyed at being used by Karl, and even more angry that this was a warning-off to a cuckolded husband rather than a threat against the US, but at the end of the day, Marlowe didn't know Dawson, wasn't in any way indebted to Dawson, and wasn't going to risk everything *for* Dawson.

Sighing, and feeling thoroughly unimpressed with himself, Marlowe turned out the lights and went to bed.

He'd find another way to fix this. One that didn't involve putting people in harm's way.

But before he could even start planning out options, he was asleep.

IT WAS GONE MIDNIGHT WHEN THEY ARRIVED AT THE ROCK Spring Trailhead, a wide expanse of empty parking lot off Ridgecrest Boulevard.

A five-mile hiking trail during the day, you could walk a forest trail that wrapped around Mount Tamalpais West Peak and follow the International Trail and Railroad Grade road, while marvelling at beautiful views of redwood forests, rolling hills, and the Pacific Ocean, through multiple ecosystems including chaparral, pine forest, and subalpine meadows.

It was a truly beautiful place by day.

But by night, though, it was empty, and foreboding.

On this night, they turned the car headlights off as they arrived, noting a couple of camper vans pulled up at the far end, lights turned off and likely bedded down for the night. There was a small dirt track to the left, however, one wide enough for park ranger trucks, and they quietly turned onto it, the single dirt track the only route they needed.

After a while, maybe a half a mile further, the car pulled to a stop; the engine turning off. But now, safe from being observed by any passing motorist, as anyone hiking at this time of night was likely performing activities just as illegal as they were, they turned the headlights back on, lighting up this particular part of the forest.

As Foster and Peters exited the car, they could now see they were in a clearing, around twenty feet from the path, leading to a series of dense, bushy areas.

Foster stretched as he straightened, his back obviously aching from the groan he gave. In his early fifties, Foster gave a world-weary impression of a man, wearing a suit and shirt but no tie. He was burly with it, and had a face you could expect to find on any nightclub door, working as a bouncer, his nose showing signs of being broken multiple times, his hair thinning and combed across, obviously dyed.

Peters, on the other hand, was the polar opposite: young, wiry and animated, wearing bright-blue tracksuit bottoms and a matching hooded top, his dyed-blond hair meticulously groomed and gelled to perfection. Even though he was a West Coast native, he gave the impression of someone from *the Sopranos*; a Brooklyn thug done good.

'Open the trunk,' Foster ordered as he held his hand up to block out the car headlights, scanning the surrounding area for movement.

'I ain't your bitch,' Peters replied sullenly, glaring back at the older man.

There wasn't much of a face-off here; after a moment Foster shrugged, as if he was used to this attitude, walking to the back of the car. Popping the trunk, he opened it to reveal a third man.

Tooley.

Bookish, middle-aged and terrified, Tooley wore a dishevelled suit, stained around the crotch area where he had, from a simple sniff of the trunk by Foster to confirm this, pissed himself.

His hands were tied together – well, that was to say they were tied together as much as you could, when the left arm was actually a multi-grip myoelectric hand prosthesis, with five movable and jointed fingers.

'Out,' Foster barked.

Silent, almost dazed, Tooley struggled to get out of the car, falling to the floor and scrabbling to his knees.

'Please—' he started, but Foster cut him off with a motion, as he leant past the begging man, pulling a shovel out of the trunk.

Tooley, seeing the shovel, shook his head.

'Oh god, please no ...'

'Come on,' Foster said, pulling Tooley up by the arm, his one remaining one, and dragging him towards the lit area of scrubland. Tooley was scuffing his feet, so Peters began pushing him, as Tooley, now realising the gravity of the situation, started pulling away.

'Jesus Christ, please ... don't—'

He punctuated the last word with a *whuff* noise as Peters, sick of the whining, punched him hard in the gut, doubling him over. Groaning, Tooley stared in shock at what he saw in front of him, shadowed by the headlights of the car.

In the bushes, out of sight from the trail, was an *already open grave.*

'Please!' Tooley begged. 'I swear, I'll disappear! I won't speak to anyone!'

Peters was tapping at his phone as Tooley started to weep. Distracted, Foster looked at the younger man.

'Are you finished with—' he started, but stopped as there was a flicker of movement to his side; Tooley, realising this was his only chance, threw himself forward, slamming through the bushes at speed.

'Shit!' Peters cried as he started after him. 'Go right!'

Tooley ran through the woodland scrub, running for his life, with Peters and Foster following hard. Crying with fear, Tooley couldn't see through the tears, and was tripping, stumbling—

Wham.

Peters charged into Tooley from the side, sending him flying to the ground.

They struggled on the floor for the moment before Foster arrived, wheezing, pulling out a gun and aiming it at the terrified man.

'Quit it,' he snarled.

It was as if this comment was the lock on a door, and the moment the words were spoken, Tooley slumped, resigning himself to be pulled to his feet by Peters.

And, quietly giving up on any form of escape, Tooley allowed himself to be brought back to the grave.

'I got mud on my hoodie,' Peters complained irritably as he wiped at his tracksuit top. 'You can pay the cleaning bill.'

'And how's he gonna do that?' a smile on his face, Foster asked the question as he pushed Tooley into the hole, the terrified, one-armed man landing painfully.

At this well-made point, Peters nodded with a hint of resignation as Foster picked up the shovel once more.

'Wait,' Peters held up a hand as, with his other, he pulled his phone back out. 'I wanna film this.'

Foster stared at the younger man as he turned on the camera app, aiming it down at Tooley.

'You're sick,' he muttered.

'Just proof of a job well done,' Peters grinned, waving for Foster to continue. And continue the older man did, shovelling a spadeful of dirt onto the man in the grave, all while Peters filmed him.

'Wait!' Tooley cried out. 'I'll make you rich, powerful even!'

More soil landed on him; Foster, not listening to the plea for leniency, was continuing his mission.

'I'll show you how the algorithm works!' his eyes wide and bright, optimistic that he could still talk his way out of this, Tooley tried to grab the shovel and halt Foster. 'I could explain everything to you! If you knew, you could make millions!'

More soil landed on him. The grave was filling. And, as Foster paused, wiping his already sweating forehead, realisation slowly dawned across Tooley's own face as he looked up at Fosters and Peters in turn.

'You ... you know already, don't you?' he asked. 'Tell them I'm sorry ...'

It was almost as if something inside Foster snapped, and he pulled a silenced pistol out of his pocket in one swift motion, shooting Tooley between the eyes, the man falling dead, his glazed expression staring off into eternity as he collapsed into the grave.

'You prick!' Peters muttered. You ruined the shot! And we were told to bury him alive!'

'Are you gonna tell them we didn't?' Foster said as he turned to Peters, who had wisely turned off the phone camera as the gun now aimed at him. 'Because it's a big hole. Big enough for two.'

'No, I'm cool,' Peters forced a weak smile.

In response, Foster tossed him the shovel.

'Good, then you can finish,' he said, stepping back and

wiping his head with his jacket sleeve as reluctantly, and moaning about getting more mud on his tracksuit, Peters continued to bury the now dead Tooley.

2

STREETS OF SAN FRANCISCO

It was just under four hundred miles to San Francisco, and Marlowe had started early in the day. He had a couple of days before the conference he was attending started, so he could have split the journey, maybe even taken in some more of the West Coast, maybe headed through Malibu or Santa Monica, but the previous night's activities had left him with a sour taste in his mouth, and he'd decided that leaping right back into work was the best option.

The conference was in the Union Square district, to the northeast of the city, so Marlowe drove instead to San Francisco International Airport, dropping the car off at the rental station; he wasn't likely to need it for the next couple of days, and even though he was hiring it under a fake name and credit card, the thought of spending three days on car hire and hotel parking for no reason went a little against his working-class beliefs.

Besides, once this was done, he was considering returning to the UK; Trix had been monitoring the recent murder at

Heston Services in West London, an explosion caused when an assassin had tried to kill him around midnight while he drove home, and the police had decided it was likely gang related, as there was no identification on the body, the DNA and dental records had brought up nothing, and Marlowe's car hadn't been picked up anywhere near.

And Marlowe had the added comfort of knowing nobody else would come after him to avenge the death; that had already happened, and Marlowe had removed that threat as well.

Or, rather, Brad Haynes had.

There was also the fact that Marlowe had learned while in New York that the assassin had been hired by his father, Taylor Coleman, a man Marlowe had spent little time with over the years, and a man who'd sent a second-rate killer purely as a message to get his estranged son to "call home".

Marlowe had obliged, and the conversation he'd had a couple of weeks earlier still rang in his head, in particular his father's words.

'I have cancer. It's eating away at my lungs. The annoying thing is it wasn't actually from smoking. It was from various carcinogenic shit I've inhaled while working on weaponry. But it doesn't matter now, the doctor says I've got weeks, months, maybe years if I'm super lucky. No one seems to know. Nobody wants to give me a solid diagnosis just in case I prove them wrong and take them to court. But chances are, by the end of this year, you'll be an orphan.'

If Marlowe was being honest, he'd considered himself an orphan for years. And the thought of Taylor, a man he couldn't even bring himself to call "Dad" dying, wasn't one that filled him with concern.

However, the reason for Marlowe's summoning had been simple and cold. Taylor had informed him, in no uncertain terms, that not only was he not being left anything in the will, but as the oldest of Taylor's children, although illegitimate, he was asked not to contest the amounts being given to his half-brother and half-sister from Taylor's actual marriage.

Marlowe had been fine with that. He didn't want to deal with them, anyway.

But then Taylor had ended the conversation with a curveball.

'I'm aware I let you down, and I let your mother down. So, when I'm gone, there'll be an item that I will send you. My last apology to you. And when you get it, I hope you use it. Class this as my last gift to you. You will never get what you hope for. Instead, you will always get what you deserve.'

This had sent a sliver of ice down Marlowe's spine. To get what he deserved could be a multitude of things, none of which were good, and this thought kept him occupied the entire journey to San Francisco Airport, and the half an hour taxi ride to the hotel. He'd tried to get ahead of this, looking into Taylor's company holdings, but it was a futile gesture, one he'd attempted many times over the years. The only new thing he found this time, and this was thanks to Trix checking into the hotel Taylor had booked into for the New York meeting, was that Taylor had stayed on a corporate account for *Arachnis Consulting*. Marlowe hadn't found anything else on this, and had guessed it was yet another shell company owned by Taylor, probably named after spiders, but he'd later learnt the "Arachnis" was an orchid, named because it *looked* like a spider, apparently.

That sounds like Taylor, he'd thought to himself on reading this. *To name a company after a flower, but only if it's a cool-*

sounding one.

Now returning his attention to San Francisco, Marlowe considered the hotel itself, the Hamilton Grand Hotel. It was a mixture of old and new; a chrome and glass skyscraper that emerged out of the roof of a far older brownstone building, on an unexciting yet expensive street to the south of Union Square. It was a five-star hotel with a variety of Michelin awards tacked onto the side, and even the most basic room was a good five hundred bucks a night. Marlowe would never have stayed here on his own dime; it was far too visible for him, especially with the company he kept and the company he wanted to avoid, but this was the job; he'd agreed to help a Senator who could, in return, make his life easier.

And even better, she'd covered the cost for the room.

He entered from the pavement, having asked the taxi to drop him around the corner. This way, he had a chance to check out the hotel's frontage as he approached, noting the paparazzi at the side, snapping at the people who came in and out. The Hamilton was known to be a favourite haunt for celebrities and politicians, probably why the place was booked in the first place, and they were looking for a salacious photo or two.

Surprisingly, or rather not so, the bearded man with unkempt hair, a brown leather jacket, and a battered duffel over his shoulder didn't even garner a second look. Marlowe didn't know whether to be insulted or relieved at this. Either way, following a cursory glance by the doorman, a slight sneer to the lips, most likely from some belief that Marlowe wasn't the right clientele for the location, Marlowe entered the hotel.

The lobby was rather understated, considering the reputation the place had: pale wooden slats for floors, chocolate walls mixed with lit glass alcoves, white seats to rest in and a long reception desk on the left welcomed him as he entered, the three receptionists behind the desks moving quickly to serve the small queue of waiting guests. Settling at the back, Marlowe waited until it was his turn, and walked over to one receptionist with a smile.

'Hi,' he said, placing the duffel down. 'I should have a room booked for me for the next two days?'

'Of course, sir. Name?'

Marlowe paused. He couldn't remember what name he'd asked Senator Kyle to book him under.

'Try Troughton,' he said. 'Or Pertwee.'

The receptionist glanced up.

'They might have accidentally used my stage name,' Marlowe explained, without skipping a beat. 'I'm performing at the conference.'

If the receptionist had been interested in this backstory, she did an incredible job of not showing it.

'John Pertwee?'

'Yes, no "h", though,' Marlowe smiled. It was a habit of his to pick semi-famous names for his hotel aliases of late; he was currently working his way through the actors known for playing *Doctor Who*, a British sci-fi show.

'Do you want to leave a card for incidentals?'

'I believe Senator Kyle is footing the bill,' Marlowe quickly replied. The last thing he wanted was leaving a paper trail. And after all, this had been one of the conditions.

'Ah, yes, thank you,' the receptionist smiled. 'Your card is in the envelope, or you can use our digital app as a key—'

'Card is fine,' Marlowe smiled once more, taking the key.

'You also have access to the Hamilton Club on the eighteenth floor, where we serve complimentary beverages and food.'

'Appreciated,' Marlowe tipped an imaginary cap to the lady, who gave a little chuckle, probably out of politeness. As he picked up his duffel, though, the receptionist cleared her throat.

'It's not my place, but as you're, well, not one of *them*—'

'Not one of them?'

The receptionist smiled awkwardly.

'You're hired to perform, right? So you're not part of the retinue?'

Marlowe nodded, understanding.

'Yeah, I see what you mean,' he said. 'What's up?'

'The security for the Senator already arrived, and last night there were ... incidents,' the receptionist explained. 'With others staying here.'

Marlowe noted the name "Becky" on her badge and leant closer.

'Are you warning me to be careful, Becky?' he whispered.

'Just don't give them a reason to kick you out,' Becky replied, mimicking a smoking motion. And, having to force his face to stay serious while inwardly chuckling, Marlowe tapped his forehead again.

She thinks that as I'm a performer, I'm smoking dope, he thought to himself. *Maybe I need to trim the beard after all.*

And, with a nod to Becky the receptionist, Marlowe walked to the elevators, and his hotel room for the next few days.

Marlowe didn't look at the slim man in the suit, pretending to read the paper. He didn't need to. He'd clocked him as he arrived, turning his head to avoid contact. Marlowe had hoped the beard and hair had actually helped him look suitably different, because the last thing he wanted was a conversation with MI5 London Section Chief Alexander Curtis.

But why Curtis was here was a question he'd need to get answered. Because if his old workmates were here, there was no way he'd be able to get to work. You can't be covert in a room full of friends.

And the same was true of enemies.

MARLOWE'S ROOM WAS A SUITE.

Well, it was probably what the Hamilton classed as a basic room, but to Marlowe, it was huge. A quick check on the website showed it was known as "executive level" and one step below "valet level", but it was more than enough.

It was a corner room, with magnolia walls and inset windows on one side, leading to the corner itself, which had floor-to-ceiling windows on either side of a desk and two chairs. To the side was a king-size bed, facing possibly one of the largest TVs he'd ever seen outside of an Ops room. The carpet was cream, the wall behind the bed terracotta, and it gave the room a fresh, clean feeling. There were the usual things a hotel would have: coffee-making facilities, an empty minibar fridge. Marlowe was amused at this, as Kyle had obviously had the drinks removed on booking, and the bathroom was brightly lit with a shower rather than a bath. Which, again, was fine as far as Marlowe was concerned. Since New York, he'd stayed in motels as he crossed the country, and this, compared to those, was a breath of fresh air.

Talking of which, although the room was great, he wasn't going to gain any intel from it, and so, after unpacking, checking the room for bugs, and finally placing his SIG Sauer pistol under the pillow, a habit he'd got into a long while before, he threw on a fresh shirt under his jacket, threw on the "do not disturb" sign on the door handle and returned downstairs. It was six by now; he was getting hungry, and he'd decided that Curtis was a problem he had to confront head on, rather than hiding in his room and ordering room service.

ALTHOUGH IT WAS STILL WHAT COULD BE CLASSED AS EARLY IN the evening, if not even late in the afternoon still, the restaurant was packed, with a forty-minute waiting time. And, deciding he could live on bar snacks and an *Uber Eat* delivery, Marlowe went into *Champions*, the side bar, grabbing an empty table in the corner, able to keep his back to both walls as he looked out into the lobby. The bar was open plan, an island where a dividing wall would usually be, and because of this, Marlowe could see all the way to reception.

He could also see that Curtis was now gone.

A server came over, a young, bubbly woman named "Tina" according to her badge, with frizzy hair who passed him a small menu for things like olives or hummus with flatbreads, and Marlowe ordered a side of fries for the moment, washed down with a Virgin Mary – a Bloody Mary without the vodka. He wanted something that wasn't a soft drink, but at the time didn't intend to drink anything alcoholic, as he didn't know what he'd end up being needed to do later in the day. And the slight hint of spice the Worcestershire sauce gave definitely woke him up after a long day of driving. Although the "Tequila Slammer" style salt dabbed around the lip of the glass was quickly wiped off.

He examined the bar as he sipped at his drink. There was a brunette woman at the bar, late twenties, perhaps, constantly checking her phone, idly playing with a hotel bar's matchbook in her other hand. It was too early to be stood up, so Marlowe assumed it was something different. She was dressed for work rather than pleasure, and Marlowe wondered briefly whether she was here for the summit in a day or two, the same one he was surreptitiously there for. He couldn't get close enough to hear her properly, but he was also sure she'd spoken with a British accent when she ordered. Could she be with Curtis? And was Curtis here with whoever was attending on behalf of the UK government?

Marlowe didn't know the ins and outs of the event; this was to be passed to him the following day when he spoke to Senator Kyle. He knew, however, she was looking to cement her position as a global leader, possibly before announcing a Presidential bid for 2024. Marlowe had removed any blackmail information Nathan Donziger and his corporation had on her quite recently and now, with a blueprint of what was out there and what could be removed, Marlowe was pretty sure Kyle had spent the last fourteen days removing any loose thread or rogue asset out there, making damned sure that if she went for the role, she was squeaky clean.

There was a man across the bar, glaring back at him, but on second glance, Marlowe realised the man was doing the same as him, scanning the bar, but in his case was doing it with the most "piss off and die" expression one could have. Even Tina was keeping her distance from him. Marlowe didn't linger on the man, but found a reflective surface on the wall to his side that, when he angled slightly to the left, he could see a reflection of the man without being noticed.

He was muscled, bulky, and had a suit on, done up even while sitting, a bulge to his left obviously a shoulder holster. He had a pin of some kind on his lapel, and he screamed "Secret Service" without even trying.

The man eventually rose, walking out of the bar, a tossed twenty-dollar bill barely enough to cover his drinks. Marlowe hadn't received his fries yet, but something about the man intrigued him so, finishing his drink, he threw down money for food, drink and tip, and quietly followed the man into the lobby—

Where another man in a tweed jacket walked straight into him.

'Bloody hell!' the man said, his accent very West London in tone. 'Nosebag?'

Marlowe froze. He hadn't been called that for a very long time. In fact, the last time he was called "Nosebag" was in the Royal Marines. He'd always been hungry, always on the scrounge for more food, and because of this, the nickname "Nosebag" had stuck.

Marlowe turned to look at the man in front of him. He was in his forties, slim and petite, a bookish air around him, pushing his thick-framed glasses back up his nose.

'Scrapper?' Marlowe could strip away the years quickly, seeing the soldier this man once was. Smaller than the others, Sergeant Warren "Scrapper" Lyons had what people called "little dog" syndrome, always kicking off fights with bigger enemies, usually resulting in Marlowe and others coming to his aid. But that had been a decade ago, when Marlowe was a far younger, and more brash man. 'What the hell are you doing here?'

'That's how you greet me after all this time?' Lyons pouted before breaking out into a wide smile. 'Bloody hell, Marlowe, you look like a hippie! What's all this beard about?'

He embraced Marlowe, as if genuinely happy to see the man. Which was confusing, really.

Because the last time Scrapper Lyons had seen Tom Marlowe, he'd tried to *kill* him.

3

WAR STORIES

MARLOWE DECIDED TO PLAY ALONG FOR THE MOMENT UNTIL HE could work out what was truly going on. Lyons seemed animated, nervous even, like he'd snorted a few lines of coke before walking into the lobby. Which, to be honest, he could have done; Marlowe knew Lyons wouldn't have been a user back in the day – you just *didn't* when in the Commandos, but it'd been a long time since then.

'Bloody hell, it's got to be, what, ten years?' Lyons was still talking. 'You still a bootneck? You disappeared overnight. I heard your mum died or something?'

Marlowe nodded, desperately trying to remember what had been stated officially when he went to work for Section D.

'No, I left a long time back,' he replied, not technically lying. 'Moved into the family business, I suppose. You?'

Lyons looked nervously around as he spoke.

'Similar, but I took a consultant job.'

'Good for you. Where?'

Lyons gave an expression of a man conflicted for a moment, but then leant closer.

'GCHQ. But mainly, I'm doing a lot of consulting with *Caliburn*.'

It was a one-word name, but with so much weight behind it.

Marlowe stared at Lyons now – Caliburn was a shadow organisation – more a "caucus for spies," loosely connected to the UK's Intelligence Service, a "spook boy's club" that ran a parallel agenda to the Government in the same way that research support groups like the ERG, or, rather the *European Research Group*, a caucus of Eurosceptic Conservative Members of Parliament who worked their own agendas. However, unlike the ERG, whose subscriptions were taxpayer-funded through the Independent Parliamentary Standards Authority's scheme of MPs' Business Costs and Expenses, Caliburn gained their funding from unused slush funds and dead spies – or, rather, the wills they'd made that bequeathed money to Caliburn after the agent's death, allowing Caliburn to work unhindered in the grey areas of international law and treaties.

Scrapper Lyons may have been a wild card in the Royal Marines, but he was definitely the type a spooky research group caucus like that would recruit, especially from the Commandos, and he knew his way around a fight, even if he needed to be saved now and then.

But Caliburn had a poor reputation; not only for the shadowy shit that would have them in front of a tribunal – if the tribunal could work out who to subpoena – but for their innovative ideas when it came to weaponry. After all, there were a lot of people, many missing, or dead now, that believed they were behind some of the worst bioweapon designs out there, for a start. Although that could be hearsay and nothing more than rumourmongering.

'Are you sure you should be telling me that?' Marlowe asked.

Lyons looked uncomfortable.

'No, not really,' he muttered. 'But needs must and all that, Nosey.'

'What, as an analyst?' Marlowe carried on, hoping the answer was "yes".

'Kinda,' Lyons replied carefully, confirming that it wasn't the case.

'I've seen some of Caliburn's work in Africa,' Marlowe stepped back as he looked Lyons up and down. 'And in Eastern Europe. Did a mission with the SAS a few years back, purely to clean up their shit, while MI6 claimed it wasn't anything to do with them.'

'I'm not part of any of that, I'm more ... research and design,' Lyons blurted, shaking his head. I do a lot of work with Brian Tooley. Remember him? He found his niche in Caliburn. Lots of secrets to play with, keep under the skin, you know?'

Marlowe couldn't recall a Brian in the unit, but it had been a good few years since he'd last served with Lyons.

'Artificial arm? Lost it in Afghanistan?' Lyons was still trying to remind Marlowe, but it didn't ring any bells.

'You here for the summit?' Lyons suddenly asked, leaning in. 'Which side are you working for?'

Marlowe didn't want to answer this; he didn't yet know Lyon's loyalties, and across the lobby, he could see the Secret Service guy speaking with someone new, a young, skinny man in a tracksuit, as the latter passed the agent what looked to be a small envelope.

'Why are you being so nice, Scrapper?' he asked. 'Last time we met, you tried to kill me with an ice cream spoon.'

'Aye, yeah, sorry about that,' Lyons rubbed at the back of his head. 'I was really screwed up around then. Thought you were shagging my wife.'

'You weren't married.'

'Yeah, as I said, I was screwed up. Not anymore, though,' Lyons looked around. 'You MI5 these days?'

'I'm sorry, I'm here on vacation,' Marlowe forced a smile, showing his beard. 'I'm out. You think anyone would let me work looking like this?'

At this, Lyons deflated slightly. He saw something out of the corner of his gaze, however, as a couple of suited men new to the lobby started towards them.

'Good to see you, anyway,' he smiled sadly. 'Even under these circumstances.'

He looked towards the bar area, as if wondering if it was worth making a run for it, but then instead leant closer to Marlowe, whispering into his ear.

'Remember, Marlowe, the truth is always in the clouds. Congratulations.'

And, this said, Lyons slid past him, moving back into the lobby, away from the two approaching men, leaving the confused Marlowe to watch after him, unsure why he'd been congratulated.

Marlowe didn't know who they were, but they were obviously after Lyons, and whether or not he'd seen the man for years, he'd still served with Lyons, broken bread with the man, and so Marlowe subtly moved into the two men's way, smiling as he did so.

'Hey, you work here?' he asked, deciding the role of "hapless tourist" could be the best option. The two men ignored him, moving around the man in their way – but stopped as Marlowe grabbed the larger of the two men.

'Hey,' he retorted. 'I asked a question.'

'We don't work here, so sod off,' the larger man said, pulling away.

'Sorry,' Marlowe stepped back, holding his hands up, allowing the two men to move on. It had only been a momentary interruption, but hopefully enough to give Lyons a head start. And it was long enough to realise one important fact here.

The man had spoken in an American accent, but it was fake. And, no matter how much he could fake it, the source of the accent was definitely British, as no American said "sod off" as a standard phrase.

Why were British thugs chasing an ex-British soldier on American soil?

It was a question he'd have to answer later, as the probable Secret Service agent, wiping his nose, was now also walking towards him.

Marlowe straightened his shoulders, preparing for a fight, but as he paused beside Marlowe, the probable agent simply nodded towards the elevators.

'Senator wants to see you,' he growled.

'I start working for her tomorrow,' Marlowe replied, mainly to see how such an answer would be taken. He had the impression the agent wasn't used to being refused.

'Fine,' the agent's mouth shrugged, nodding at this. 'I'll get them to cancel your room for the night. Grab your things. You can come back tomorrow.'

Marlowe grinned. The agent had expected this response. Which meant he'd read up on the man he'd been told to collect.

'Take me to her,' he smiled, glancing off to the back of the lobby, where Scrapper Lyons had last been seen. He wanted to go after him, make sure he was okay.

But Scrapper Lyons was always okay. And Marlowe had been beaten up enough times coming to his aid.

And so, placing his one-time squaddie colleague out of his mind, Marlowe followed the agent off to the elevators, the Presidential Suite, and Senator Kyle.

THE AGENT HAD IGNORED MARLOWE FOR THE JOURNEY UP TO the Presidential Suite, but Marlowe hadn't ignored him. The closeness of the elevator carriage was an opportunity to get close and personal without the other person getting annoyed. And, being this close, Marlowe was gathering a lot of intelligence.

'Worked for Kyle long?' he asked conversationally.

'Yes,' the agent replied.

'Were you in New York when I was?'

The agent looked at Marlowe, and his eyes narrowed.

'Do you mean was I there when you broke into her hotel room? No,' he replied icily. 'If I had been, you wouldn't be here now. You'd be dead.'

Marlowe shrugged, unconcerned. The fact the agent had to emphasise the point meant he didn't think Marlowe was quick enough to understand. Which was fine by him. He preferred to be underestimated.

'What's your name?' he carried on, noting the elevator approaching the top floor.

'Mister eff off,' the agent said, and actually chuckled at his bad joke. The elevator stopped, and the agent motioned for Marlowe to leave.

'Ladies first.'

'No, you first, I insist,' Marlowe smiled, holding a hand out, but as the agent started out of the carriage, Marlowe stepped forward, bumping into him as they both reached the exit.

'Sorry, I didn't think you'd actually do it,' Marlowe stepped back.

'Just get the hell out,' the agent muttered.

Marlowe, smiling, complied.

The suite was designed and painted very much like his own room, but it was far larger. And the door led into a hallway that, in turn, led into a living space, floor-to-ceiling windows on two walls, a two-seater sofa and chair set up in the middle, surrounding a coffee table.

Sitting on the chair, rising as Marlowe arrived, was Arizona Senator Maureen Kyle. A middle-aged woman, heading more towards the upper end of that description, her hair was short, spiky and a mixture of black and silver, in a natural, salt and pepper style. She wasn't slim, but she wasn't overweight either, settling more for a middling, "healthy but not too healthy" kind of look.

Marlowe knew she was a widow; her husband had died three years earlier in a helicopter crash. It had been believed that Nathan Donziger, the industrialist who had blackmail information on her, had done this, but when Marlowe had stolen the file Donziger had on Kyle, back in New York, he had found none of this in the notes.

'Mister Marlowe,' Senator Kyle held out a hand to be shaken and, this done, indicated with her arm a spot on the sofa for him to sit. 'You're here early. Good. You can start early.'

'I don't think I can,' Marlowe shook his head sadly. 'You've already broken our deal.'

'Oh?' an eyebrow rose quizzically.

'When we met in the hotel that night—'

'You make it sound so normal,' Senator Kyle replied, the smile on her face not matching the tone in her voice. 'But let's call it as it was. When you broke into my suite in the middle of the night ...'

Marlowe conceded the point.

'No matter how we met, it doesn't change the fact that I said for you to fire your agents and bring in a new security team, as the ones you had worked for Donziger.'

'And I did.'

Marlowe nodded at the agent he'd travelled here with.

'Your man there said he'd been in your service for a long time, since before New York.'

'And he wasn't in New York,' Kyle replied. 'He wasn't part of this. Ford's the best I have, and I kept him on.'

Marlowe settled back into the sofa.

'If he's the best you have, then you have a problem,' he drawled. 'He's not up to it.'

'You son of a—' the now-named Ford snarled as he moved in on the sitting Marlowe. However, this had been prepared for, expected even, and as he reached for his target, Marlowe slid out from underneath him, twisting as he did so, grabbing Ford's arm and wrenching it back.

One of the other Secret Service agents in the room went to assist, but Senator Kyle held a hand up as Marlowe brought Ford to the floor, the agent grimacing in pain.

'He's too amped up on cocaine to be useful,' Marlowe

said, keeping pressure on the arm. 'And he's not diligent enough to wipe it from his nostril when he's done. His hands have been twitching and clenching since I met him, and his pupils have been more dilated than they should be.'

'Bullshit! Lies!' Ford screamed.

'A drug test could prove me wrong right now,' Marlowe replied, looking at Senator Kyle. 'I'm sure the Senator has a kit around. Random testing of agents is still the norm, right?'

'Let him go,' Senator Kyle sighed, sitting back in her chair. 'I've known about his habit for years. I choose to ignore it as he's, well, useful in other ways.'

Marlowe pulled away as Ford fell to the floor. Now he knew what Ford had meant earlier, when he said if he'd been there, the outcome in the New York hotel would have been different.

He meant in the bed, beside his employer and lover.

'And this?' he asked, pulling out the envelope he'd seen Ford given earlier, the envelope he'd taken when bumping into Ford while leaving the elevator. He chucked it over to Senator Kyle, who opened it, revealing a wad of banknotes.

'Who gave him this?'

'Man in a tracksuit.'

Senator Kyle now rose.

'Bribe money?'

Ford wisely kept quiet. Marlowe did the same, watching the scene play out.

'What do you know about this weekend?' Senator Kyle suddenly spoke.

'You're talking at a Veteran's Summit tomorrow night,' Marlowe replied carefully. 'But that's not why you're here. You're brokering some kind of deal with the British Government.'

'And how do you see that?'

'Because I've seen MI5 agents in the hotel,' Marlowe looked directly at Kyle now as he continued. 'In particular, a Section Chief of the London Unit that deals with Whitehall and the Government. For him to come, it has to be a member of the Government, even of the Cabinet, that's coming to speak to you. Not Baker, the PM's too high a role to expect to attend a talk for an Arizona Senator, but Harriet Turnbull, the Defence Secretary, or maybe the Home Secretary, Joanna Karolides, they could come here on a dozen different reasons. Especially if they were pushing to be the next PM after Baker, probably when the next election hurts him, and knew you were considering making a play for the Presidency.'

Ford, rubbing at his arm, glared up at Marlowe as he continued.

'Is that why I'm here?' Marlowe snarled. 'To be your own private MI5 agent?'

Senator Kyle tossed the money onto the coffee table.

'I bought your loyalty when you decided that helping me helped your own cause,' she pointed out. 'Be honest, Tom. Your own people don't give a shit about you. Your only option to get out of the shit hole you've thrown yourself into, a life of fake names and constantly looking over your shoulder, is to throw your cards in with me.'

'You used me,' Marlowe shook his head. 'As what, bait? You want me to spy on my own people?'

'Caliburn,' Senator Kyle whispered the word, her eyebrows rising as she spied Marlowe's expression. 'Oh, you know it. Good.'

'The sword King Arthur drew from the stone—'

'Don't play me for a fool,' Senator Kyle walked to the side

cabinet, pouring a generous measure of bourbon out into a glass. 'You're better than that.'

'Caliburn. Shadow caucus-slash-research group with Government ties and funding,' he rattled off the details as if giving a debriefing. 'Accused of atrocities and black-bag actions around the world, never proven, disbanded officially two years ago.'

'And are they really disbanded?'

'No,' Marlowe knew with a certainty. 'Partly because how do you disband an organisation that doesn't really exist and is nothing more than a really well-organised WhatsApp group, but mainly because I spoke to an operative from them less than half an hour ago.'

Senator Kyle paused, the tumbler to her lips.

'They're here for me?'

'You tell me,' Marlowe was quickly realising the rules of engagement here were changing. 'The man I spoke to wasn't what I'd call a specialist. More a techy type.'

'Caliburn wants to kill me,' Senator Kyle explained. 'Many of them are within MI5 and the British Civil Service. Over the last year or so, they stopped being a taxpayer-funded ghost protocol and became a more military version of the Freemasons. And they want more than anything to stop my meeting with Karolides.'

'So we stop them,' Marlowe shrugged. 'But I'd start with better guards.'

Senator Kyle looked down at Ford.

'The man he gained this from, did you see him? Would you recognise him?'

Marlowe nodded.

'What was it for?' Kyle asked Ford.

'Tomorrow's itinerary,' he reluctantly admitted. 'But not for you, for the Brits. I'd never go against you.'

'Have you done it yet?' Marlowe asked.

After a nod from Senator Kyle, Ford shook his head.

'Not yet,' he said. 'Too many things in the air. This is just an advance.'

'Then you're lucky,' Senator Kyle motioned for one of the other Secret Service agents to grab Ford, pulling him to his feet. 'Because you're going to arrange for Mister Marlowe to meet with them tomorrow.'

'One thing,' Marlowe said as he started towards the door. 'I'll look into it, but I suggest you stay in your room and surround yourself with loyal bodies.'

Senator Kyle, paling a little at the comment, nodded, as Marlowe walked out of the room, heading towards the elevators and his own room once more.

There was something going on here he didn't like. His own people, here with the Government and having clandestine meetings with Kyle – that seemed too coincidental. And Caliburn being mentioned twice in the same night by two different people? That wasn't by chance.

The doors opened, and Marlowe entered the elevator, pressing the button for his floor. But after a couple of floors, it stopped, opening the doors to allow another guest in.

The woman who entered was young, no older than early twenties, peroxide-blonde hair poking out from under a baseball cap, the matt blackness of it matching her oversized hoodie.

'Alright, Marlowe, can we talk?' she said with a smile, keeping her face from the view of the elevator camera.

'Trix, what the hell are you doing here?' Marlowe exclaimed – the last he'd seen of Trix Preston, she was getting on a plane from New York, looking to regain her career in Section D.

'Getting you the hell away from whatever bloody mess you've gotten yourself into,' she snapped in response. 'And convincing MI5 that you weren't just hired by the CIA to kill a serving officer.'

'Which officer?' Marlowe turned to face Trix now. 'Curtis?'

'No, you idiot. Warren Lyons.'

Marlowe felt his stomach flip-flop.

'You think I'm here to kill him? Does Curtis think this too?'

Trix stared long and hard at Marlowe, before pressing another floor's button.

'You need to come chat to Curtis,' she said. 'Because there's no future tense about this. We got the call five minutes back.'

She looked away.

'Warren Lyons is already dead.'

4

RAISE A GLASS

'YOU'VE GOT SOME NERVE BEING HERE,' CURTIS MUTTERED AS he glared across a hotel bedroom at Marlowe, now standing by the entrance door, returning a gaze back to the London Section Chief.

The room was basic: one bed, a sideboard with a TV on top, an armchair and a desk to work on. The windows were floor-to-ceiling but sparse, more wall than glass, and the view was of the building across the street.

'My room's better than yours,' Marlowe mused loudly to himself. 'Guess they were right when they said the Civil Service budget for travelling is shit.'

He looked from the window back to Curtis.

'You burnt me,' he said with a minimal amount of venom in his voice. 'Left me out to dry. I needed to find new allies.'

'I burnt you because someone needed to take the blame on the NOC list,' Curtis grumbled once more, mentioning a list of spies that Marlowe had helped retrieve a few months back, a list that Marlowe had kept a lie within, in order to save an innocent woman. 'And if I recall correctly, you were the one that said to do it.'

'Yeah, fair point,' Marlowe walked over to the bed, perching on the edge. 'Does your minibar have anything in it? Mine's been emptied. Bloody Americans.'

'No,' Trix said, currently sitting behind the desk, already working on her laptop, now plugged into the ethernet port.

'And why's she here?' Marlowe asked Curtis, pointing at Trix. 'Last I heard, she was on her way back to Wintergreen.'

'Wintergreen didn't want her,' Curtis replied. 'Section D is for all intents and purposes closed. And so Preston here needed something new to do, and I asked her to come back to America with me. After all, she did work with Senator Kyle's blackmailer.'

'In a roundabout way,' Trix muttered loudly, opening a strip of chewing gum and tossing it into her mouth as she worked.

There was a knock at the door, and Curtis rose, walking past Marlowe, opening it. In the doorway was a young man, in his mid-thirties, black spiky hair over a dress shirt and jeans.

'Marlowe, meet Casey,' Curtis said as he walked back to his chair. 'As in surname. You don't need to know his first name.'

'Everyone knows yours,' Casey shook Marlowe's hand. 'Tom Marlowe, the guy who almost killed the President, and blew up the Thames.'

'I seem to recall I *saved* the President when I blew up the Thames,' Marlowe raised an eyebrow.

At this, Casey shrugged.

'I heard it was a team effort,' he said, nodding at Curtis.

'And that the Section Chief had a way larger role in it than your fans claim.'

'I have fans now?' Marlowe looked expectantly at Curtis, who grimaced.

'The Kirks, Wintergreen, a few others,' he said. 'In a roundabout way, it's why we're here.'

He leant back, reaching for something on his lap, and Marlowe knew with no doubt that it was a gun aimed at him.

'Did you kill Lyons?' Curtis asked, his hand hidden.

Marlowe shook his head.

'I didn't even know he was here,' he said. 'He bumped into me out in the lobby.'

'What did he say?' Casey leant closer. 'How did he react to seeing you?'

'Honestly? Like an old friend,' Marlowe frowned. 'I haven't spoken to the man for years, and the last time we saw each other it ... well, it didn't end in an optimal state—'

'He tried to kill you with an apple corer,' Trix added.

'Ice cream scoop,' Marlowe corrected. 'But here he was, a few years later, acting like nothing was wrong between us, and treating me like the groom at a wedding.'

He looked back at Curtis.

'Lyons was alive half an hour back, because that's when I saw him.'

'Where did he go after that?'

Marlowe paused from answering, his lips thinning as he considered the situation.

'Trix said you thought I'd been hired by the CIA to kill him.'

'The thought had crossed our minds,' Curtis walked over to the minibar now, pulling a can of beer out of it, opening it with a *hiss* as he returned to the chair. 'We heard the Americans wanted him gone.'

'You said there was nothing in the bar,' wounded, Marlowe glared at Trix.

'No, I said there was nothing for *you*,' Trix loudly chewed her gum as she smiled at him. 'Did I lie? Nope.'

Sighing, Marlowe turned back to Curtis.

'So if the US wanted him gone, then why were British agents hunting him?' he asked, almost innocently.

'The only British agents here right now are in this room,' Casey said in response. 'Oh, and you. But you don't really count anymore.'

Marlowe spun to face him.

'Bollocks,' he replied. 'Lyons was one of yours, wasn't he? Or was he rogue?'

'Why would you think he was rogue?'

'Because he told me he was working for Caliburn.'

'Caliburn is an old wives' tale for shit spies to blame when their ops go bad,' Casey leant back onto the bed as he replied, with the slightest of sneers on his face. 'The only reason he'd tell you that was if he thought you were one as well. Are you?'

'Make your mind up,' Marlowe snapped, rising to his feet. 'I can't be a member if it's an old wives' tale. And as for the others, the two men who were following him spoke with British accents, even though they tried to hide it.'

'You spoke to them? Why?'

'Because I ran interference on them to give Scrapper a few more seconds,' Marlowe was tiring of the conversation.

'You assisted a known rogue agent?' Curtis still had his hand under the table, returned to the weapon most likely hidden there after returning with his drink.

'One, he's not a rogue agent to me,' Marlowe counted off his fingers. 'I didn't even know he was in the Service. We were soldiers together. Two, technically I'm a rogue agent too, according to dickless there, so that idea goes out the window. And three, you're damn right I helped him. We fought together. Bled together.'

He turned his attention to Casey.

'Your man here looks more worried about having his next pedicure, than who he's fighting next—'

He didn't finish as Casey, angered, threw a punch at him. It was telegraphed, though, and Marlowe was ready for it, grabbing the arm as it swung past his head, sliding out of the way as he used the momentum to flip Casey over, the younger man landing with a painful thud onto the hotel room floor.

'You done?' Curtis sighed.

'No,' Marlowe growled. 'Who killed Scrapper, and where?'

'You don't want to know the how?' Curtis leant closer, hunching over the desk.

'For God's sake, Curtis, just pull the bloody thing out,' Marlowe let go of Casey's arm. 'I know you have a Glock or something. And I'm not in the mood right now for games.'

'Warren Lyons was killed in a corridor through the back doors,' Trix said, now pushing away the laptop. 'The two men you saw who were following him, they caught up with him as he was running for the delivery area, with nobody around.'

Curtis looked over at her.

'Marlowe?'

'Nowhere near it,' Trix shook her head. 'Just as I said. He was in a lift going up to the penthouse when it happened. Cameras confirm it.'

She turned the laptop around to show a CCTV image.

'That doesn't look like a traditional camera,' Marlowe leant closer, looking at it. The image was in colour and well defined, showing the door and the shutters beside it.

'It's not,' Trix said. 'I went around the whole place earlier today, placing our own cameras up. I'm sure the CIA did the same thing, but I covered entrances and exits. This was one of them.'

On the screen, they saw Lyons run for the door, pulling at it as he realised it was locked. He tried the shutters, but then slumped as he turned around, chuckling.

A voice, someone off camera, spoke.

'What the hell do you think you're doing, eh? Didn't you hear us calling?'

'That's the man I spoke to,' Marlowe said. 'The one in the lobby.'

'Where's the data, Warren?' the voice continued.

In response, Lyons laughed, shaking his head as he replied.

'In the clouds. Look at you both! You don't even know what you're hunting! Did you think I'd have a notebook? A flash-drive?'

He took a deep breath, as if steeling himself for the worst.

Marlowe almost didn't want to look as Lyons continued.

'So tell McKellan to go fu—'

He didn't finish, the sound of a silenced pistol echoing softly as Warren "Scrapper" Lyons was shot in the head.

'Bastards!' Marlowe shouted, looking at Curtis. 'This was you!'

'Marlowe, you don't—'

'*Bullshit!*' Marlowe had spun around now, moving towards the Section Chief. 'McKellan. You heard him. That's Sir

Walter McKellan, isn't it? MI6 Deputy Director or something?'

'We don't know this,' Curtis rose, and finally the Glock 17 in his hand was revealed. 'We're on the back foot, just like you. Did Lyons say anything to you before he left?'

'Go to hell!'

'Marlowe!' Curtis shouted now, and the intensity of his voice halted everyone in the room. As Marlowe turned, he realised Casey had grabbed the ice bucket from the side cabinet, and was about to smack it across the back of his head, the younger man now pausing as well.

'We were sent here to protect the Home Secretary,' Curtis continued, his voice calmer now. She was told there was a credible threat to her life this weekend if she carried on with this meeting. The name Caliburn had been mentioned.'

'McKellan was never a fan of Joanna Karolides,' Marlowe reluctantly accepted. 'You think he could be Caliburn?'

'I think he probably is, but why kill one of his own?' now it was Casey who asked.

'Because Lyons was telling everyone he was Caliburn?' Trix suggested. 'And it sounds like he stole something.'

'Something he gave you,' Curtis finished the thought, nodding at Marlowe. 'Maybe he gave you something without you realising. Help us, Tom. Help us avenge him, and we'll get you reinstated.'

Marlowe went to reply, but found he was momentarily speechless by the offer.

'You'll reinstate me into MI5, just like that?' he glanced at Trix, noting quietly that she wasn't agreeing with this. If anything, she seemed just as surprised at the offer as he was.

'I can make it happen,' Curtis replied. 'As we discussed

earlier, it was only your selfless act of misguided chivalry that had you burnt in the first place.'

Marlowe looked at each of the British agents in the room. He trusted Trix with his life, but he didn't know the full story of why she was there yet. Curtis was a career officer who'd spent most of their relationship hunting him, and Casey was an upstart who Marlowe really wanted to punch.

'Give me the night,' he said. 'I need to think about it. Where's the body?'

'Already off site,' Curtis replied. 'We thought it best.'

Marlowe nodded. The last thing MI5 wanted was an asset found dead in the hotel of an obviously important meeting. Especially if it came out it was rogue British agents that killed him.

'I want to be kept in the loop, Curtis,' he said, moving to the door. 'I want to know who did this. I'm not talking about Caliburn, I want the man who pulled the trigger.'

'Join the queue,' Curtis muttered as Marlowe walked out of the hotel room.

Alone in the corridor, Marlowe took a deep breath. This was supposed to have been a simple mission, to sit in the shadows and watch for enemies.

But now enemies seemed to be everywhere. And he had a chance of regaining his Service status, probably by betraying the Senator who'd brought him here in the first place.

A Senator who believed Caliburn wanted to kill her – at a meeting with the British Home Secretary, convinced Caliburn wanted to kill *her*.

For a pretty much ignored research group, they were getting a lot of unwanted attention right now.

And right now, Marlowe needed a drink.

THE HOTEL BAR WAS THE SAME AS IT'D BEEN WHEN HE LEFT IT an hour earlier, but this time he didn't walk to a table in the corner, instead heading straight for the bar.

Sitting on one of the high chairs along the edge, Marlowe nodded to the bartender.

'Whisky, neat,' he said, pointing at one of the many bottles on the back wall. The bartender poured a generous measure into the glass, passing it over. And, as Marlowe nursed the glass, he considered the last words Warren Lyons said to him, trying to make sense of this.

'GCHQ. But mainly, I'm doing a lot of consulting with Caliburn.'

'Are you sure you should be telling me that?'

'No, not really, but needs must and all that, Nosey.'

What did Lyons mean by that? "Needs must" was slang for doing something you needed to do, while at the same time not liking the fact you were doing it. Was he unhappy he was working with Caliburn, or rather that he was telling Marlowe about it?

'I'm not part of any of that, I'm more ... research and design. I do a lot of work with Brian Tooley. Remember him? He found his niche in Caliburn. Lots of secrets to play with, keep under the skin, you know? You here for the summit? Which side are you working for?'

Marlowe pulled out his phone, checking his social media pages. His old Royal Marine Unit had a group page on one of the social media sites, but there was no Tooley on there. He couldn't check right now, but he was pretty sure even Trix wouldn't find one on the Navy records. So why would Lyons have given that as a name?

'Remember, Marlowe, the truth is always in the clouds. Congratulations.'

Marlowe was about to rise from the chair when a woman sat down beside him. It was the brunette who'd been checking her phone earlier, the one Marlowe was sure had spoken with a British accent.

'Don't go back to your room tonight,' she said, while pretending to read the bar's cocktail menu.

'Sorry?' Marlowe wasn't sure he heard correctly.

The woman now turned to look at him, placing the menu down.

'I said, don't go back to your room.'

Marlowe gave a smile, wondering if she wasn't here for the conference, but more for the attendees there. A more "personal" option for loneliness.

'I don't mean to be rude, but I'm not looking for what you're offering,' he said, testing this hypothesis. If she was indeed a hooker, she'd nod, rise from the chair and go find another mark.

Instead, she looked out across the lobby.

'Don't go back to your room, Mister Marlowe.'

'So you know me,' Marlowe nodded, looking at her. 'And how would that be?'

'Warren Lyons was a mutual friend.'

'Was?'

'Please don't treat me like a fool, Thomas,' the woman sighed. 'I know they killed him. There was a body removed fifteen minutes ago.'

'And you know this how?'

The woman now twisted on the chair, fully facing Marlowe now.

'Because I helped create the protocol the British Government use when removing dead assets,' she said. 'Kate Maybury. I worked with Warren.'

Marlowe's eyes narrowed.

'MI5, MI6, GCHQ or Caliburn?'

'Does it matter?' Kate asked. 'To many out here, they're the same, mostly. But for transparency, I work day-to-day at a Government subsidiary in London, so yes.'

'Government subsidiary in London? That's code for security services. What are you? I don't recall you from MI5, so are you MI6? GCHQ?'

Kate didn't reply to this, and Marlowe rose to leave, dropping a ten-dollar bill for the drink.

'I'm not interested in what's going on here, but I hadn't seen Lyons for years, and as much as I'm saddened by what happened, and I will find out who did it, I want nothing to do with Caliburn, the Government, or whatever shadow agency you're part of.'

'Mister Marlowe, I don't know why you think I'm here—'

'I don't know, and I don't care,' Marlowe shook his head. 'Have a good night, Miss Maybury. Sorry for your loss. But it's open season on rogue agents right now, and I'm getting my head down. I suggest you do the same.'

And, this stated, Marlowe finished the glass of whisky and left the bar.

HE'D DECIDED AS HE RETURNED TO HIS ROOM THAT IT WAS probably best to take the advice he'd given Kate and keep his own head down. His plan was to find out what he could through his own skills, and only call on Trix if it was truly necessary – after all, he still didn't know where she stood on this.

He stopped as he reached his room, however.

The door was slightly ajar.

Marlowe reached for his SIG Sauer, silently cursing his stupidity in leaving it under the pillow. Carefully, he moved closer, pushing the door open. There was a slight smell of stale cigarette smoke—

The hand that grabbed Marlowe was burly, and the grip was harder than he'd expected as he was pulled into the hotel room, the force of the pull almost throwing him into the back of the sofa in the process. As he collapsed against it, Marlowe saw that the room was a mess, and pretty much completely trashed. The only thing still standing was a table lamp on the office desk, which itself had been left alone, although the drawers had been pulled out.

The man who'd grabbed him had been standing behind the door, as if expecting him to arrive. He was muscled, his hair thinning and in a side parting, as he aimed a gun, a six-chamber pistol at him. He also smelt of cigarettes, which explained the smell Marlowe had picked up as he entered.

'Where is it?' he growled as, from the bathroom, the man in the tracksuit who Marlowe had seen in the lobby walked out, drying his hands.

'Where's what?' Marlowe asked, unable to resist himself, wincing as the track-suited man kicked him hard in the side.

'He said where is it, bitch!' the younger man yelled, as the burly man grabbed Marlowe by the shirt, hoisting him up, gun rammed into Marlowe's face.

'We know you met with Lyons,' he snarled. 'We know he passed the data to you.'

'What data? I don't know what you're talking about!'

The burly man let go of Marlowe as the track-suited thug punched him hard in the gut, doubling him over.

'Thomas Marlowe. Burnt MI5 spy, working for anyone who pays. Why help him? He tried to kill you with a cheese knife. You're not part of this.'

'It was a sodding ice cream scoop, and you're making a big mistake,' Marlowe held his hands up, warding off another potential attack from the tracksuit guy.

'So you know nothing about the algorithm? Fractal Destiny?'

Marlowe frowned.

'Now you're just adding words together—' he started, but the gun was aimed at his face once more.

'We know he didn't have it when he died, and we know you're the only one he was close to,' the gunman finished. 'So you have three seconds to give us it, before I shoot you in the face as well.'

5

GUN FIGHT

Marlowe didn't have a clue what was going on, or who these men were, but he knew he needed a way out of here, and fast.

Luckily for him, it came as a knock on the door.

As the two men paused, momentarily distracted, Kate walked in, already talking.

'Look, I've tried to be nice—' she started, but then paused in the entranceway in horror at the scene in front of her.

And it was all Marlowe needed.

Grabbing the lamp from the table, he slammed it into the gunman's head. However, as he fell back, blood streaming from a wound on his skull, the younger, track-suited guy now came in at Marlowe, a blade in his hand.

Marlowe deflected the first slash, still holding the lamp in his hand, using it like a baton, blocking slice after slice with it, before swinging it up, catching the knife man on the jaw, staggering back as he dropped the blade. Marlowe was about to go for it, but was yanked back as the burly, bleeding man grabbed at the lamp's cord, detached from the wall now in the fight, using it as a garrotte around Marlowe's throat. Dropping the lamp, Marlowe grabbed at the cord around his neck, pulling hard at it, feeling the plastic cable bite into him as the man grunted behind him, pulling harder – before loosening the cable with another, more painful grunt as Kate, pulling a painting from the room's wall, slammed it down onto the back of his head.

As Marlowe stumbled back, the track-suit thug moved in again, grabbing Kate in anger, hands around her neck. Marlowe went to charge at him, but the burly man, now furious, his shirt collar covered in blood from where the glass of the frame had cut into the back of his neck brought the pistol back up, aiming at Marlowe, who, changing target now, dove directly at him, spearing the larger man in his midsection, the two of them going down, both struggling to gain control of the pistol.

The pistol fired, once. Staggering back, blood oozing from his chest, the burly man stared in horror, before collapsing beside the bed.

Marlowe turned to tracksuit guy now, the pistol spinning to aim at him now, but the man had already risen, having picked up his fallen blade, holding it to Kate's throat as he pulled her up as a shield.

'Drop it or I waste her!' he cried out in desperation.

Marlowe watched him for a moment, then glanced at Kate.

'Do it,' he replied casually. 'I don't care.'

If the track-suited man had expected an answer, this definitely wasn't it, as he waved the blade more threateningly.

'I'm serious, man!' he cried out, licking his lips, glancing around the room, looking for ways out of this—

He didn't get the chance to do anything else. Kate rammed her heel down hard onto his foot, the stiletto heel having nothing to block this except for trainer material. It obviously hurt a lot, and the man screamed, letting her go—

That was all Marlowe needed, as he fired one shot, point blank into the track-suit top, the man falling down beside his partner.

There was a moment of calm and tranquillity in the room, but this was soon broken by Kate shouting.

'*Do* it?'

Marlowe was moving over to the bed, checking under the discarded pillows with a groan. The gun he'd placed there earlier was gone.

'You work for the Security Services,' he replied. 'I assumed you could look after yourself. You know, field training and all that.'

Kate grumbled as she went through the two bodies, pulling out phones, wallets, everything she could find.

'As an *analyst at GCHQ*,' she hissed. 'Not a bloody spook.'

'Sorry,' Marlowe apologised sheepishly, as he picked up the hotel room phone, pressing a button.

'Don't call the police!' Kate rose at this. 'How are you going to explain this?'

Marlowe looked back at the bodies, fallen beside the bed.

'The guy in the tracksuit, he gave one of Senator Kyle's agents an envelope of money,' he explained. 'I thought it was a press thing, or an asset gathering thing, but considering they just tried to kill us, I'm now wondering if it's more than that.'

He growled as he listened to the receiver.

'Get me the Presidential Suite,' he said. 'Yes, it's bloody important.'

Kate picked up a pillow, pulling the case off it, throwing the phones, wallets, and keys she'd found into her makeshift sack. After a few moments, Marlowe slammed the phone down.

'No answer,' he said. 'There would be an answer.'

He finally noticed Kate's new accessory.

'What are you doing?'

'Gathering intel,' Kate shrugged. 'As I said, I'm an analyst. We analyse things. Do you have anything in the room safe?'

'No, I've barely had time to unpack,' Marlowe shook his head.

'Good. Grab your bag,' Kate was already moving towards the door.

'Why?' Marlowe grabbed the bag, taking one last look at the two dead assassins.

'Because you're not coming back,' Kate finished as she moved into the corridor. 'Come on, let's go check on your Senator.'

THE MOMENT THEY ARRIVED AT THE DOOR TO THE Presidential Suite, Marlowe knew something was wrong.

It was quiet.

'The hotel should lock down by now,' he said as he looked down the corridor, back to the elevators. 'Two gunshots, people must have heard.'

'They'll go check first,' Kate had paused beside the door, holding the pillow bag filled with items like it was some kind of cosh. 'Only when they find the bodies would they call the police. Or, with a hotel filled with spooks, probably someone from the CIA or NSA.'

Marlowe pushed at the door before knocking, and wasn't surprised to find that it opened. The lock to the side, the simple card reader that you placed a hotel room card against was broken.

'Shit,' he said, checking the gun as he entered. There were four bullets in the chamber, and he'd fired twice already. If this was Ford, then he'd only need one clear shot to take him down – but he'd have rather had more bullets.

He'd rather have his own gun if he was being honest.

The hallway to the suite was empty, and there was no sound to be heard.

No. Scratch that.

There was a faint, wheezing breath from the main living area. Marlowe demonstrated quietly to Kate to stick with him as he slid into the main room—

To see Senator Kyle, her chest seeped in blood, lying on the floor.

She wasn't dead; the bullet wound was high, and to the right. But she was bleeding badly, and without medical attention soon wouldn't be here for long.

'Call an ambulance,' Marlowe said, kneeling beside her. 'Kyle, can you hear me?'

But Senator Kyle was unconscious, her breathing laboured.

'This is recent,' Marlowe said as he looked back at Kate, now picking up the phone. 'You need—'

The gunshot was loud; the glass pitcher beside his head exploding was louder. Marlowe spun to see Ford, a gun in his hand, aiming at him, drawing a bead on his next shot. Marlowe fired back, diving behind the sofa as bullets *spanged* into the wooden frame, cursing himself as he did so.

Ford hadn't been paid to give information. They had paid Ford to kill his boss.

Marlowe knew that there was at least one small silver lining to his current predicament; Ford must have aimed high by accident, or maybe Kyle moved as he shot her, or the wound wasn't a kill shot. He probably waited to see if anyone heard the weapon, and was about to move in for the kill when Marlowe arrived. Which was shitty timing on Marlowe's part, but at the same time damned lucky for Senator Kyle, who was currently being ignored by her assassin.

Or the plan was to wait until Marlowe turned up, and then kill them both, blaming him for the murder.

Marlowe decided that, although probably the most likely, he really didn't like that one.

The newer problem, though, was that Kate hadn't finished her call, and had dived for cover the moment Ford arrived.

Ford had also realised she was there, and had turned to shoot at her instead, as Marlowe rose quickly, firing into Ford's back. However, Ford must have heard him and spun around again, because the bullet didn't hit its mark, and Ford returned his attention to Marlowe, firing the gun again. As Marlowe instinctively ducked, tossing the now empty pistol at Ford in an act of desperation, he felt the bullet whistle past his ear. He had the sofa in between him and his attacker, and he knew the moment he tried to vault it, he'd be caught with another bullet – but Kate, picking up the phone from the table, slammed it into the back of Ford's head with a scream of rage.

Ford stumbled, the gun falling from his hand – there was

something wrong with the motion, something fake, or rather deliberate, but Marlowe didn't consider this as he now jumped the sofa, diving for the gun, grabbing it by the grip and bringing it up—

But Ford was gone, the door to the Presidential Suite swinging open.

'Dammit!' Marlowe snapped. He went to rise, to chase after him – only to find Kate blocking the way.

'She needs our help more,' she said, running over to Kyle, still breathing, pressing down on the wound. 'We need to put pressure on this.'

'Call the ambulance, I'll do that,' Marlowe walked over now, but Kate shook her head.

'If they weren't locking down the place, they'll do so now after the gunfight you just had,' she said. 'And currently you're holding the gun that someone used to shoot a US Senator.'

Marlowe looked down at the gun in his hand – he realised why Ford's hand had looked strange now.

The man had been wearing a latex glove. A glove to hide his fingerprints on, what Marlowe could now see clearly, was his stolen SIG Sauer, the one taken from under his pillow.

Shit. This was deliberate.

He could hear sirens now; Kate was right, and the authorities were coming.

'You need to get out of here,' he said, moving in, and gently pushing her to the side. 'They'll take me either way. This was created to throw blame on me.'

'So run!'

Marlowe shook his head.

'I'm an ex-British Secret Service agent found with a dead,

or almost dead US Senator, shot with my gun. I can't go on the run. I need to clear this.'

'They'll stick you in a black site and you'll rot in there for years!' Kate exclaimed. 'You want to clear yourself, then help me.'

Marlowe stopped, staring at Kate. In everything that had happened, he hadn't actually asked why she was there, and why she'd gone to his room.

'Why me?' he asked. 'Why did you talk to me out of everyone there?'

Kate pulled her phone out, ignoring the smears of blood she left on the screen as she showed Marlowe a single message.

FROM: WARREN LYONS

Speak to Marlowe he has the code

'What bloody code?' Marlowe shook his head. 'I didn't get anything from him!'

'Warren was here because there's a threat out in the world which could end everything, and we need to stop it,' Kate looked back at the door, before pointing back at Kyle, who, now Marlowe had been performing some battlefield dressing, was regaining a little colour. 'It's bigger than this, Marlowe. And Caliburn is behind it.'

'But Kyle—'

'Will wake up in hospital in a few hours,' Kate was pulling Marlowe now. 'And when she does, she'll tell people it was Ford who tried to kill her. You'll be cleared. But while you rot in a black site waiting for that call, Caliburn is going to set fire to the world.'

Marlowe pulled out his phone, dialling a number, hoping it was still active.

'Bloody hell, Marlowe, do you ever visit a place and not turn it into shit?' the half-amused, half-concerned voice of Trix Preston echoed through the speaker.

'I'm being set up,' he replied.

'Oh, so it's a Tuesday,' Trix's voice had a touch of sarcasm to it now. 'We've got gunshots in the Presidential Suite. That you?'

'And the ones in my room,' Marlowe looked back out of the door, towards the elevators. 'I need an exit strategy, and fast.'

'Dude, I can't—'

'Dammit, Trix, I'm being set up for the attempted murder of a US Senator!' Marlowe hissed. 'Do you want me to be taken by Curtis?'

'It wouldn't be Curtis,' Trix said ominously, and Marlowe could hear her working on the keyboard as she spoke. 'Okay. You're lucky, as we've just been linking to the service elevator cameras. Kyle wanted a secret meeting, and we looped some footage to make it look empty. I'll just start the loop now.'

'Who was the secret meeting with?' Marlowe glanced at Kate as he spoke.

'Sir Walter McKellan.'

'Shit,' Marlowe placed his SIG Sauer into his duffel, still beside the doorway from where he'd dropped it when entering. 'I didn't realise McKellan was here as well.'

He couldn't help noticing that on the utterance of the surname, Kate froze, her expression turning into one of fear.

'Just get out, you have about a minute before someone works out it's a loop,' Trix replied. 'The carriage shows an empty area, but there's a jump in the numbers as it moves up them. Someone will notice if they watch it long enough.'

'You're a star, Trix.'

'Lose this number, Marlowe.'

Marlowe disconnected, now looking back at Kate.

'I don't have a car, and I can't stay in the hotel. I've got CIA, NSA, FBI, MI5, MI6 and rogue agents now after me. So, unless *you* have a car—'

Kate rummaged in the pillowcase, pulling out a car key fob.

'I don't, but the guy in the suit who tried to kill you did,' she said. 'It's probably in the car park.'

Marlowe glanced back at Senator Kyle and swore to himself.

'Come on,' he said, pulling her away to the elevators. 'Trix will make sure they get medics up here, while we get to the car park through the service elevators.'

The service elevators, used mainly by staff for maintenance and cleaning were through a set of double doors, and as Marlowe and Kate entered the now opening carriage, Marlowe saw the light on the other elevators, on the other side of the corridor and through the still open doors blink on – people, likely agents were about to arrive.

Marlowe wanted to return to the room, claim his innocence, but he knew it was a lost cause, and as the doors closed and the elevator started hurtling towards the ground floor, he leant back, into the corner of the carriage, hoping that Trix had done her magic on the CCTV, but, if she hadn't and had deliberately betrayed him, anyone looking through the CCTV camera above him would only see Kate.

'I wasn't his contact, or anything,' he said. 'I didn't know Warren would even be here.'

'I know you weren't,' Kate was irritated, watching the numbers drop on the screen as she spoke. 'I was. He saw I was being watched in the bar, went to the next option.'

Marlowe remembered Ford sitting in the hotel restaurant, while Kate was at the bar.

'Ford was watching you?'

'Had been for about an hour. But I didn't know who he sided with. Well, until now, anyway.'

'And the next best option was me?'

'Yeah, probably because he knew you,' Kate nodded. 'I've shown you the text, but I couldn't talk to you then because you were pulled to see the Senator. And by the time I could speak to you, I'd already worked out your room was being turned over.'

'Hence the warning,' Marlowe wanted to bang his head against the elevator wall. 'So, you worked with Scrapper?'

'We had similar aims.'

'Fractal Destiny.'

Kate's eyes widened, and she instinctively backed away from Marlowe.

'How did you know—'

'The goon in the suit asked me about it. What is it?'

Kate took a moment to calm herself, but her lips were thin now, as if the conversation she was about to have was distasteful to her.

'An algorithm,' she explained. 'A series of events that, if placed in the right order, can destabilise anything, from a small corporation to a large country. Well, it's more of a neural network if I'm being brutally honest, but for lay men, it's easier to call it that.'

'Jesus.'

'The neural network changes depending on the size of the target, but there's always a set amount of steps. Caliburn developed it to help them, well, "get things moving" when they needed things to be – but they didn't realise what they had until later.'

Marlowe shook his head, instantly understanding the enormity of the situation.

'It's a kingmaker device.'

'Yeah. Any company or country that goes against them? Gone. Ultimate power. And this is something Sir Walter McKellan shouldn't have.'

'McKellan? Not Caliburn?'

Kate stared at Marlowe.

'They're the same thing,' she said. 'Your friend who sorted the CCTV, she said McKellan was going to meet with Kyle, right? That's why there was a faked footage scenario in play?'

She shook her head.

'That was in case you didn't make it to the room. McKellan shouldn't be here when MI5 is already taking point. And there's no way he'd be meeting Kyle, Karolides would have a fit. So, they did this so they could claim you still performed the act, but the footage hid you.'

As Marlowe considered this, the doors opened out to the car park, and Kate and Marlowe quickly made their way out, Kate clicking the key fob as they did so.

'How many steps in the neural network?' he asked.

'Fifteen, maybe sixteen if needed,' Kate clicked and heard a beep across the car park floor. 'But they've already activated it. Currently, we're on step six. Well, we were. The death of a high ranking political figure was step eight, so we could be there right now if Kyle dies.'

'What's the target?' Marlowe pointed at a black Mercedes Saloon car, its lights now flashing.

'The destabilisation of East and West relations, primarily in Eastern Europe, the collapse of NATO and the whole Eastern seaboard falling into nuclear fire,' Kate replied.

'Then we need to stop it.'

Kate paused beside the car.

'There is no it, Marlowe. That's the problem,' she explained. 'It's out in the air. All we can do is learn the choke points and try to divert them. Make the alternatives too large for the neural network to work.'

Marlowe turned to face the analyst, a slow realisation moving across his face.

'That's why you worked with Tooley.'

'He was the one that learned it was running. He made a virtual copy and hid it somewhere, but then he dropped off the radar. I came here to find him.'

'But Warren Lyons needed to pass you the data first.'

Kate nodded, looking to the ground as she did so.

'Yeah,' she replied sadly. 'He didn't give you anything, did he? Say anything?'

Marlowe thought back to the meeting.

'We spoke, he mentioned Tooley, which was odd, because he acted like we were old friends, but I don't think I've ever met the man. He even mentioned a prosthetic arm, but it didn't ring any bells.'

Marlowe paused, remembering.

'There was one odd thing. He said, "Remember, Marlowe – the truth is always in the clouds", before he ran.'

'The truth is in the clouds?' Kate was climbing into the passenger seat of the car now, as Marlowe tossed his duffel into the back seat, before sitting in the driver's seat. 'Then what?'

Marlowe pressed a button, hearing the engine start up. It was a soft purr, and Marlowe felt a little more at ease. In a car, he could escape. In a car, he could gain distance on his enemies – whoever they were.

'Then he congratulated me and left, heading to his death,' he finished sadly, as he pushed the car into Drive, and started out of the car park, leaving the hotel, his fellow agents, and a close-to-death US Senator behind.

6

SPECIAL OPS

Curtis hadn't expected anyone from MI6 to appear on what was obviously a Whitehall mission. He also hadn't expected them to take over a mission in the middle of an operation.

But, the one thing he really hadn't expected was to find that Sir Walter McKellan had created a fully operational Ops room in a business suite on the second floor of the hotel.

'About time you arrived,' McKellan said as Curtis entered, looking around in confusion. For a simple hotel suite, this now looked like James Bond's wet dream.

They had placed banks of computer screens up on racks against the wall, the boardroom table moved to the side to support them, the remaining space filled with desks, with operatives unknown to Curtis working on even more laptops, ignoring McKellan as he approached.

Sixties, old school British and straight from the cover of a Le Carré novel, everyone knew McKellan to be a vicious looking, lean man in a tailored suit. He'd been MI6 for most of his career, starting off in the military, but no matter how hard he had tried, Curtis hadn't been able to pierce the veil on where he'd served.

Which meant nasty shit. Black ops shit from an early age.

So god knows how bad he is now, Curtis thought.

He'd only been within McKellan's radar since they had promoted him to Harris's old job, and so far, whenever MI5 and MI6 had been commanded to play nice with each other, he'd decided he wasn't really a fan of the man. And, that McKellan was here either showed a lack of faith in Curtis, or a knowledge of something worse to happen that hadn't been passed down the line.

On one screen was CNN news, showing a video of Senator Kyle. It was archive footage, showing a strong woman in her late fifties waving to a crowd.

'... As the Democrats and Republicans both face a tough midterm, with voters expressing distrust with their elected representatives, Republican Arizona Senator Maureen Kyle has asked for more transparency within governmental departments ...'

Curtis winced. The news cycle would change rapidly the moment it was released that Kyle was now the target of a botched assassination attempt.

On another screen was the CCTV footage of the hotel's lobby and the edge of the open bar area.

'It looks like you started without me, sir,' Curtis replied, keeping his tone polite, even if he wanted to scream at the meddling older man. 'What's going on?'

McKellan, in response, looked over at one of the people at the laptops, a young woman, no older than Trix, over-ear headphones half on her head.

'We're hunting the man you let die on your watch,' he

said, pointing at a screen. There, walking into the lobby, was the late Warren Lyons.

'We're not hunting Marlowe?' Curtis was surprised.

'We're MI6,' McKellan said, with more than a hint of irritation. 'We can multitask, unlike your people at Box. But it's all connected.'

He looked back at the woman.

'What do you have?'

In response, she shrugged.

'Nothing. Sorry.'

McKellan moved closer to the screen, peering at it.

'What do you mean, nothing?'

'I mean literally nothing. It's not on him, inside him ... if Lyons had the data, it's gone.'

'What data?' Curtis asked, feeling as if he'd missed a briefing or two.

'Above your pay grade,' McKellan didn't even look at him as he spoke, still watching the screen.

'So she can know and I, the London Section Chief, can't?'

McKellan now turned to stare at Curtis, and it wasn't a good stare.

'Listen to you, saying words like they mean something,' he sneered. 'London Section Chief. You're not even Deputy Director level, Mister Curtis. When you are, then come and tell me what to do, okay?'

He looked around.

'How's *your* tech girl?' he asked cordially, but with a fake smile on his lips. 'She helped Kyle's assassin escape. You know that, right?'

'First, I don't know what you mean, and second, last I heard, Kyle was still alive.'

'For the moment,' McKellan looked back to the woman, who had raised her hand.

'You don't have to raise your hand, Hill.'

Hill, reddening, forwarded through the footage, and on the screen Lyons moved faster through the lobby.

'Now, we know our men got there around ... here. See?' Hill paused the tape. On the screen, in the corner, they could see the two agents entering the lobby.

'That girl,' McKellan pointed at a brunette at the bar. 'She's watching him. She looks familiar, too.'

'She's not the one. Watch.'

On the screen, they watched Lyons pause, turn and then walk into Marlowe.

'There's his contact,' McKellan said, as he looked at Curtis. 'Tom Marlowe. Here on the request of the US Government. The man you burnt, and who killed Lyons.'

'No sir,' Curtis shook his head. 'We have footage showing him in the elevator to Senator Kyle at the same time.'

'Was this from Miss Preston? The woman who also faked the footage in the service elevator?' McKellan replied, his voice close to a growl now.

'If I recall, sir, that footage was doctored for your visit later.'

'One I now won't be making because of Marlowe.'

The door opened, and Curtis saw Casey enter the room, Trix beside him.

'I didn't call you,' he said, confused as to their arrival.

'I did,' McKellan replied, nodding at Casey. 'I've decided Mister Casey will be temporarily seconded to MI6 to work on damage control on a top-secret joint-ops command I've just created to head, while the two of you return to London.'

Before Curtis could say anything, though, Hill looked up from her monitor.

'Lyons sent a single text to a burner phone shortly before he was caught. It read "Speak to Marlowe", so I think we can confirm he's working with him.'

'I can't believe that,' Curtis shook his head again, thinking back to the meeting earlier that day. 'We confronted him on this, even gave him a get out, said it might have been passed to him without his knowledge. But he had nothing. We gave him a night to consider it, offered him a way back into Box.'

'And he then went off books and shot a Senator,' McKellan muttered. 'That doesn't look good on you.'

'Only if he did it,' Trix argued. 'And I'm still not sure about that. Kyle could recover, and if she does, she can ID the killer.'

McKellan turned to stare at Trix, his expression unreadable.

'Did I ask the kiddie corner for opinions?' he enquired mockingly. 'How about you keep quiet until you're old enough to drink?'

Trix reddened at the insult, but Curtis stepped forward.

'Preston has a point about the Senator,' he said.

'Sure,' McKellan mocked. 'But to do that, she has to survive.'

Hill motioned her hand again to gain the attention of the two men, but quickly dropped it.

'You were right, we found the woman,' she said. 'Kate Maybury. GCHQ, but in the London Office.'

McKellan turned back to Curtis.

'Does your woman know where he went?'

'My woman?' Curtis was appalled. 'Do you, by chance, mean my associate?'

'I'm right here,' Trix said icily. 'Or don't you speak to people still young enough to do their job well?'

McKellan didn't reply, instead just sniffing with irritation as Curtis held a hand up.

'Look, sir, I don't think Preston here would have compromised her—'

'You worked with him in Wintergreen's team, right? And then came with him to New York?' McKellan sneered at Trix before looking back at her superior. 'Please, tell me what else you don't think Trixibelle Preston would do.'

'I wouldn't work for Caliburn,' Trix muttered. 'Unlike some people in this room.'

Before McKellan could reply, Curtis turned to her.

'That's enough,' he retorted. 'Go get your things, we leave on the next flight.'

'But, sir—'

'That's enough!' Curtis snapped. 'I don't want you doing anymore off-the-books deals. Get your things and wait for my call.'

He looked back at McKellan who, enjoying what he saw, just shrugged, turning back to Hill, pointing at Marlowe as he did so, currently on the CCTV.

'If he's in the hotel, I want him,' he snarled. 'If he's not, I want to know where he is, and how we can intercept him before the bloody Yanks do.'

McKellan glared at Curtis for a long moment, while Casey turned away, finding something else to look at rather than being involved in the unfolding scene.

'You and your *woman* can go home while I fix this bloody mess,' he said. 'Preferably before the Republican Senator for Arizona dies of gunshot wounds.'

THE CAR HAD EXITED THE CAR PARK WITHOUT ANY ISSUES, AND Marlowe kept the route he was driving at random, heading away from the busier parts of the city.

Kate, sitting beside him, was listening to one of the phones.

'What are you doing?' he asked, glancing briefly to the side.

In response, Kate looked at the wallet in the other hand, checking the ID.

'I'm listening to mister ... Foster ... that's the guy who wore the suit jacket – I'm listening to his voicemails.'

'Why?'

Kate disconnected the call.

'Because I want to know who he was, and who he worked for,' she explained.

They drove in silence for a moment before Kate continued.

'Were they your first? The men in the hotel room. You know, with the gun.'

Marlowe shook his head.

'Unfortunately not,' he said. 'Recently it's become a bit of a habit, as weird as that sounds.'

He went to continue, but something in Kate's demeanour stopped him. She'd started listening to the other phone, and her expression was now one of cold fury.

'Tracksuit guy got this yesterday,' she said, turning the phone onto speaker. 'This is in his voicemails.'

A voice spoke out through the speakers; a British accent.

'Tooley's getting skittish, acting odd,' it said, the voice

unemotional and detached, as if ordering food. 'Get rid of him.'

Kate was already tapping on the screen, bringing up the car's sat nav system. Once up, she scrolled through the addresses. She stopped at the second one.

'What's Mount Tamalpais?' she asked.

'A forest reserve or something a few hours north, I think,' Marlowe furrowed his brows as he thought. 'I saw it on a map as I drove from LA.'

'There's a pinned location in the sat nav. Last night around midnight, this car, Mister Foster's car, stopped there, at the Rock Spring Trailhead, off Ridgecrest Boulevard. Half an hour later, it returns to San Francisco.'

'Midnight?' Marlowe glanced across. 'A drive to the middle of nowhere only to return? That doesn't sound ominous at all.'

Kate was still going through the second phone, but paused in horror as a video started showing.

'He filmed it,' she whispered.

'Filmed what?'

Kate shook her head.

'Not while you're driving,' she breathed, almost a sob. 'But there's a video here of Brian Tooley in a grave, in the middle of the night.'

She was watching it, the light from the screen illuminating her horrified face, but as Marlowe was driving, all he could hear were the words spoken.

'I'll show you how the algorithm works! I could explain everything to you! If you knew, you could make millions!'

'You ... you know already, don't you?'

'Tell them I'm sorry ...'

There was the sound of a silenced pistol, and Kate turned off the video, placing it in her lap as she looked out of the window.

'They shot him,' she said.

Marlowe stared ahead, frowning.

'He said he'd show them,' he said. 'Not explain, not tell. He'd *show* them.'

'You can't show an algorithm,' Kate argued. 'Not unless you have it to hand.'

'But they'd have searched him before burying him, surely,' Marlowe glanced at her.

Kate bit at her lip as she stared off.

'Did Lyons tell you anything else?'

'Lots of secrets to play with, keep under the skin, you know?'

'Yeah,' Marlowe replied, remembering. 'He said he dealt with secrets, kept under the skin.'

'Under the skin ... inside his arm? The fake one? He's still wearing it in the video.'

'Maybe we should go look,' Marlowe nodded at the sat nav. 'Let's check the last location he was seen.'

Kate pressed the most recent journey on the sat nav, and the directions to the Rock Spring Trailhead came up.

'It's a couple of hours,' she said. 'And it's late in the night.'

'You have a better time for digging up bodies?' Marlowe kept his eyes on the road. 'Because I don't.'

'Okay then,' Kate settled back into the seat. 'So, what do you want to talk about for the next couple of hours?'

'Actually,' Marlowe's face was dark and brooding. 'I'd really like you to tell me everything Scrapper Lyons ever told you about Brian Tooley.'

It was almost midnight by the time they reached the empty parking lot off Ridgecrest Boulevard. The wind had picked up, and there was a threat of rain, but currently the sky was cloudy, but dry.

'This is where the sat nav said they stopped,' Kate peered out of the windscreen. 'Actually, no, that path there.'

The "path" was a single dirt track that led for another half a mile, arriving at a clearing, the road stopping as if someone had simply built a track for vehicles and then, after a while simply decided they couldn't be bothered anymore.

Kate stared out into the headlights-lit landscape.

'I think it matches the video,' she said as Marlowe, turning off the engine but keeping the lights on, climbed out of the car, standing in the windswept night.

'We really are in the middle of nowhere,' he muttered. 'No wonder they thought it was a great place to hide a body. I wonder how many others are buried around here?'

'Let's see what Mister Foster has in the boot,' Kate said, popping the rear of the car and, as it opened, reaching in and pulling out a shovel.

Taking it, Marlowe moved away from the car, staying in the lit area as he walked around, examining the ground.

'Now, if I was burying a body, where would I ...'

He paused, looking at a small cairn of stones.

Kate walked over as he stared down.

'That looks like a hastily filled in grave to me,' she said. 'You want to start?'

Nodding, Marlowe dug into the ground, as Kate moved away some of the larger stones.

'How well did you know him?' she asked as she did this. 'Lyons?'

'Not well. I mean, we were in the Royal Marines together,

but it wasn't *Band of Brothers* or anything,' Marlowe admitted. 'Until he bumped into me in the lobby, he hadn't crossed my mind in years.'

He carried on digging now, finding the ground easy to dig into, a sure sign someone had been here before, turning over the soil in the exact same spot.

Kate had stopped asking questions, perhaps because the severity of the situation had finally hit her.

And, after about ten minutes of digging, Marlowe paused as the shovel hit in against something.

'Hold on,' he said as, in the light of the car beams, he crouched to his knees and scrabbled in the dirt.

After a moment, part of a suited arm was found in the shallow grave, the rest of the body still buried.

'Is it the left one?' Kate asked. 'That's the fake one.'

Nodding, Marlowe leant in and, taking hold, pulled harder at the arm. After a struggle, it came free in his hands, the sleeve around it falling off as he pulled it away.

'Got it,' he said, staring down at it. It was modern, a multi-grip myoelectric prosthesis with what looked to be a fully functional robot hand on the end, far from the basic hook hands films like The Fugitive showed back in the nineties.

'Jesus, that's some Star Trek level shit right there,' Marlowe said, turning the prosthesis in his hands. 'You get this level on the NHS?'

'Actually, I think you get close these days,' Kate nodded. 'And people now customise them with 3D printers. It's incredible.'

'You can say that again.'

'Okay, now we have it, let's get out of here,' Kate pulled at Marlowe's arm in turn.

However, Marlowe didn't move, now staring back at the

grave where, under the dirt, were the remains of Brian Tooley.

'We should call MI5, or GCHQ, whoever he worked for,' he said. 'Let them know about this.'

'The moment we do, Caliburn knows,' Kate shook her head. 'We can tell them the moment we've stopped the bad guys. How's that?'

'It'll have to do,' Marlowe stared down at the body.

Kate stood awkwardly to the side.

'If you want to say some words or something ...' Marlowe let the words trail off.

However, Kate shook her head.

'He was a humanist, I think,' she said. 'I don't think he'd want me speaking words over him.'

Marlowe stood up silently, the arm still in his hand.

'I saw a motel a mile or so back,' Kate said, pointing back the way they'd come. 'We should see if we can get a room until the morning. But first we'll need to make a stop.'

'Why?'

Kate pursed her lips.

'If Kyle died, then I reckon the entire country's law enforcement is probably after us now,' she said. 'We need to go shopping.'

Nodding at the wiseness of the suggestion, Marlowe tossed the shovel back into the car's boot, closing it down before climbing back into the driver's seat.

And, with Kate sliding in next to him, he reversed the car back down the dirt track, away from the disturbed body of Brian Tooley.

He hadn't reburied the body, because at some point soon, he'd tell people where to find it, and the man could have a proper burial.

When that would be, however, Marlowe had no idea.

All he cared about right now was making it through to the morning without being captured, or killed.

7

OPEN ALL NIGHT

THE ROMANTICALLY NAMED *STARLIGHT INN* WAS A TYPICAL rest-stop motel, composed mainly of a car park with three sides of chalets, allowing the residents of the chalets to park in front of the one they'd rented for the night. It was cheap, uniform, and undistinguishable from a million other such motels across America, except for the fact that Foster's hired car was now parked outside chalet number nine.

Inside the chalet, Marlowe was in the bathroom, shirtless, working on his beard with a shaver. He'd liked his beard; it was something he never really had while in the service, but he'd really let it go of late, and now, using the shaver from his duffel, he was trimming it down to a way-more manageable length, while also removing the "hipster" impression he'd been giving of late. He'd also worked on the back of his hair, using the trimming tool to bring it down into a shorter cut. It was a good cut – not because he was a secret hairdresser, but because he'd done this so many times while on a mission before.

Sometimes you have to grow your hair out for this very

cause; a drastic cut after a mission success would be the easiest way to instantly change your appearance, and it was easier to cut hair than to suddenly grow it.

They'd arrived shortly before one in the morning, giving a sob story of a flat tyre causing a break in the journey and a very early start the following day. The night manager hadn't cared, and was more than happy to take cash for the room. Marlowe didn't even think they'd been entered into the visitors' book, which made sense. The management had probably left already, wouldn't be back until midmorning, and by then the guests would be gone. Nobody would be the wiser, and the night manager had a hundred bucks in his pocket.

They'd stopped at an all-night store before arriving though and had bought hair dye for Kate and some food and drink for the pair of them. Marlowe hadn't eaten since the journey from LA, and Kate claimed she'd only arrived from the UK that day, and her only food had been an economy-flight meal. So, they'd gathered some items, and then bought take out from a twenty-four-hour drive-through burger joint on the Panoramic Highway.

It might have been the adrenaline pulsing through his body, but Marlowe had never eaten a better tasting burger.

Emerging from the bathroom, he looked across the motel bedroom at Kate. She was in a vest, a towel around her head, drying her now-dyed-black hair, while staring down at the stolen prosthetic arm resting on the top of her bed.

'I had a look at it while you were in there,' he said, nodding his head at the bathroom. 'I couldn't see anything on it.'

Pausing her hair drying, Kate placed the towel down and picked up the arm, turning it around in her hands.

'Tooley wouldn't simply scrawl on it in marker,' she said,

looking back at Marlowe with a smile. 'Trimming the beard makes you look younger.'

'Younger? I'm in my thirties,' Marlowe growled.

Kate grinned.

'Oh,' she replied with mock concern.

Marlowe shook his head at this.

'Well, now I feel way older,' he muttered. 'So, why did you join Caliburn?'

'I didn't,' Kate placed the arm back down, turning her attention to the shirtless man in front of her. 'I joined a group of people to share ideas after university. They didn't tell me that Caliburn, or at least a sub caucus of Caliburn, funded it. And when I left and moved to Whitehall, I was already under their watchful gaze.'

She spat the last words, as if they were distasteful to her.

'And Warren Lyons?'

'We talked, became friends. When he learned about the neural network, he came to me with his concerns.'

She looked back at his bare chest.

'Do they hurt?' she asked, and Marlowe had to look down to work out what she meant.

The warmth of the shower had reddened the puckered skin his bullet wounds had given to him almost a year earlier. At the start, they were all he could think of, but now he barely noticed them, even when more visible than usual.

'More of an itch,' he said. 'A reminder they're there, you know?'

'Had you been shot before them?'

'Grazed, but nothing serious,' Marlowe walked over to the bed now, picking up and examining the arm. 'This was my wake-up call, I suppose.'

He stopped, looking at her.

'How did you know they were all at the same time?'

'They've healed the same,' Kate reddened. 'Older ones wouldn't have puckered as much under the water. I might have been checking you – *them* – out.'

Marlowe chuckled as he clicked the arm back, exposing the hydraulics inside. Kate watched him as he stared into the mechanisms.

'Do you want some alone time?' she asked, amused.

'Secrets under the skin,' Marlowe replied. 'That's what Scrapper told me: "Lots of secrets to play with, keep under the skin". Maybe it was more than a slang phrase?'

He pressed a lever inside the hinge mount.

'There's a hinge, or some kind of catch here that does nothing,' he explained, working at it. 'It's not that big and—'

He stopped as it broke off in his hand.

'Oh, well done,' Kate shook her head.

'I think it was meant to do that.' Placing the rest of the arm down, he concentrated his attention on the fake metal hydraulic hinge. Then, after a moment, he realised it was screwed together, and pulled his penknife out of his duffel and began unscrewing it. Eventually, he pulled the top off the fake hinge, pulling out a piece of paper.

'That's not usual for a fake arm,' Kate took the offered paper, opening it up and looking at it. 'It's an address in Paris. A security box and the access code to get into it.'

'So we go to Paris,' Marlowe rubbed at his chin, already working on the problem.

'Be serious,' Kate snapped back. 'We're on the West Coast of America and we're wanted for treason by now. How the hell are we going to Paris?'

Marlowe went back to his duffel, dropping the penknife

back in, and pulling out a box. In it was a recently bought pay-as-you-go burner phone, still in its wrapping.

'I call a friend and see if I can get a lift,' he said.

HILL WAS STILL AT HER DESK, TIRED, GOING THROUGH TRAFFIC camera footage in five-second bursts, in the same way someone would look if they were clicking through TV channels.

Click. *No.*

Click. *Not there.*

Click.

Suddenly, she stopped.

Frowning, she clicked back to the previous channel.

On the screen was the car – the one Marlowe had been seen driving out of the hotel in. They'd lost it in San Francisco, but now, on a freeway north, the licences matched and they had him again.

'You beauty,' she said to the screen as she woke up, clicking buttons, following the car as it made its journey through the night suburbia of northern San Francisco.

Without looking away from the monitor, as if scared it'd disappear the moment she diverted attention, she waved her arm to attract the attention of one of the other MI6 officers, also staring at their laptop screens. Eventually, one looked over at her.

'What?'

'Get McKellan! Now!' Hill cried. 'I have him.'

Rising quickly, the officer ran out of the room as Hill carried on clicking cameras, stalking the car on her screen.

Eventually, rubbing his eyes, woken from sleep, McKellan entered.

'Report,' he grumbled.

'The car they stole was licenced to a Mister Foster,' Hill nodded at the monitor screen.

'Never heard of him. Should I have?'

Hill shrugged.

'Until we find him, I don't know,' she said. 'However, I just found Foster's hire car. They're north of the Golden Gate Bridge, a few miles into Marin County on the Panoramic Highway. Looks like they've gone to ground in a motel.'

Now awake, McKellan stared at the screen.

'Raise a team,' he ordered. 'I want them picked up before dawn.'

'Sir, dawn's in a couple of hours.'

McKellan glared down at Hill.

'Then you'd better hurry,' he said, a hint of anger mixed with sarcasm in his voice. 'And check the police bands.'

'Sir?'

McKellan was already walking to the door.

'Because I don't want the local plod catching Marlowe first,' he growled.

'YOU HAVE SOME NERVE CALLING ME,' THE VOICE OF SASHA Bordeaux said down the phone. Or, rather, the voice of the CIA chief who called herself that, as *Sasha Bordeaux* was a comic book character.

'Didn't have a choice,' Marlowe said, staring out of the motel room window. 'Thanks for taking the call. How's Kyle?'

'Senator Kyle is in the ICU,' Sasha replied. 'She's in an induced coma after you apparently shot her.'

'It wasn't me,' Marlowe shook his head, aware Sasha couldn't see the action. 'It was her agent, Ford.'

'With your gun?' Sasha's voice was incredulous. 'The same SIG Sauer you've used before?'

'That was taken from my room,' Marlowe argued. 'I think by either a man named Foster, or one named ...'

He checked the other wallet.

'... Peters.'

'Foster and Peters,' Sasha repeated. 'And how do we find them?'

'Shouldn't be hard, I left them both dead in my room,' Marlowe replied, perhaps a little too flippantly. 'It was self-defence, Sasha. I didn't attack the Senator.'

There was a long pause down the line, and for a moment Marlowe wondered if the call had disconnected.

'In your room.'

It was said as a statement rather than a question.

'Yeah. Why?'

'Marlowe, they went through your room with a fine-tooth comb the moment you ran,' Sasha replied. 'They found nothing. There's nothing out of place there. No bodies, no bullet holes, nothing.'

Marlowe felt a slight *whooshing* noise in his ears, and he instinctively grabbed at the back of a chair to keep himself upright.

'That's not possible,' he said. 'Sasha, I swear to you. I fought and killed two men in that room. We took their IDs. Their weapons. They were there!'

The last part was almost shouted, and Marlowe had to force himself to calm down.

'We?'

'I have a GCHQ analyst with me,' Marlowe said carefully. He really didn't want to give away too much here. 'She's being hunted, too.'

'What do you need?' Sasha eventually asked.

'Do you believe me?'

'Actually, and surprisingly, yes,' Sasha said. 'You're a dick, Marlowe, but you're an honest one. And the fact you have a woman in need with you, who you're obviously helping, ticks all your white knight boxes. So, you get one lifeline. What's it to be?'

'I need to get to Paris,' Marlowe said.

'Marlowe, there are better and nearer countries with non-extradition treaties—'

'Fractal Destiny.'

The two words immediately paused Sasha.

'Oh, so you have heard of it. Good.' Marlowe shifted the phone as he continued. 'This is all connected to that, Sasha. It's started. And the answer is in Paris.'

'Stay near this phone,' Sasha sighed. 'I'll see what I can do. But this is off books, yeah? CIA isn't helping you. And this is only because you did me a solid in New York.'

'I appreciate it,' Marlowe said, disconnecting the call. He hadn't realised it, but he'd been holding his breath during the call, and his chest was tight. Forcing himself to relax, he tried some deep breathing exercises.

Senator Kyle wasn't dead.

That was good news, at least.

After a couple of long minutes, there was a beep from his phone, and Marlowe stared down at it with a smile. Sasha Bordeaux worked fast because the message was from her.

Get to San Rafael Airport by 7am ask for
Steve Trevor

Marlowe grinned. Steve Trevor was yet another DC character.

'Hey, do you know San Rafael Airport?' he shouted to Kate, now in the bathroom.

'I think it's about half an hour north,' she said. 'About thirty miles. Why?'

'We need to be there for seven,' Marlowe looked at his watch. It was almost five am now.

Kate was in the bathroom, her shirt back on, using the trimmer part of Marlowe's shaver to work on her black hair. It was almost done, but incredibly rough. Marlowe walked over to her, taking the razor from her hand.

'Here, let me do that,' he said, looking at Kate through the mirror.

'You think you can do better?'

Marlowe grinned, stepping back to examine her handiwork.

'Looking at this? I know I can.'

Carefully, he pulled back her vest, exposing her neck as he worked on the hair, the clipper taking off thin shavings of hair from each pass, slowly shaping the back of it. As he did this, he thought with a smile how doing someone else's hair was much easier than doing his own.

Kate, meanwhile, was blushing a little, the blood rising to her cheeks and shivering slightly as the edge of Marlowe's hand touched her neck.

He paused as he traced his finger along a small white scar on the back of her neck.

'Your scar looks like a flower,' he said.

'It is a flower,' Kate nodded. 'But it's not a scar.'

She turned to look at him.

'It's a black-light tattoo,' she explained. 'Invisible under regular lighting and only appears under UV light because of the fluorescent compounds in the ink.'

'Looks like an orchid,' Marlowe stroked the tattoo again; it was only an inch in length.

As he said this, though, Kate tensed.

'How did you know that?' she asked. 'It's not that great a sketch.'

Marlowe flushed.

'Arachnis,' he replied. 'It's the name of my Dad's company. *Estranged* Dad. Whatever. Anyway, I looked into what the name meant, and learnt it was part of the Orchid family, although it's named because the flowers don't have bulbs, and are thought to resemble spiders.'

Kate relaxed at this, and he carried on cutting slowly, almost sensually, as his fingers brushed her neck softly.

'But while looking into it, I saw a lot of orchid images. It's not too hard to see it here.'

Enjoying the moment, probably for the first time in a while, she shut her eyes, relaxing.

'It's just a flower,' she said, her voice now a purr. 'Means nothing.'

Marlowe smiled. He hadn't meant to try to seduce her, but there was no denying that Kate Maybury was a beautiful woman.

There were worse things to be doing right now.

Outside the motel, two San Francisco police cars pulled into the parking lot, stopping for a moment in the entranceway, as the two men inside each peered through the windscreens.

Eventually, they nodded towards the black Mercedes, both cars now driving up to the chalet where Marlowe and Kate were staying the night.

It was approaching dawn now, though, and the sky was lightening as the lead car flicked a switch, its blue and red lights now flashing.

With the other car following suit, the two squad cars drove silently in.

As Marlowe continued to work the razor on her, Kate's hand reached back, touching his thigh. She bit her lip, flushing again as a slight moan passed her lips.

As she did this, he stopped what he was doing, the razor now resting on the sink's edge, as she now turned slowly, looking up at him.

There was no need for words. No need for subtlety.

Quietly, softly, they moved closer, their lips about to meet …

From the window, blue and red lights lit up the room, pausing them in their motion.

Kate turned from Marlowe, realising what this meant.

'Oh, shit,' she said. 'They found us.'

OUTSIDE OF THE MOTEL CHALETS, THE TWO CARS STOPPED, THE officers now jumping out of the vehicles, their guns already out, running to the motel door.

This was a bust. And nothing was going to stop them as they stopped at the door to the chalet room, nodding to each other.

Then, as one, two of the police officers used their feet to kick in the door, while the other two moved in behind them, guns aimed at the two people inside.

'Police! Freeze!' the lead officer cried. 'You're under arrest!'

8

STOWAWAYS

KATE HELD A HAND UP, PAUSING MARLOWE AS HE GRABBED HIS duffel, throwing the prosthetic arm into it with one hand as he pulled a fresh t-shirt on with the other.

'Shh,' she whispered as the noises next door could be heard. 'It's not us they're here for.'

Marlowe slowly moved to the window, pulling aside the curtain the slightest sliver to see the red and blue lights of two police cars, parked next to Foster's Mercedes, the officers now pulling out a teenaged boy, in only his underpants, his hands cuffed behind him.

'You can't do this, dude!' he screamed. 'We have rights!'

Marlowe looked back at Kate, already pulling her jacket on. With her black hair in a bob, and with a pair of thick-rimmed glasses on, she looked nothing like the woman he'd arrived with. His hair was shorter, his beard thinner, but Marlowe also knew how to shift his stance to look shorter, to adjust his gait to give the impression of an older man.

The police might not be for them, but at the same time, it

wouldn't be long until someone realised the two strangers in room nine were driving a car used in a murder.

Marlowe almost wanted to go outside and kiss the half-naked teenager. His timely arrest, as well as the second youth being pulled out, had refocused him on the mission at hand.

'We need to drop the car,' Kate said, moving to the door. 'They'll use it to find us.'

'You want to leave now?' Marlowe was surprised. 'Why not wait until they leave?'

'Because we don't know how long it'll be,' Kate replied. 'They might have CSI turn up. Or FBI. Someone might check the car and boom, *we're* in the shit. Better to bluff it now and get out.'

'Without a car, and with a thirty-mile journey to the airport,' Marlowe pursed his lips. 'That's difficult. Any suggestions?'

Kate shrugged.

'We're in the middle of nowhere, but I've seen trucks go past on the highway,' she said. 'I reckon we can get one to the 101 and then catch a lift north. Shouldn't take more than a hour, tops, and we have that if we leave now.'

Marlowe pulled a recently bought hoodie over his head and grabbed his duffel, pausing as he looked at the window.

'You think MI6 will find us?' Kate asked.

'Oh, I don't doubt it,' Marlowe smiled. 'In fact, Sasha's probably already told them she spoke to me.'

'Then why set us up an escape if she means to turn us in?'

Marlowe walked to the window, checking out of it.

'Oh, she wants us to escape, as it'll piss off her opposites in London, and give her some drinking stories for Washington,' he said. 'And she'll give us time to get away before she lets MI6 know how we did it. She'll play the clueless card, say

MI6 didn't tell her they were running an op, so why would she go to them, all that sort of thing. She'll want to cover all bases first.'

'You sound confident about that.'

'It's what I'd do.'

Straightening, he glanced at Kate. She no longer had a pillowcase as a bag, and now used a tote bag, grabbed from the same store they'd bought the dye.

'Come on, then,' she smiled.

Opening the door, they walked out of the chalet.

One of the police officers standing outside the door looked over at them.

'Sorry to disturb you,' he said, forcing a smile as he nodded at them.

'Not a problem, early start,' Kate said, in a more than passable West Coast accent. She peered past the officer, into the room, curiosity getting to her in the same way that anyone normal and not running from the authorities would act. 'Everything alright, officer ...?'

'Wolfe, Ma'am. And it's nothing. Just some drug dealers,' Officer Wolfe replied. 'Nothing to worry about.'

Kate gave a relieved smile.

'Good, we thought we'd slept through something bad,' she said. 'Have a good day.'

'You too, ma'am,' Wolfe tipped his cap as Kate and Marlowe walked away from them, heading for the highway. As they reached the entrance, Kate saw a truck approaching and held out her hand, waving it down.

As it stopped beside her, the driver leant out of the window, noting the police in the parking lot, the lights still flashing.

'Everything okay?' he asked.

'Yeah, we're surviving,' Marlowe stepped forward. 'Bastards stole our car. Police caught them before they could get others, but now we're screwed and late for our flight.'

'I'm not heading that way,' the driver gave a regretful look.

'Could you at least take us to the 101?' Kate asked. 'We can grab an Uber from there.'

'I can do that,' the driver opened the door. 'Come on up. It's only ten, fifteen minutes.'

'Thanks!' Kate exclaimed with delight as they climbed into the cab of the truck. And, after the two of them got settled into their seats, the driver nodded, took one last glance at the police outside the chalets, and started forward again.

As the truck left, Officer Wolfe, watching the door, looked back to the entrance to the parking lot, watching the morning sunrise. It was cloudy, but the light held a kind of warmth that the officer liked, shutting his eyes, letting it warm his face.

He must have stood like that for a couple of minutes while the other officers checked the chalet for drugs, or spoke to the two teenagers in the squad car – they claimed they'd been set up, that the drugs were already in the room, but this wasn't a surprise. They always said that.

It was a few minutes more before two black SUVs pulled up in the motel car park at speed, screeching to a halt a few yards away from him.

By now, the day was moving on, the evidence was secured, the perps under arrest. Miles, one of the other officers, walked over, pointing his thumb at the new arrivals.

'What are the odds this is FBI, trying to take our bust?' he asked.

However, before Wolfe could reply, an older man in a

tweed suit jumped out, confused and furious at the same time, as he turned his gaze from the car outside number nine to the squad cars, to the officers watching him with bemusement.

'What the hell's going on?' he snapped, and Wolfe noted with a little confusion to the situation that the man spoke with an accent. Maybe British, maybe Australian. He could never tell the two apart.

'And you are?' he asked in response, noting the other suited men appearing from the SUVs. The old man showed an ID impatiently.

'McKellan, Secret Service,' he said, and although Wolfe wasn't sure he believed the man, he had an ID, and that probably meant he was real. 'Where's Marlowe?'

Wolfe frowned at this. Neither of the teenagers, nor any of the officers there, had the name Marlowe.

'Who?' he asked, looking around, noting the motel's night manager was now emerging from his office. He hadn't come out before this, probably because he didn't want the hassle of knowing what was going on, but the new arrivals had probably worried him; this wasn't the usual bust situation, after all.

'Man and a woman,' McKellan continued, making motions at his face as he spoke. 'Man had a big bushy beard, woman has mousey hair.'

'Didn't see anyone like that,' Wolfe wondered if the older man meant the couple that left a few minutes earlier, but there was something about his demeanour that made Wolfe want to take his time giving the answer.

McKellan, obviously not believing this, started pointing at the black Mercedes out front.

'They came in that,' he continued. 'Which chalet?'

Now it was the night manager who spoke.

'Number nine,' he said, pointing at the door beside the police officer.

'And you didn't see anyone leave?'

'Well, sure,' the officer replied uncertainly now, looking at Miles for support. 'But the guy had a small beard, only stubble, really, and the woman had black hair.'

'Lord, give me strength,' McKellan moaned, looking back at the night manager. 'Key. Now.'

Fumbling at the ring of keys on his belt, the night manager held up a single key. And, at McKellan's insistence, he opened up the door, stepping back from it as McKellan waved to one of his agents to enter the room.

'If they didn't leave by the car, how did they leave?' McKellan growled.

'By foot, I think,' Wolfe replied, wishing he'd paid more attention.

'Where?'

'Over there, to the entrance,' Wolfe continued. 'I think they hitched a ride.'

'You *think?*' McKellan, furious, punched the wall in anger, cradling his hand as the agent who went into the chalet returned, a car fob in his hand.

'Empty, except for this,' he said, clicking it. With a beep, the Mercedes unlocked.

'Check the car,' McKellan snapped. 'Check every bit of the car. I want to know where they went before they came here. And check the traffic cameras – I want every van, car, lorry, whatever came through here in the last half hour. I want licences, where they were going, everything!'

Wolfe cleared his throat.

'Can ... um, can we do anything?' he asked.

It was as if McKellan had forgotten he was there, and this sudden question had laser-focused the old man's attention back on the officer.

'No, I think you've done enough here,' he said, forcing a thankful expression onto his face momentarily. 'You just keep on doing, well, whatever in God's name you're doing, and get the hell out of our crime scene.'

'Um, sir, I don't care who you are, this was our crime scene first, and State law says—'

'Oh, for Christ's sake! I don't care!' McKellan cried out to the sky. 'Can somebody *please* find our missing traitors? Please?'

THE TRUCK DRIVER WAS AS GOOD AS HIS WORD, TAKING Marlowe and Kate to the Manzanita Park and Ride lot, where they were able to catch a 150 bus into the San Rafael Transit Center and then a taxi the last five miles, arriving half an hour early.

San Rafael Airport wasn't an international hub; it wasn't even a domestic one of sorts, with a few hangars and only one runway to its name. Most of the planes were smaller than two or four-seater light aircraft, primarily Cessnas.

'This is getting us to Paris?' Kate asked, uncertain. Marlowe, as equally uncertain, shrugged his shoulders.

'Let's see what this Steve Trevor says,' he replied, walking towards the closest hangar, and the only one that seemed to be open at this time in the morning.

A man, wiping his hands with an oily rag, walked out of the hangar doors to meet them.

Steve Trevor was as aptly named as Sasha Bordeaux was.

That said, he looked nothing like the Steve Trevor in the comics. The tanned, blond, muscled boyfriend of Diana Prince, aka Wonder Woman, was nothing like the stranger who faced them. This man was overweight, with black, greasy hair, and the startings of a moustache peeking out from under his nose.

'You Linda's friend?' he asked, and, as Marlowe paused, he grinned. 'Probably used a different name with you. With me it was music, so she named herself Linda Ronstadt.'

'Comics,' Marlowe replied. 'Named herself Sasha Bordeaux.'

'That explains the whole "Steve Trevor" bullshit,' the man smiled, holding his hand out. 'I'm Garcia. I was told you need a flight to Paris?'

'Yeah, if you can,' Marlowe looked around, frowning. 'Although, I don't know if these can make the trip.'

Garcia laughed, as if this was the funniest joke in the world.

'Yeah, I see that. No, Mister Comics, it'll be in two parts, though.'

He pointed across at a four-seater Cessna, ready to go and fire-truck-red.

'We have a small plane here that will take us down to Oakland International. It's about forty miles, so we'll be there easy in twenty minutes or so. And then once there, I can get you on a freight plane across into Europe.'

'Freight plane?' Kate glanced nervously at Marlowe. Garcia, picking up her concern, flashed another smile.

'Yeah, we do a lot of work with people like FedEx and UPS, and one of the hubs is Oakland,' he explained. 'It won't be hard to get you in, and once we get through the security, something I'm an expert in, we can put you on one.'

'And how do we get out the other side?'

'I'll have someone there,' Garcia was returning to the hangar, tossing the rag onto a table. 'You're not my first rodeo, Mister Comics. I do this all the time. Well, not *all* the time. But often when I'm asked to, we've brought assets in and out of the country on a regular basis this way.'

He walked to the plane, indicating that Marlowe and Kate should climb in.

'How long you been working for the CIA?' Marlowe asked as he helped Kate up.

'I don't,' Garcia shrugged. 'I work for Linda. And I have done ever since she got me out of the Colombian Cartels.'

'What did you do there?' Kate asked, but then shook her head. 'Let me guess. Smuggled things and flew planes.'

Garcia clambered into the plane in front of them, already flicking switches.

'See?' he grinned. 'It's like we've known each other for years.'

THE FLIGHT TO OAKLAND HAD BEEN QUICK; ALTHOUGH GARCIA had said it would be so, Marlowe had assumed this was bluster, but the plane wasn't up in the air for over ten, fifteen minutes tops before it was already heading down, landing in the far corner of Oakland International. There was a truck waiting for them, the FedEx logo on the side, and a man who Garcia called "Luis" explained he was "like a brother" to him. And, shaking their hands, and refusing any kind of payment, explaining that "Linda" would recompense, he was already refuelling, preparing to return to San Rafael. Luis, meanwhile, kept them hidden in the back of the van as he drove out into the Freight Transport hub, and within half an hour of arriving at the airport, Marlowe and Kate were being escorted quietly up the cargo ramp, and into the bowels of an Airbus A300.

'Are you sure we'll be okay here?' Marlowe asked, looking around the hold.

'Oh, absolutely,' Luis smiled in the same way Garcia had. 'It's gonna take about eleven hours in total, though, so I suggest you settle in.'

He pointed to some seat benches along the side.

'Sometimes we have cargo that can't leave the sight of, well, whoever needs to keep an eye on it, so there's seating and seatbelts and all that shit here. And they don't depressurise. Although it gets a little cold, so I hope you have some coats.'

Marlowe shook his head, and Luis sighed theatrically, passing out two winter coats branded with a local freight company.

'That'll keep you toasty,' he said, handing them across. 'I also hope that you've picked up your own water and snacks, because we don't offer an in-flight service here.'

'I'm guessing you have something for us in there too?'

Luis smiled, passing a cool bag over.

'Subs and soda,' he said. 'Try not to drink too much as there aren't any toilets down here.'

Marlowe passed Luis a hundred-dollar bill for his help, and unlike Garcia, Luis took it eagerly, giving them a nod and a small wave as he stepped back, allowing the cargo door to raise up, as Marlowe and Kate settled down in the half-lit cargo hold to rest up. Marlowe was already arranging a makeshift bedding area, finding some bubble wrapping to use as a mattress of his new bed.

'You intend to sleep?' Kate was stunned. 'How can you even think about sleep?'

'I haven't slept since yesterday,' Marlowe said, patting down the wrapping. And even then, he'd spent a lot of the night before on top of a Los Angeles roof, so it was probably closer to two days since he'd gotten more than a few hours' kip. 'I think we need to get some sleep if we can, as we'll need to be ready the moment we land.'

He paused, thinking to himself.

'Tooley was based in San Francisco. Why would he have a drop box in Paris?'

'He wasn't based in San Francisco,' Kate replied, sitting on one of the seats and strapping herself in. 'He was only over here because of the meeting between Kyle and Karolides. Tooley was actually based in London, but he visited Paris quite a lot.'

She considered this for a moment.

'I think he had a boyfriend, or girlfriend, or whatever, over there. Makes sense his go bag would be there. It's easier to get into Europe from France than it is from England these days.'

Marlowe nodded. Kate was right; unlike running from London, where customs and border patrol were now ramped up, it was far easier to go off grid in an EU country these days. All Tooley needed to do was pick up his go bag from his Paris drop box, and then hop on a train. He could be in Eastern Europe within a couple of hours.

'What do you think he's got hidden in it?' he asked. 'Just his backup? Or something about Caliburn?'

'I don't know,' Kate admitted. 'I didn't know him as well as Lyons did. I'm hoping it's something that can help us, but we won't know until we get there.'

Marlowe nodded, rolling up another section of bubble wrap as the plane started moving. 'Make yourself something comfortable, and settle down. You're gonna need the rest,' he said. 'If it's anything like today, we're not gonna be stopping until it's finished.'

Kate grinned impishly.

'Hey,' she said, a little more huskily than she'd intended. 'In the motel there was a moment ...'

Marlowe, now lying on the mattress with his eyes shut, smiled.

'Moments come and pass,' he said. 'Let's not worry about that right now.'

'Shame,' Kate replied, settling in as the engines rose and the plane began to taxi. 'Eleven hours is a long flight. We could get ... bored.'

Marlowe turned away, hoping she wouldn't see the flush of his cheeks.

'Let's try sleeping first,' he said. 'We can discuss how to keep ourselves occupied later on.'

'Spoilsport,' Kate grumbled, but her next words were drowned out as the engines roared, and the A300 took off, heading towards Paris ... and answers.

9

DON CORLEONE

'THEY TOOK THE BLOODY ARM.'

McKellan stood beside the half buried body of Tooley, raising his head to look across the scrubland. After they'd found the black Mercedes, it'd been a simple job to check through the sat nav details to see where it had gone, a journey that led the two SUVs into the middle of nowhere, just in time to piss off the early morning hikers and dog walkers as they drove at speed down a dirt track, to frankly the most pointless place in existence.

And, to make matters worse, he'd gotten his patent-leather brogues covered in mud.

Now, he returned his withering gaze to Hill, kneeling down beside the unearthed grave, peering at the stump of the arm that poked out of the ground, the suit jacket crumpled around it.

'I know they took the bloody arm, I can tell that from here,' he replied irritably. 'I don't need bloody forensics to tell me that.'

'Good, because I'm not forensics,' Hill rose and walked off.

McKellan grumbled to himself, looking up at the sky and forcing himself not to scream.

I should have sent Casey here, or Curtis, he thought to himself. *Let them run around the middle of nowhere.*

'The sat nav said they came here almost directly after escaping the hotel,' he muttered. 'They came here, took the arm, and then went back to the motel. Why?'

'Because they needed a shower?' Hill suggested. 'Or some sleep?'

'Are you deliberately trying to piss me off?' McKellan snapped. 'Because if you are, you're doing great. I mean, why take the arm?'

'Tooley was rogue,' Hill mused. 'The sat nav showed the car coming here the night before, and I'm no forensics, as I've already said, but the smell coming from that grave says to me he's been dead a good day or two.'

McKellan dabbed his nose with a handkerchief at this.

'Marlowe wasn't in San Francisco by then,' he said. 'Although he could have come up here the night before, and then checked in yesterday. Can we find out where he was?'

'His friend Preston might be better there,' Hill replied. 'He'd be off the grid, using fake names and old legends. She'd know which ones he's likely using.'

'Is she in the air yet?' McKellan looked at his watch. It was almost eight in the morning. 'No, it'll be later in the day. Find her. See what she knows.'

McKellan stared back down at the body of Brian Tooley. He'd worked with him a few times over the years. He knew the secrets the stupid old bastard kept.

If this was anything to do with Senator Kyle ...

He looked back at Hill, now on the phone.

'Ignore Preston,' he shook his hand, waving off her reply. 'Stay here with a car, get the body exhumed and taken to a morgue. Any morgue. I don't care where. Find a friendly coroner and get me a full detail on time, cause, bloody well everything of death.'

'And you, sir?'

'I need a plane back to London ASAP,' McKellan was already walking back to the second car.

'Why?' disconnecting the call, Hill glanced back at the body, trying to work out how this decision had come to pass.

'Because someone is probably going to be killed by the end of the day,' McKellan finished ominously, before climbing into the SUV, nodding to his driver.

'Get me back to the hotel, and damn the traffic cops,' he ordered.

THE SAINT FRANCIS MEMORIAL HOSPITAL HAD ONLY STARTED its morning turnaround when Trix arrived. The night-time shift was ending, the drunks, party goers and whatever else that'd end up there in the early hours of the morning were now sorted, triaged and processed, and the day was starting afresh.

It wasn't that busy as Trix walked through the main lobby, looking for the ward, where she knew Senator Kyle would be under guard. But at the same time, Trix knew that with an active Senator fighting for her life, the place was likely to be filled with security agents, and a US Secret Service contingent currently nervous about British spies. The chances were anyone with an English accent was likely to be targeted the moment they spoke, and so Trix kept this at the front of her mind as she walked up to the main reception desk.

The woman on the desk looked up expectantly, and Trix smiled, trying on her best West Coast accent.

'I'm looking for Senator Maureen Kyle,' she said. 'I was told she would be somewhere here. Maybe intensive care?'

The receptionist looked her up and down and smiled.

'Journalist,' she decided.

At this, Trix gave her best mortified look.

'You think I'm a reporter? No, I'm her ...' Trix paused. 'I'm her daughter. Um, I mean daughter-in-law. Yes.'

The receptionist smiled.

'Of course you are, honey.'

Trix leant closer.

'I'm just looking to make sure she's okay,' she said softly. 'I was told she came in this morning. Gunshot wound. ICU. That's why we're worried.'

'Fine.' The receptionist checked on the screen while typing in some details. 'She's here. But she's not in intensive care, so I don't know why they told you that, if they told you anything at all. She's in one of the wards.'

'Oh,' this surprised Trix. 'I was under the assumption she was in a medical coma.'

The receptionist checked some more details.

'No, she looks like she's fine.'

The receptionist smiled as she looked back at Trix.

'I think the information from your editor was wrong,' she stated.

'I couldn't possibly comment,' Trix replied with the slightest hint of a smile, deciding that perhaps "reporter" was a better option than "British spy trying to find out about an American asset," when the chips fell. 'Which floor is she on?'

'I'm afraid I can't tell you that.'

Trix sighed and pulled out a twenty-dollar bill, placing it on the table.

'Maybe now you could tell me?'

'Daughters usually pay more for their mothers.' The receptionist smiled, still taking the bill from the counter with a practised ease.

'Well, then it's just lucky that I'm a daughter-in-*law*,' Trix replied.

The receptionist considered this, and then nodded towards the door at the other end of the corridor.

'Two floors up, and then third on the right,' she said. 'I'll warn you though, she has a lot of Secret Service wandering around. You're not gonna get far.'

'That's fine, maybe I'll get information on my mother-in-law from them,' Trix straightened, glancing around the lobby before leaving the counter. She took the back route, however, moving towards the rear service staircase, rather than taking the more obvious elevator and walking through the main entrance, directly into the waiting agents.

As she did this, her hip started buzzing. Pulling out her phone, she looked down at it, grimacing.

It was a call from Curtis.

Sighing audibly, she answered it.

'Where the hell are you?' he asked.

'I'm in my hotel room,' Trix replied, walking away from the crowded lobby, looking for somewhere quieter. 'You know, packing for London.'

'The hell you are,' Curtis replied. 'I'm standing in your hotel room right now.'

Trix winced.

Busted.

'I'm at the hospital,' she admitted. 'I'm checking in on Kyle and then I'm straight back, I swear.'

She leaned against the wall, phone to her ear.

'There's something fishy going on here, boss, and you can see it too, I know you can,' she whispered. 'I needed to see with my own eyes what we're being fed from MI6 and McKellan.'

'McKellan has gone,' Curtis replied. 'Turned up, grabbed his things, left for London. He's probably on the same plane as you are. Or, would have been, if you'd gone.'

'I packed hand luggage only,' Trix started up the stairs now. 'I can still make the plane.'

'You'd better,' Curtis snapped, and the phone went dead.

Well, at least he didn't tell you not to check on Kyle, Trix thought to herself, keeping to the wall, to not alert any agents on the third floor.

She needn't have bothered when she arrived.

There was no security there.

Walking through the doors, she looked around, wondering for a moment if she'd even arrived at the right place. About a dozen yards from her, she could see a nurse's station, complete with a computer screen. A nurse was sitting there, working through something on it, and from her expression, she didn't seem to think anything was wrong with this scene. And so, deciding she was probably the best point of contact, Trix walked over to her.

'Hey,' she said, flashing a badge before placing it back, still trying the US accent. It was a basic-looking badge, and one she always carried with her; it indicated to the person seeing it, of some kind of high-level and generic US agency, mainly as most civilians didn't know what a badge looked like outside of the movies. 'Where's the security for Senator Kyle?'

The nurse looked up and noted the badge, as it was flipped back into Trix's pocket. This done, she then looked around, as if realising for the first time she was alone, and shrugged.

'No idea,' she said. 'I think they were all called away about ten, maybe fifteen minutes ago.'

She gave a "more than my pay grade" gesture.

'I don't think she needs them, to be perfectly honest. She's been demanding breakfast since she got here, even though the doctors had her down as "nil by mouth" on the forms.'

'She's speaking?' Trix was surprised. 'She's not in a coma?'

'You're the third person to ask me that,' the nurse shrugged. 'She's not been in a coma since she arrived. God, she was screaming and yelling when she got here. I suppose a gunshot wound does that, though. Poor woman probably hurts like hell.'

Mentally evaluating everything she knew, Trix nodded around the ward floor.

'Which room?'

The nurse nodded behind Trix to a glass window almost opposite the nurse's station. 'Thanks,' Trix smiled, walking across the floor and up to the door, but stopping briefly as she noticed the chair next to it. Now empty, but with today's newspaper on it, someone had been sitting here quite recently – and they'd gone, possibly in a hurry, around ten or fifteen minutes earlier.

That's not good.

Opening the door, she drew a breath to steady herself, and then walked in.

Senator Kyle was lying on a hospital ward bed; her eyes were shut as if sleeping, and a television in the corner was showing the morning news.

'Senator Kyle?' Trix said softly, repeating slightly louder. 'Senator Kyle.'

Kyle opened one eye, looking across at her.

'I know you,' she croaked, her throat dry. 'You're Marlowe's friend.'

'I am, Ma'am,' Trix passed Senator Kyle some water, which the older woman took and drank gratefully. 'I came to make sure you're okay, as we've heard worrying things like, well, that you're in a medical coma and you're unlikely to survive.'

She glanced around, looking back out of the door.

'However, it seems the rumours of your death have been greatly exaggerated.'

Senator Kyle laughed weakly at the obvious Mark Twain reference.

'I'm doing okay,' she said. 'And I'll be looked after here, so don't you worry. Tell Marlowe I appreciate what he did.'

'How'd you mean?'

Senator Kyle shifted painfully on her bed, wincing as she moved the shoulder.

'Well, I'm guessing he's the one who stopped me from being killed,' she replied. 'I heard he was seen in the room, or something.'

Her face darkened.

'I also heard he's now on the run. Poor bastard – must be hell being blamed for something you didn't do.'

'So you're confirming Marlowe didn't shoot you?' Trix turned her phone on to "record" as she asked the question.

'God no,' Kyle smiled. 'It was my own agent, Ford. Son of a bitch has worked with me for years, and then out of nowhere pulls out a gun, and tries to kill me.'

She looked up at the television, her eyes narrowing as she saw the news chyron scrolling across the bottom.

SENATOR KYLE FIGHTS FOR LIFE AFTER ASSASSINATION ATTEMPT

'I was lucky,' she admitted. 'I was a little suspicious of Ford after talking to Marlowe earlier that night. But I didn't expect him to try to kill me. My suspicions saved my life, as I dived to the side, and he caught me in the shoulder.'

She then rubbed at her head, and Trix noticed the staple in the hairline for the first time.

'I went down hard and smacked my head against the table. I was out. Next thing I know, I wake up and I'm in an ambulance, being taken to hospital.'

'Lucky break.'

'For me, yeah,' Kyle said. 'Not for Marlowe. I understand they're looking for him?'

'They are, Ma'am,' Trix said. 'Have you told anybody about this, about Ford being the assassin?'

'Oh, hell yes,' Senator Kyle exclaimed. 'As soon as I woke.'

Trix felt a cold sliver of ice slide down her spine.

'We've not been told anything, Senator,' she intoned. 'And going on the basis that MI5 and MI6 pretty much know everything, I would say this means nobody's been passing it on.'

At this revelation, Kyle frowned.

'Are you telling me they didn't tell you I was awake?'

'No, Senator, I'm telling you that as far as the world is concerned, you're currently in a medical coma after a rogue British agent tried to kill you. And because of this, you can't speak, or tell anyone this is incorrect. Meanwhile, the CIA,

NSA, Secret Service, MI5, MI6, hell, probably half a dozen made-up organisations as well, all have a "shoot to kill" order on Marlowe.'

Senator Kyle stared silently at Trix for a long period before finally speaking.

'Somebody's changing my narrative, and I don't like that,' she said.

'I don't like it either,' Trix replied. 'But what I also don't like is that you don't seem to have any security right now, while there's a rogue think tank named Caliburn that's trying to kill you.'

For the first time in the conversation, Senator Kyle noticed there was nobody outside, as Trix moved over and closed the room's door.

'There was someone there literally a few minutes ago,' she whispered. 'I spoke to him, I was asking for a mug of strong coffee. They said I wasn't allowed any.'

'There's nobody there now.' Trix looked out of the room's window, out onto the ward's floor, noticing the nurse at the counter. She was watching Trix back through the window, but then stopped as another nurse, an older woman, walked over, tapping her on the shoulder and pointing to the door with an almost apologetic look back at Trix.

The nurse rose, leaving her station empty, and followed the older nurse out.

'Shit,' Trix said, looking around for some kind of weapon. 'Your security has been removed, and now the witnesses are leaving. There's only one reason someone would do that. We need to get you out of here. Can you walk?'

'He didn't shoot me in the leg, hun,' Senator Kyle was already climbing out of her bed. 'I am connected to this gurney thing, though.'

Trix went to reply, but stopped; she could see the elevator across the ward. The lights were flashing – someone was on their way up.

Pulling out her phone, she dialled a number quickly, crouching down, looking around for anything that she could use to defend herself with.

Curtis answered on the second ring.

'You've seen her?' he asked, straight to the point.

'I'm with her now, and she's completely awake,' Trix replied. 'But that's not why I'm calling. Have you seen that scene in *The Godfather* where Michael Corleone goes to see his dad, and finds all the police had been moved?'

'Yeah, it's a classic.'

'Well, we're about to re-enact that here at the hospital,' Trix whispered. 'We've got no security, we've got a very alive Senator, and we've got assassins on the way. How fast can you get to me?'

'Ten minutes at best,' Curtis was already moving from the sounds of his laboured breath down the line. 'We can get someone there quickly, but you're gonna have to hold the fort until we do. What weapons do you have?'

'I didn't think I was going to need any. But don't worry. I can get this done. Just get someone here ASAP.'

Trix disconnected the call, looking back at Kyle.

'We might not have time to run,' she said. 'We might need to stay and fight. I'll find you something to hold – and if they get past me, you take them out and get out of here as quickly as you can.'

'You're a field agent?' Kyle was confused. 'I got the impression you weren't, back in New York.'

'I'm just a computer girl,' Trix smiled, looking around. 'What I'm really good with is electronics ...'

She trailed off, reaching under the table and pulling out a plastic box. Inside was a defibrillator, one of the portable versions that ambulances had on board.

Turning it on and hearing noises in the ward, Trix pulled the pads away. It was going to take a few seconds to charge, but currently this was all she had.

'Stay in the bed,' she whispered. 'Pretend you're asleep. Hopefully, when they come in, they won't realise we're waiting.'

Moving to the side of the door, the pads warming up in her hands, she crouched. She could hear the faint whine of the defibrillator as it charged, hoping the noise from the television would drown it out. She glanced up through the window, keeping as low as she possibly could and flinching back down as a suited man walked past, aiming for the room's door. He didn't need to ask the nurse where Senator Kyle was, like Trix. Someone had already told him. His gun was ready to be fired, held in his hand as he slowly turned the doorknob.

Trix glanced across at Senator Kyle, who was already lying in bed, her eyes shut. Trix was impressed; It took a lot to pretend to be asleep when a man was about to come in and kill you. Often people would want to see it happening, they'd want to make sure that they could get out and, of course, if he walked in and found her staring at him, waiting for him, he'd know something was wrong immediately.

The door slowly opened, and the gun moved into view as the guy walked in, weapon raising and now aimed at the believed asleep Senator Kyle.

'Nothing personal—' he started, his voice turning into a scream as Trix leapt forward, slamming the two pads into his side.

'Clear!' she shouted, as she pressed the buttons.

The charge from the defibrillator hurtling through his body affected him in the same way that a taser would; he arched back, his eyes rolling into his head, and the gun falling to the floor as the assassin collapsed to the ground. But by then Trix was already dropping the pads before they could charge again, picking up the gun.

It was a Glock 17, a standard issue weapon for many places. It didn't give any clues as to where the man came from, but she didn't need any clues.

She knew who this man was. She had heard his voice when he had shot Lyons in a back room on a CCTV camera.

'He's one of mine?' Kyle whispered, her eyes half open.

'No Ma'am. I'm afraid he's one of ours,' Trix said, peeking through the door, seeing a second agent walking around. 'I think that guy's there to back him up in case something goes wrong.'

'Well, he's about to realise it,' Kyle muttered. 'What now?'

Before Trix could reply, the man watching the door decided the waiting was boring, and started towards the room.

Trix prepared herself and, as the man walked in, and with two hands supporting the gun, she fired.

It was a point-blank shot, but even with that, Trix wasn't the best of shooters. The bullet hit the assassin in the hip, though, and he went down screaming. Cursing, Trix quickly moved forwards and rather than shooting again, she slammed the butt of the gun into the side of his head, knocking him out.

'Ma'am, we need to get you somewhere safe,' she said, passing the second gun over to the Senator.

Senator Kyle, however, shook her head.

'There's nowhere safe,' she replied. 'If these guys can get to me here, they can get to me anywhere.'

'Do you know anyone you trust?' Trix was watching the elevator, before returning to the two downed men, pulling out lengths of bandages and using it to tie their arms behind their back. 'Because once my people arrive, you need to get somewhere nobody can find you.'

'I know someone who can help,' Senator Kyle nodded. 'But first, let's concentrate on staying alive until your people get here. How does it end in *The Godfather*?'

'They stand outside, pull their collars up and look menacing with their fingers in pockets pretending they're guns.'

Kyle shook her head as she heard this.

'Yeah, that won't work here,' she said, clearing the chamber and loading a new bullet from the magazine. 'Let's just use real guns instead.'

10

LOCKBOX

THE FLIGHT FROM SAN FRANCISCO TO PARIS HAD TAKEN JUST under eleven hours in total, and Marlowe had slept for at least half of that. The rest of the time had been spent awake, but alone, as circumstances meant that while he was awake, Kate had finally got to sleep.

Marlowe knew Paris was about nine hours ahead of the West Coast, and so, following the details he knew of the flight time, it was now around six in the morning of the following day. There weren't any windows to confirm this, so Marlowe whiled away the hours checking his duffel bag. He assumed they'd be smuggled out of whatever hub they were travelling to, courtesy of the CIA, but there was a chance they'd have to go through Paris detectors, and walking out with a stolen gun in his hand wasn't the best of looks. He didn't really know what was waiting for them when they landed; Senator Kyle could be dead, the CIA might have changed their mind about helping him, and they could have a furious armed reception waiting for them, which wasn't good.

Marlowe could feel the plane decelerating slightly, and

felt the shift in pressure. It was about ten and a half hours into the journey, so the final twenty or so minutes would feel like this, and he ignored the slightly unsettling sensation in his stomach as he continued to check his bag. He'd brought everything with him when he went to San Francisco, as he didn't have a bolthole in LA he could store things in, and so the duffel still had items from the East Coast, when he'd been in New York, as well as his Fairburn Sykes knife and some ammunition.

There were some changes of clothes, which he took advantage of, and a couple of thousand dollars' worth of bills. He also had half a dozen fake credit cards under four unique identities, and around a dozen bullion coins hidden in the duffel's lining, gold one-ounce "Britannia" coins from the Royal Mint, worth about two thousand dollars each, and easily transportable across borders.

Basically, he was good to go if things went south. And he'd be in Paris, where he had allies. Well, people he used to work with, and he was sure he had a bag left with at least one of them. Worst-case scenario, he could take one of the identities and go back to the UK—

No.

Marlowe stared down at the ID cards in his hands.

The chances were that even though he'd used a couple of these while in the US, MI5 and MI6 knew about these identities, even if Trix hadn't given them up. Each one could be on a dozen lists, waiting for him to use them. Unfortunately for Marlowe, if he wanted to get to London again, he either needed to clear his name, or find an alternate supplier of fake IDs, something he'd meant to do after being burnt, but pushed to the back burner the moment he went to the US.

Of course, and luckily for Marlowe, he knew someone who did just that.

There was also Tooley's arm, taken from the motel; not needing it anymore, he took it out of the bag, securing it in some side netting beside his seat.

That'll confuse the next person cleaning in here, he thought to himself wryly.

There was movement from the side, and Kate opened an eye blearily.

'You snore,' she moaned.

'Engines,' Marlowe smiled. 'You're mistaken.'

'Liar,' Kate grabbed a bottle of water from the bag and drank it down greedily, the air having dehydrated them both. 'How long?'

'Soon,' Marlowe was already gathering his items together. He made sure Kate didn't see the coins or the dollars – not because he didn't trust her, but because they were his, they were personal.

They were his past.

The engines were gaining in noise now, and there was a whine underneath them as the wheels extended out for landing. Strapping themselves in, they waited for the plane to land, and Marlowe was actually impressed at how smooth it was.

Although they'd do their best because of the cargo, and he didn't mean the stowaways.

'Do you know where we're landing?' Kate asked.

Marlowe shrugged.

'I'm guessing Charles de Gaulle,' he replied. 'It's the biggest.'

'I hope they have a plan,' Kate muttered.

Marlowe almost replied, telling her about the time the CIA gave him a gun instead of a cavity search in JFK, but knew it'd probably worry her. Analysts weren't field agents usually, mainly because they, well, analysed things. And sometimes that wasn't the best of plans.

The plane stopped, and Marlowe gathered his things, waiting by the cargo entrance. After a few minutes, the door lowered, and a blonde woman stared up at them.

'CIA send their regards,' she said, waving them to follow her to a black car waiting on the tarmac. 'If you'll follow me?'

'You're CIA?' Marlowe asked as they followed her, but the woman shook her head.

'I'm Fischer, Paris Embassy,' she said, her accent showing she was definitely American rather than French. 'I just owe a favour, one that had me up at five in the morning, so you're welcome.'

She nodded to the back doors as she climbed into the driver's seat.

'We have diplomatic plates, so you're safe for the moment,' she said, starting the car. 'But we need to move, so hurry up.'

'Is there a toilet we can use?' Kate asked. 'It's been a long flight.'

'Hold it a while longer,' Fischer replied, already driving. 'I'll be dropping you off on the outskirts of Paris, so you can find a McDonald's or something.'

She turned to look at Marlowe.

'Oh, my friend said you'd want to know, Senator Kyle is alive and well, so we think,' she smiled. 'Apparently, one of your MI5 buddies saved her ass. Our mutual friend wanted you to know it was your *not* assistant.'

Marlowe chuckled at that; the last time he'd seen Sasha face to face had been in New York, and at the time, she'd commented that Trix Preston was "anything but your assistant," when it was suggested.

So Trix had got Senator Kyle out. That was good. He could trust her.

Could he?

Marlowe shook the thought from his head. He was so busy fighting bloody ghosts, he didn't know who he could trust anymore. Caliburn was a glorified boys' club, nothing more. They had delusions of grandeur, sure, but it was Spooks trying to find ways to be more "spooky."

It was a gang for *Walter Mitty* wannabes. Unfortunately, someone hadn't passed Caliburn the message, it seemed.

Fischer had been as good as her word, and after driving out with no issues from the FedEx hub, she took them to Saint-Denis before stopping the car and suggesting politely they get the hell out, but not before passing them a couple of hundred euros in small notes. After all, dollars weren't used in France that often, and the Bureau de Changes hadn't opened yet.

Marlowe took the money gratefully and, with Kate beside him, found himself on the Rue Jean Jaurès, a small shopping parade just off the Basilique de Saint-Denis with, conveniently, a couple of coffee shops.

Settling in the quietest one, Marlowe and Kate ordered breakfast, eating and drinking ravenously as they did so. After all, Marlowe had now been on the run for over twenty-four hours, and apart from a rather stale sub from a cold bag and a take-out burger, this was his first proper meal in much longer.

'What do we know about the Paris address?' he asked.

Kate leant back in her chair, shrugging.

'Only what we got before we left the motel,' she replied. 'It's a small security deposit company in the financial district, La Défense; has links to London, so it's probably filled with bloody spies.'

Marlowe shuddered.

'If I recall, that's out to the west,' he said, pulling out a map of the Paris Metro he'd picked up from a rack of flyers as they entered. 'We'd take the train from here to Gare Saint-Lazare, and change there for the train to La Défense. Looks like about an hour.'

'Good,' Kate munched on her breakfast. 'We don't want to be there first thing, because we don't want to look eager. And the staff will be fresh.'

'I think we're okay there,' Marlowe was looking now at the piece of paper with the box details on. 'It looks like it's a blank name box. You know the number and the password, you get in. They probably have tons of them.'

'Still, gives us time for more food,' Kate finished her plate. 'I don't know about you, but I'm famished.'

THE *SECURETRADE* SECURITY DEPOSIT OFFICES WERE EASY TO find, and, made from chrome and glass, looked more like an Apple store than a bank.

Marlowe secreted his SIG Sauer and duffel in a safe place outside, just in case there'd been metal detectors inside, but instead, a single reception desk faced Marlowe and Kate as they entered, a smiling receptionist sitting behind it.

Marlowe looked around; there were three cameras, all aimed directly at him, but the baseball cap he was wearing should have hidden the bulk of his face from them. And, to the left, by a door, was a burly guard in a security office.

'Bonjour,' the receptionist smiled.

'Sorry, do you speak English?' Kate asked.

The receptionist nodded, with the resigned smile of someone who was being forced yet again to speak a non-native language in their own country.

'Please excuse my friend,' he said in fluent French. 'And forgive my accent. It's been a while. But although I can understand your beautiful language, she cannot, and I'm stuck with that.'

He finished with a wink, and the receptionist brightened.

'Good morning, and welcome to SecureTrade,' she said, her English accent and pronunciations miles better than Marlowe's French. 'Are you a customer?'

Marlowe and Kate looked at each other, then back to the receptionist, speaking simultaneously.

'Yes,' Kate replied.

'No,' Marlowe replied.

Kate looked at Marlowe, shocked he would say that.

He looked sheepishly back at her before turning back to the receptionist.

'That is, our employer is,' he explained, reaching into his pocket. 'We've been sent to examine his box. I have the details.'

The receptionist didn't even bat an eyelid at this, giving Marlowe the impression this was a common occurrence.

'That's all we need,' she waved for the paper. 'The number?'

Pulling it from his pocket, Marlowe passed the receptionist a slip of paper.

'Everything's on there,' he said.

The receptionist frowned as she looked at it.

'You wrote this?'

'I did,' Kate replied cautiously, looking nervously at Marlowe. 'Is there a problem?'

'Yes,' the receptionist looked back at Kate now, showing the number on the top line. 'Third number in. Is this a seven or a four?'

'Oh, a four,' Kate, visibly relieved, squinted at the number. 'Sorry.'

This decided, the receptionist returned to the keyboard, typing in the number with practised ease. Marlowe glanced at Kate, winking at her.

'I don't think she likes you,' he smiled.

'It's because you suck all the oxygen out of the room with your charm,' Kate muttered back. 'All that "your beautiful language" bollocks.'

'You understood?'

It was Kate's turn to smile now.

'Unlike you, I don't have the boyish urge to show off to everyone on how clever a boy I am,' she replied, giving a simple, apologetic while mocking shrug.

Her data entry finished, the receptionist looked back to Marlowe.

'Account and passcode match,' she smiled. 'If you'll follow the guard to your left, he'll take you to a private viewing room.'

'Thank you,' Kate replied, her French flawless. 'And I apologise for my workmate's candour, he can't help flirting with every woman he meets.'

And, this said, and the receptionist blushing now, Marlowe and Kate followed the guard out of the lobby and in through a small, but well-designed door. Even from the movement, Marlowe could tell it was a heavy, likely metal one.

The door led into a viewing room, or at least this was what Marlowe assumed it was. In reality, it was a small space, no larger than a double-sized changing room, a table in the middle, and with a red cloth that could be pulled across the door, giving privacy. Marlowe glanced up at the corners and noted no security there either. Either SecureTrade was very moral with client security when checking their boxes, or they had superb tiny cameras hidden in the folds of the cloth.

The guard indicated for them to stay where they were, and walked back out of the room, the heavy door closing behind him.

'You know, if this was a trap, and we put in the wrong details, that was a really easy way of being captured,' Kate muttered, partly to herself.

'You're such a people person, a real ray of light,' Marlowe smiled in response. 'Sometimes you have to roll the dice.'

'I should have let you come in alone,' Kate continued to mutter. 'No, then you'd have been alone in here if it wasn't a trap.'

Marlowe went to reply, but paused as the door opened again, and the guard returned, this time carrying a medium-sized aluminium box. Nodding to them both, he placed it on the table, unlocking it with what looked to be some kind of RFID card attached to his belt.

'When you are done, lock up the box and leave,' he replied in English, his accent worse than the receptionist. And, this explained, the guard left the two of them alone.

'Are you sure you don't want to tell him how beautiful his language is too?' Kate mocked. Marlowe, however, decided the best course of action would be to ignore her, and instead moved over to the box, pulling up the flip top aluminium lid, exposing the contents inside.

All that was inside the box, however, was a black canvas holdall.

Marlowe recognised it instantly; he had one of these himself. A backup bag, often known as a "go" bag. He'd even used one a few weeks back, kept secure in a store off Kings Cross. It was a bag you could literally grab and go when things got too hot. Money, weapons, ID, that was all you needed to get somewhere safe, and fast. His own duffel was a slightly glorified version, with his cards and bullion coins within.

Kate leant over now, pulling the bag out of the aluminium box, placing it carefully onto the wooden table beside it.

'You want to do the honours?' she asked, nodding at Marlowe.

'You don't want to do it?' Marlowe was surprised, but then smiled darkly. 'Oh, wait. You think it's booby trapped.'

'It's what I'd do.'

'You have a bag like this?' Marlowe asked, examining the zip for any secret threads. 'I thought it was mainly a field agent thing.'

'I don't even know what kind of bag it is,' Kate said. 'I'm guessing this is something you understand better than me. I just hope it links to Fractal Destiny.'

Straightening, deciding the bag was safe to open, Marlowe took the zip and pulled gently, opening up the top. And, once this was done, Marlowe and Kate carefully peered inside.

Within the bag was a treasure trove for spies.

Wads of dollar bills, and a similar amount of UK tender greeted them, at least a couple of grand's worth of each. Under those were a selection of blank passports, UK, EU and US based, and an equal amount of ID cards, none of which had names or photos within.

At the back were still-in-plastic burner phones, simple ones, mainly for sending messages and taking calls, a couple of credit cards, complete with names and signatures, and in the middle was a small, black projector of some kind, linked to a base unit with a power cord, and four extendable stands coming out of each corner.

'Jesus,' Kate whistled, picking up one wad of dollars, riffling through it. 'Did he rob a bank or something?'

'It's Tooley's backup bag,' Marlowe explained, taking the dollars from Kate and placing them back into the bag, zipping it back up. 'He knew they were catching up. This was his new life, his bargaining chip.'

He looked to the door, wondering once more if someone was watching them right now.

'Come on, let's get out of here before someone checks on us,' he suggested, pulling the new bag onto his shoulder.

'And then what?' Kate asked.

Marlowe shrugged.

'We find a hotel, one that takes cash, and we hole up while we work out what to do next,' he said. 'The box. Is it Fractal Destiny?'

Kate didn't reply, her expression one of confusion.

'I'll be honest, Marlowe, I didn't think it was a physical item,' she admitted. 'So, if that is Fractal Destiny, I have no idea how to make it work.'

'Cool, so let's work it out over room service,' Marlowe

shifted the bag on his shoulder as he started for the door. 'But let's get my gun and the other bag back first.'

'You think we're going to need a gun?'

Marlowe nodded.

'I think, seeing what Tooley left here, we're going to need more guns than I currently have,' he said. 'I think we're about to have every agency on the planet coming after us.'

11

HOMECOMING

STANDING BESIDE A CONTROL DESK, SIR WALTER MCKELLAN looked up at the door as Trix and Curtis entered, an expression of someone who'd smelt a rather pungent and nasty smell on his face.

'I thought I told you to go back to your MI5 offices and forget about all this?' he muttered. 'Instead I get back to London, to *my* side of the Thames, to hear you've gone off script and started attacking agents in a hospital—' this first line was to Trix, '—while *you* then arrived and proceeded to lose a sitting US Senator to God knows where.'

'Good to see you too, Walter,' Curtis replied. 'And if I'm not mistaken, I'm MI5, not MI6, so I don't report to you.'

'I have a Government mandate to be whichever bloody agency I damn well want to be, at any moment, and you'd be well advised to remember that,' McKellan growled. 'Come on then, report.'

Curtis looked as if he was about to continue his fight, but Trix straightened.

'I didn't think the Americans were being truthful about Kyle,' she said.

'Of course they weren't being truthful,' McKellan grumbled. 'They're American. They've been pissy with us since 1776.'

'Either way, I checked in on Senator Kyle,' Trix, unabated, continued. 'I'd—we'd been told she was unresponsive and close to death. In fact, she was quite conscious and quite coherent. Although her taste in hospital TV was a bit pedestrian. The problem was, however, that I arrived just before a kill-squad did.'

'CIA?' McKellan stopped what he was doing and fixed his gaze on Trix now.

'Yes, sir,' Trix nodded. 'And no, sir.'

She passed her phone across, two images showing on it.

'These are the two men I took down—'

'You took them down? I thought you were just a glorified hacker?'

Trix ignored the insult.

'Yes, sir,' she continued. 'As I was saying, these were the two men. The first one is the image you see at the top of the screen. MI6 trained, based out of Los Angeles. Nigel Holden.'

'I know Holden,' McKellan nodded. 'I also know he wouldn't have done this—'

'Sir, I recognised his voice,' Trix interrupted. 'And I checked the CCTV footage of Warren Lyons' death on the flight back. It's the same man.'

'So, before you tell us he wouldn't do such a thing, ask if he'd also not kill a British asset,' Curtis added helpfully. 'And I'll point out here he's your team, not ours. No Box agents trying to kill Senators, it seems.'

'Christ,' McKellan muttered. 'If Karolides finds out about

this, she'll have a field day. She'll audit the entire bloody Intelligence Service. Me *and* you.'

'That might be a good thing, sir,' Trix replied. 'We might find who's loyal, and who's sharing their masters.'

'Sharing their masters?' McKellan nodded. 'Oh. You mean Caliburn. I'd tread carefully there. You seem to push the narrative that it's a treasonous secret society, but I've been a part of it for three decades – and we've never once acted against the Government or the Crown.'

'UK or US based?' Curtis asked. 'Because if it's the latter, you're branching out.'

McKellan frowned at the question.

'It's always been a UK research group,' he muttered. 'Why would we—'

'The second image is Peter Doherty, NSA agent, Boston,' Trix added. 'He wasn't even supposed to be in San Francisco this weekend. He wasn't part of the arrangements, wasn't seconded to the Senator. In fact, his superiors thought he was on vacation.'

'You spoke to his superiors in the NSA?' McKellan was appalled.

'No, Senator Kyle did,' Trix flashed a winning smile. 'While she arranged for a close protection unit to take her to a safe house.'

She nodded at the phone.

'Oh, swipe to the left, please, sir.'

McKellan did, and a recording played.

'So you're confirming Marlowe didn't shoot you?'

'God no, It was my own agent, Ford. Son of a bitch has worked with me for years, and then out of nowhere pulls out a gun, and tries to kill me. I was lucky – I was a little suspicious of Ford, after talking to Marlowe earlier that night. But I didn't

expect him to try to kill me. My suspicions saved my life, as I dived to the side, and he caught me in the shoulder. I went down hard and smacked my head against the table. I was out. Next thing I know, I wake up and I'm in an ambulance, being taken to hospital.'

'Lucky break.'

'For me, yeah, not for Marlowe. I understand they're looking for him?'

'They are, Ma'am. Have you told anybody about this, about Ford being the assassin?'

'Oh, hell yes. As soon as I woke.'

McKellan looked up from the phone at Trix.

'Marlowe isn't the traitor we think he is,' she said. 'We need to find Ford, and—'

'Ford's dead,' McKellan waved across the room, and for the first time, Trix and Curtis noticed Casey as he rose from his desk, walking over. 'Tell them, Mister Casey.'

'Ford was found about seven hours ago,' Casey explained. 'We were all in the air around then, I'm guessing. News came in from MI6 assets about three hours back. He shot himself with his own gun while hiding out in a hotel room. Had a written confession in his own hand when they found him.'

'So, what, he escapes Marlowe, runs to his room, writes a confession, kills himself and it takes a whole day for someone to work this out?' Curtis shook his head. 'That's suspicious.'

'It is, but it's not *us* suspicious,' Casey replied. 'We were out of the hotel before he died, according to the time of death. It was quite recent when they found him, the gunshot overheard.'

'So that's a lead we can't use,' Trix glared at the monitor in front of her, as if expecting it to argue back. 'So what's next?'

'What's next is you follow bloody orders and go back to

work, leaving the grown up work to MI6,' McKellan snapped. 'You've done nothing of note here—'

'I saved the Senator!'

'Wasn't our job to do that.'

'I proved Marlowe didn't kill her!'

'Ford's letter proved that.'

'I fought agents trying to kill her!'

'You fought assets we could have questioned,' McKellan growled. 'And now they're under the care of the CIA, so we won't learn a damn thing.'

He went to continue, but there was a noise from outside the door, what sounded like some kind of growing argument, and it burst open, revealing an agent trying futilely to hold back a small, bulky woman in her late forties, Greek in looks, from entering.

'Remove your dog, Sir Walter, before I neuter him,' Joanna Karolides smiled.

'Home Secretary, what a pleasure,' McKellan smiled, but the humour failed to reach his eyes, that watched her with a fair amount of suspicion. 'If we'd been told of your visit—'

'You would have shredded the files?' Karolides raised an eyebrow. 'Don't play me for a fool.'

Trix tried to hide her smile. She liked this woman already. Especially as it was obvious McKellan didn't.

'What do I owe this visit to?' McKellan wasn't playing.

'The chaos you left in San Francisco for a start,' Karolides replied. 'Almost killing Senator Kyle—'

'We also saved her,' McKellan quickly interjected. 'Miss Preston here did that.'

Karolides looked at Trix now, as if realising for the first time there were other people in the room.

'You're Charles Baker's little project, aren't you?' she

asked, and although it was phrased bluntly, Trix got the impression it wasn't deliberate.

'Ma'am?'

'Section D. That's you, right? Wintergreen's band of merry miscreants?'

Trix felt her cheeks flushing.

'She was,' Curtis cut in. 'Now she works for me on the MI5 London desk, Ma'am.'

'Well, at least we have some friends on *that* side of the river still, then,' Karolides replied, glaring at McKellan. 'Kyle wanted more transparency in government oversight, and I want the same. Rattlestone and their ilk have stained the Security Service, and I'm sick of hearing worrying rumours about other little boys' clubs like Caliburn.'

Trix saw McKellan visibly bristle at this.

'Home Secretary, Caliburn isn't anything more than a collective consciousness, like the groups within the Conservatives, like the ERG,' he replied stiffly. 'And we have always been a friend to all governments, including this one—'

'We have enough friends, thank you,' Karolides cut McKellan off with a wave of her hand. 'And secret gang or not, you're a *public servant*, Sir Walter. It's a requirement you be a friend to the Government.'

She sighed.

'Tell your people to book you a holiday. A long one. I'm here to serve you notice – your services are no longer required.'

There was a long moment of uncomfortable silence.

'Are you sure about that?' McKellan replied softly, his voice unemotional and cold. 'You've got some large and unpopular bills going through over the next few weeks. You fail to deliver, Baker will have you out, and another, more malleable replacement will be snuggling down in your chair before you know it.'

'I'll pass those bills,' Karolides returned the ice-cold response. 'I'm certain of it.'

'Then come back then, Home Secretary, if indeed you still have a job,' McKellan turned away from Karolides, returning his attention to the surrounding monitors. 'Until then, if you'll excuse me, I have work to do. The safety of the nation never sleeps.'

Karolides looked back at Trix.

'I'm sad to see you working for him,' she muttered before turning around and storming out of the office. 'I'd expected better from the London office.'

As the door slammed behind her, McKellan let out an explosive sigh of annoyance, before glancing at Casey.

'Get her out of here before I kill her myself,' he muttered, as Casey ran quickly out of the room, following Karolides.

Curtis nodded to Trix to follow him before looking back at McKellan.

'Whatever's going on here, I don't want it landing on my lap, *sir*,' he said as courteously as he could muster, before turning to the door.

McKellan didn't even respond, already watching the monitors.

'We need to be cautious around McKellan,' Curtis said as they made their way back to his Thames House offices. 'For someone to talk to the Home Secretary like that, shows you have the belief you're untouchable. And for all we know, he is.'

'We were told there was a credible threat to her life this weekend, if she carried on with this meeting, right?' Trix mused. 'Maybe McKellan did all this to save her?'

'What, try to kill a Senator just to stop the Home Secretary from attending?' Curtis almost laughed, but stopped himself as he paused in the corridor. 'Actually, that kind of scorched earth technique is pretty much on brand for him. But it was more likely he found a way to let others do his dirty work.'

He leant closer to Trix, lowering his voice.

'Holden was one of his,' he said. 'And by killing Lyons, he was taking out Caliburn assets. Now this was either because he'd been told to, because they were causing problems *as* Caliburn, or because they were causing problems *for* Caliburn. Do your thing, find out where his loyalties were. Give me lists of people he spent time with; anyone who could have connections to both McKellan and Karolides.'

'You think this could have been her?'

Curtis rubbed at his chin.

'You're the Home Secretary,' he mused. 'You're told there's a credible threat against you. So, rather than go, you send a team to take out the person believed to be the threat.'

'Senator Kyle?'

Curtis shrugged.

'I'm spit balling,' he replied. 'But Karolides isn't an angel, either. She's a Tory Cabinet Minister, she's got her own skeletons in her cupboard. Added to the fact she wants Baker's job when they finally have an election, and he invariably loses. Or, he wins, and she ducks back down and waits. She has time. Either way, she could be using Caliburn as a smokescreen.'

He watched Trix for a moment, his eyebrows furrowing as he noticed her concerned expression.

'Second thoughts, Preston?'

'No,' Trix pulled out her phone, typing on it. 'There was a phrase on the screen McKellan was looking at. It was a fraction of a second, but I saw it before his tech closed the window. It said, "Fractal Destiny." Do you have any idea what that means?'

Curtis shook his head.

'Fractal sounds techno, though, so go have a chat with Q-Branch, see if they know anything. You know, boffin speaker to boffin speaker.'

'You know the technical team hates being called that,' Trix smiled.

At this, Curtis shrugged.

'MI6 now call theirs it, so they'll just have to get with the times,' he turned, walking off towards his office. 'Check it out, check Holden out – you know what? Check every bloody thing out. Because currently we're massively underwater here.'

'Casey?'

'Keep him out of the loop,' Curtis rubbed at his chin. 'He was seconded by McKellan less than twenty-four hours back, and he's already looking at home there. Something doesn't feel right. We'll treat him as MI6 until he becomes MI5 again.'

'And Marlowe?' Trix cried out after him.

Curtis turned, his face one of regret.

'He's on his own,' he said. 'We just have to hope he's intelligent, and stubborn enough to bloody well stay alive, wherever he is right now.'

12

THE MATRIX

MARLOWE HAD DECIDED THAT UNLIKE THE MOTEL THEY'D settled for the previous night, a swanky hotel would be enough of a complete contrast that, if he was being hunted in Paris right now, nobody would even consider it.

It was a strategy he often used, and probably owed more to his childhood watching James Bond and Harry Palmer movies than actual operational procedure, but he'd always found that when he stayed in an utter shitehole, he was always found quicker than when he stayed at a multi-level chain hotel.

And, they gave whatever fake ID he was using at the time loyalty points.

Usually going for a suite, Marlowe had pulled himself back a little from his usual extravagance though, and had booked a simple room on a middle floor, under one of his older fake identities, one not created by MI5. In fact, the only person who'd pick up on "David Rimmer" was Trix, and that was partly because they were names from two characters in her favourite show, *Red Dwarf,* Dave Lister and Arnold

Rimmer, mashed together, but also because she'd created the ID in the first place.

Marlowe really hoped she was still on his side.

The moment they arrived in the room, locking the door behind them, Marlowe had resisted Kate's suggestion to order room service, wondering for the first time how she could still be so hungry after their effective double breakfast, and instead had opened Tooley's bag, removing the black box and extending the four stands. He'd originally thought these stood like tripod legs, but now he'd realised these were more like surround speakers, and, connected by some kind of Bluetooth technology, they created a kind of working space, the black box now on the bed, directly in the centre of this.

He couldn't take full credit though, as much of this had been Kate's idea, once she'd had a good look at it.

'Are you sure about this?' he asked as he positioned the last stand. It rose about four feet into the air, matching the others, and as he stepped back, he wondered if he needed to find some sort of power switch for each stand, too.

'Not really, but there's a lot here that feels familiar,' Kate explained. 'From the design, its next-gen tech. Probably some kind of holographic recall device.'

She pointed at the stands.

'You see? The sensors in the corners create a virtual cube.'

Marlowe held his hands up in a confused half-shrug.

'You should talk to Trix about this,' he chuckled. 'I have no idea what you meant after the word *holographic*.'

Kate sighed, grabbing the power cable and placing the UK plug into an adaptor provided by the hotel. Now able to use it in a French socket, she plugged it in.

'Is something supposed to happen?' Marlowe asked.

Kate shrugged.

'I don't even know if the damned thing has a power button,' she said, lifting up the box and peering at the underside. 'And Tooley forgot to leave a user manual with it, so—'

She stopped as the box started speaking, almost dropping it in the process.

'Caliburn holocrom active. Satellite Wi-Fi active. Accessing cloud drive.'

Marlowe moved closer, pointing at the four stands, which had now lit up.

'It's doing something.'

'Cloud drive protected,' the box continued. *'Enter password, using the prefix "keyword" on entry.'*

Marlowe stared at Kate in confusion.

'It wants a password?' he asked in surprise. 'What password?'

Kate tapped at her lip as she thought about this.

'Well, the box was created by Caliburn, because that's where Tooley stole it from,' she said. 'Maybe we're overthinking it.'

She looked back at the box.

'Keyword, Caliburn,' she said clearly.

There was a long pause, and then a defiant *beep*.

'Incorrect,' the box replied, almost mockingly, although Marlowe admitted that could just be his own opinion. *'You have two attempts remaining.'*

'Okay, how about—'

Kate stopped speaking as Marlowe silenced her by placing his hand over her mouth.

'We can't just say anything,' he hissed. 'We have two more opportunities, and after that, we might be locked out.'

'Okay then, so what do *you* think it is?' Kate pulled away

from the hand. 'And I wasn't going to state the password, I would have had to start with Key—'

She stopped herself this time.

'You know what I mean,' she muttered. 'I would have said the key-thing first.'

Marlowe nodded, staring down at the box. There had been nothing else in the bag that linked to any password, and there hadn't been any papers with random words written on it, either.

'Would Lyons have known it?' he asked.

'Absolutely,' Kate nodded. 'They were thick as thieves, the two of them. In fact, it was one reason Lyons was meeting me there.'

'If that's the case, then think. This must have been the data Lyons was giving you.'

'Lyons didn't speak to me in the end, remember?' Kate folded her arms. 'He spoke to you. And then he texted me, telling me to speak to you, remember?'

Marlowe straightened, frowning.

'He didn't say anything!' he exclaimed irritably. 'He—'

He stopped as he remembered the conversation.

'Remember, Marlowe, the truth is always in the clouds. Congratulations.'

'The clouds,' he muttered, noticing Kate's confused expression at this. 'Lyons, when he spoke to me in the lobby. His last message to me was that "the truth was in the clouds," and it is.'

He pointed at the box.

'A cloud drive. The data of which is out there, on the cloud.'

'And then you said that he congratulated you,' Kate

looked excited as she turned back to the box. 'Keyword. Congratulations.'

Marlowe had gone to stop her, but he was too late, and before he could speak over her, the box was already replying.

'Incorrect. You have one attempt remaining.'

Kate looked hurt as she stared back at Marlowe.

'You said—'

'I did, and he did,' Marlowe shook his head as he worked through the phrase. 'But when he said it, I was confused. Scrapper was Jewish, you see. Made a big thing of his surname, Lyons, all the time we served together. He always called himself the "Lion of Judae" and he *never* said "congratulations." He'd say ...'

He turned to the box, taking a deep breath. If he was wrong about this, then everything would collapse around him, and Fractal Destiny would be unstoppable. Apparently. He didn't even know what this box did.

'Keyword. *Mazel tov*.'

Nothing happened, and for a moment Marlowe felt a sinking sensation in his stomach as he waited for the device to power off, or even send some kind of locator distress signal out, ruining their day really fast.

Instead, however, the edge of the box glowed, as previously hidden LEDs in the seams slowly increased in intensity. The stands hummed with power, and Marlowe, wondering for a second whether this was actually some kind of self-destruct countdown, took an actual step backwards before the stands burst into light, projecting a three-dimensional wireframe image between them, one that covered the room.

'Jesus,' Marlowe muttered to himself as he stared at the scene in front of him. 'It's like *Minority Report* met *Iron Man* and had a baby.'

He wasn't wrong; as he stood in the middle of the hotel room, it was as if there was a light-created virtual room within it, line-art in style. Three of the walls were blank, with shimmering lines of code flashing up and down them randomly, but on the wall directly in front of Marlowe was, well, the best way for him to explain it would be to call it a wall board, filled with pieces of paper, visually replicating how this would look in the real world, while nothing more than files tacked onto a virtual wall and digitally created.

'It's like a three-dimensional desktop,' he said, looking at the imagery. 'Why so detailed?'

'Because it's not just an image,' Kate explained, pointing at the stands. 'Look. Each of them, above the projectors, have cameras. It's like a VR set. You know, like the PC games.'

Marlowe looked blankly at her.

'I like playing FIFA,' he suggested. 'Is this like playing FIFA?'

'Okay, absolutely not,' Kate sighed. 'So, when VR gaming took off, there was a standard style to it. The headpiece had a camera, and that created your "area" to play in. When you moved your hands, the helmet camera caught the motion and changed the game depending on what you did with it.'

She pointed at the stands.

'The more high-end kits had things like those,' she continued. 'Cameras to take in the entire space, so that as you walked around a room, you literally had the whole thing change around you based on what the cameras saw. You could play games where you had a bow and arrow, and if you reached for the quiver behind you, the camera behind would pick this up and your hand in the game would have the arrow in it. Simple commands. Pinch. Move. Pick up. Drop.'

She now pointed at the wall of stuff.

'The projector means we don't need helmets, and the cameras relate our position in the "room" to the box's CPU. It means we can utilise everything we see. Each piece that's tacked virtually on the wall can be clicked, moved, enlarged. And the room is probably based on Tooley's actual office.'

She showed this by pulling a piece of paper from the wall, using her two hands, both pinched between index finger and thumb to open up wider, enlarging the piece of paper, and Marlowe stared in wonder as it turned into a three-dimensional newspaper in her hand. Pictures of Senator Kyle and the Home Secretary Joanna Karolides appeared beside news reports of the Middle East, the current Democratic and Republican Party poll reports, notes on upcoming UK by-election expectations, the Stock Exchange ...

'They're like little browser windows,' he marvelled.

More than that, though, it was a conspiracy theorist's dream; a wall filled with possibilities and "what ifs".

'A friend of mine told me about wallpaper once,' he said, picking up his own piece of line art real estate, turning it in his hand. 'It's wired up so there's a charge through it, and you can use your entire wall as a HD OLED screen. You don't need to buy a TV, you could literally open a window on the wall, play the video through it, and by sliding your arms out on each corner, make it as large or as small as you wanted.'

'I'm guessing the TV manufacturers wouldn't be happy with that,' Kate replied.

Marlowe shrugged.

'This was a few years back, and nothing ever came from it, so maybe the TV manufacturers are more powerful than we thought.'

After staring at the wall for a moment longer, he turned back to Kate.

'So this is it?' he asked. 'Fractal Destiny?'

'Yeah,' Kate said, but Marlowe heard a slight note of uncertainty in her voice.

'You sure?'

After a moment, Kate shook her head.

'I think it's more a window into where Fractal Destiny lives,' she said. 'It's not this box, but this box can link to it. Stream from it.'

Marlowe nodded at this. It made sense that a cloud-based neural network wasn't locked to a box in a bag in a security deposit vault, after all.

'How does it work?'

'It's a virtual room. Touch the file you're interested in, expand, edit or delete it. Very user friendly.'

Marlowe, having already worked this part out, was already moving files around, examining them.

'You said they'd already started, that Fractal Destiny was already in action,' he asked, looking back at her. 'How far is Caliburn from what they want?'

'When I left? They were on stage six, I think,' Kate rubbed at her neck as she considered this. 'By now, probably stage seven or eight. Although I think eight was the death of a high-ranking political figure—'

'And Senator Kyle didn't die,' Marlowe finished the sentence. 'And how do we stop it?'

'We can't. Once it starts, the algorithm within the neural network will constantly adjust, no matter what we do.'

'Turn it off?'

'It'll run in the background.'

Marlowe was looking annoyed at the box.

'Disconnect it from the network?'

'It'll find another network,' Kate replied mournfully. 'It's a level five crypto-masher. It goes through network passcodes like a knife through butter. It could hack the NSA's servers in five minutes if you so wanted to.'

Forgetting where he was for a moment, Marlowe went to punch the wall and overbalanced as his fist went straight through it.

'There must be something,' he snapped as he regained his composure.

'Not really—' Kate had started to speak, but then stopped, her eyes widening as, working through whatever idea she'd now had, she paced the room.

'Actually, there still has to be someone to fulfil each task, right? The human element?' she suggested.

'You mean Caliburn, or whoever's in the room doing what the neural network requires,' Marlowe was understanding where Kate was going with this. 'The Agent Fords of the world.'

Kate nodded.

'If we want to stop the neural network, then we need to stop them,' she smiled. 'It doesn't matter what number it's reached, if it doesn't have the physical, real world element to fulfil what it needs to do next.'

She looked at the box on the bed.

'I wonder if it's voice commands too,' she mused. 'It took voice for the password, after all. Computer, identify Fractal Destiny stages seven to nine.'

'Stage seven,' the computer spoke. *'European Union crisis talks about world debt. America is isolated. Stage eight. American Senator assassinated on US soil. Stage nine. Dow Jones Index slumps to all-time low—low—low—'*

'What's happening?' Marlowe turned from the virtual wall.

'It's changing in real time,' Kate replied. 'It's altering the neural network, as the American Senator wasn't assassinated.'

There was a *beep*, and the computer restarted speaking.

'Adjusted parameters,' it continued. *'Stage seven. European Union crisis talks about world debt. America is isolated. Stage eight. UK Cabinet Minister assassinated on British soil. Stage nine. City Financial Index slumps to all-time low. Dow Jones follows.'*

'See,' Kate moved to the bag, pulling out one of the burner phones, opening it up. 'It's altered the parameters and changed the US attack to a UK attack. Either way, it still destabilises the Dow Jones, which is what is probably needed for stage ten.'

She opened up the virtual newspaper again, showing Marlowe a news page browser.

'The world debt talks were last week in Geneva,' she said. 'And with Kyle still alive, it's creating alternate paths.'

Returning to the virtual wall, she flipped some files around, looking for something in particular.

'If I was McKellan, and if I wanted to kill a UK Cabinet Minister, I'd kill two birds with one stone,' she said, pointing back at the image of Joanna Karolides that they'd seen earlier. 'I'd take out the Home Secretary.'

'Why her?' Marlowe asked. 'Apart from the fact she was meaning to speak to Kyle?'

'Because she's a massive pain in McKellan's arse,' Kate was still swiping files around, hunting for something as yet unseen. 'She's been trying for more transparency in government and the agencies they outsource to for years. She helped dismantle Rattlestone, and she's one House of Lords Bill away from cancelling anyone with Caliburn affiliations from working in the Security Service, claiming it's a massive conflict of interest.'

'I bet McKellan would see that differently,' Marlowe pulled out his phone, googling Karolides. 'There's an article here from the Daily Mail, talking about how there's a bit of an uproar about her attending a Veteran's Ball tomorrow night in Kensington.'

Kate smiled at Marlowe, staring at a phone in a holographic room.

'Bloody luddite,' she said. 'You could have found that here.'

'Yeah, but it's all hand wavey when I could just type it with my thumbs,' Marlowe tossed the phone onto the bed. 'London. That's where they'll do it. What happens if we stop it?'

'It'll be like we saw here,' Kate replied. 'The device creates a new stage eight. But after two changes, it'll be looking at further down the line options. It might even have to add new stages to get to where it needs to be. And by then we'll have time to change things.'

'So we need to get into the ball,' Marlowe smiled. 'Which also involves returning to London. Where I'm possibly still wanted for murder—'

'Sorry?' Kate's eyes rose at this.

'Long story, more self-defence,' Marlowe shrugged. 'But even with that, MI6 will be hunting me for treason still, maybe even MI5 too, and even if they're not, Caliburn will want to shut me up. And they'll also want to kill you, so that might be a little difficult.'

He grinned.

'So we make it up as we go along. It's worked so far.'

'That involves getting into London first,' Kate pulled the

plug from the socket, and the entire three-dimensional virtual room winked into nothingness. 'And if you haven't noticed, we don't have passports that would let us in, and I don't think your CIA friend is going to want to keep helping us without something in return.'

Marlowe shook his head, rummaging in the black bag they'd taken from Tooley's vault, and pulling out a couple of the passport blanks.

'Don't worry,' he smiled. 'I know someone who can sort that.'

13

THE FORGER

WHEN ASKED TO DESCRIBE A FORGER, MOST PEOPLE WOULD probably think of a young man or woman, surrounded by technology and image-altering software, working deep into the night as they alter digital watermarks onto specially treated paper, while listening to ambient sounds through their headphones, working long hours to create these important documents.

What they probably *wouldn't* expect was a middle-aged, dumpy woman with wiry grey hair, chain-smoking cigarettes while working in the most dingy and mould-ridden location you can think of – but that was *exactly* what Helen Bonneville was, and where she was working, as Marlowe and Kate were escorted in by a muscled black teenager in a puffer jacket, an obvious pistol in his inside pocket.

'Thomas,' she said familiarly, rising from her chair and giving Marlowe a hug. 'It's been too long. I heard you've been fired. Again. What's going on?'

Marlowe smiled.

'Kate, meet Helen Bonneville,' he said. 'She knew my mum, so I've known her since I was a kid. She might not look much, but she is by far one of the best forgers I've ever had the honour of meeting.'

'Listen to you. "Honour of meeting,"' Helen mocked. 'Good God, are you trying to shag this woman or what?'

Marlowe sighed.

'She also has a language selection that defeats most soldiers I've ever worked with, as well,' he continued. 'So I apologise in advance for her rather advanced form of Tourette's.'

Kate laughed.

'Pleasure to meet you,' she said. 'I've never heard of you, but that's probably a good thing in our industry.'

'Ah, so you're a spook as well,' Helen returned to her chair, sitting back in it as she observed the new arrival. 'That explains why he's brought you with him.'

She glanced back at Marlowe, the slightest hint of a smile on her lips.

'Usually it's because he's in trouble, or he needs an identity to get out of something he doesn't want to do.'

She raised an eyebrow at Marlowe, mockingly.

'Have you got something here that you need to get out of that you don't want to do?'

'Yes and no,' Marlowe replied honestly. 'It's more of a "need an identity to do something that needs to be done" kind of thing.'

'Ah, so it's back to being Kevin Costner again,' Helen nodded.

'Kevin Costner?' Kate raised an eyebrow.

'Ignore her, she drinks,' Marlowe pleaded.

'*Robin Hood, Prince of Thieves.* Bloody film, it fair ruined toddler Thomas, made him want to be one of the good guys. Work for the law.'

'And your problem with that was?' Marlowe argued.

'Costner played Robin, and he was the bad guy,' Helen sniffed. 'The Sheriff was the good guy. He's even named "Sheriff," for goodness' sake. Have you ever even watched a sodding Western?'

She glanced at Kate morosely.

'But the victors write the stories,' she said. 'Just look at poor bloody Richard Plantagenet and Shakespeare. What do you need?'

Marlowe had struggled to keep up with the rapidly drifting subjects, but straightened now he was on firm footing again.

'Two identities that can get the two of us into London, or at least to the UK,' he explained, reaching into his jacket pocket. 'Once I'm there, we can work out our next stops.'

'And you can't use *your* passport because ...'

'Because MI5 burned me.'

'Fair point, but that doesn't explain why you can't use your passport anyway—'

'Because Marlowe and I are currently being chased by half a dozen agencies on treason charges. Well, we believe they are, at least,' Kate smiled winningly. 'We had some issues in America, and because of those, we had to find alternate ways to arrive in France. And now we need to get back into England before anybody realises we've left America.'

'Right ...' Helen clicked her tongue against the roof of her mouth as she pondered this, now understanding a little more about what was going on. 'So you need passable IDs that can get through customs, or maybe St Pancras on the train – I'd suggest you use the Eurostar, so you'd prefer something that could get through that security ...'

She sighed.

'Problem is, my love, to get you into the UK, I'd need a couple of passport blanks. Since they changed up the style and the biometric recommendations, I've found it a little harder to get hold of such things.'

'Then how about we pay you in blanks?' Marlowe suggested, pulling out a handful of varying ones from his inside pocket. 'These, for example? You make us two passports, you can have the rest.'

Helen whistled to herself as she stared at the blanks in Marlowe's hand.

'You know how much those are worth?' she asked.

'Yes, but I also know how much two passports from you are worth,' Marlowe flashed a grin. 'I'd much rather go for the full service and give you something in return than expect your usual and pay for it.'

Helen grinned back, taking one blank and staring at it, turning it over in her hands.

'This is good work,' she said. 'Looks like it's from the source. Hard to push back on it once we have the right information here.'

Kate glanced at Marlowe before replying.

'Knowing the man who it came from, it probably is,' she said.

Helen placed the blank on the table, already opening up a file on her screen.

'Can it be done?'

'Oh, it can be done, there's no issue there,' Helen replied, eyes still glued to the screen. 'But that's not the question you want answered, is it? It's not so much a "can it be done," more a case of "when it can be done," if I'm being honest.'

She turned back to face Marlowe.

'When do you need it by?'

Marlowe nervously rubbed at his beard.

'We kind of need them as quickly as possible,' he said. 'We need to be in England by tomorrow.'

'Tomorrow?' Helen almost fell off her chair. 'That's less than twenty-four hours' turnaround!'

'I wouldn't have come to you if I didn't think you could do it,' Marlowe said softly.

'Flattery will get you everywhere,' Helen tapped on her lips with a pen. 'You really need this, don't you?'

'It could be life or death,' Marlowe continued.

'Oh, don't be so dramatic.'

'I'm not. There's a strong possibility the Home Secretary, Joanna Karolides's life is on the line, tomorrow evening.'

'Home Secretary?' Helen's voice grew colder. 'Well, if that's the case, Thomas, let's say my rate has just gone up.'

Marlowe went to reply to this, but as he moved to speak, Helen held up a hand.

'Not what you think,' she said. 'Joanna Karolides is one reason I'm working in France still.'

She rose, walking over to a printer as it spat out a sheet.

'We had a falling out a few years back,' she explained as she picked the sheet up, inspecting it before tearing it into three pieces and tossing it into a waste bin. 'I found it better to go to the EU than stay in London working with her, so you get an idea of how lovely she was as a boss.'

She returned to her chair.

'And then she was one of the crew who created Brexit, thus abandoning me to the French government as the walls around jolly old England rose up. So, if I'm doing something that's going to get her saved, I want credit when you do it. I want that miserable old bitch to know I saved her life, and I didn't leave my chair to do it.'

Marlowe smiled at this.

'So basically, if you give us an ID that gets us into the UK, and if we somehow managed to save the woman who is being targeted for assassination, and – in the process – save the Western world, by the way, you would like credit for doing this?'

'Oh, don't get me wrong, my love, I don't want to be the main star of it,' Helen shook her head. 'I just want my part in the whole shebang to be recognised.'

Marlowe nodded at this.

'I can guarantee, Helen, that I will do everything I can – before they drag me off and put me in some black site in the middle of nowhere – to make sure they all know you helped me do what I needed to do.'

'Well, if it's going to involve me being taken to a black site, I'd prefer to keep my name out of it,' Helen grinned, already returning to the blanks, peering hard at the pages. 'Do you have names in mind? Or would you prefer me to make you them?'

'I'm guessing you've already got some IDs that actually exist, that you can adapt?'

'I do,' Helen sighed. 'Unfortunately, I don't have stupid names. So you're going to have to have a more pedestrian one this time.'

'I'm fine with having pedestrian names,' Kate interjected.

'Fine, then. Come back tomorrow. I'll get this done.'

'What's the quickest you can get these ready?'

Helen considered the question.

'Well, I need you to take some photos, and we can do that now, as I have a wall over there for that. I then need to hack into the system to make sure it all fits the IDs I'm considering, maybe alter a few little details to match things I know about you, Thomas. Scars, things like that.'

She slowly spun in a circle on her chair as she went through the process in her mind.

'I'd need to sort out your biometrics before we do anything else,' she mused. 'Realistically, I'd have to bring a guy in to do that. I'm assuming you wouldn't want him knowing what's going on, or who you are, why you're doing this – all that sort of spooky spy shit, so that'd take up time. Earliest I'd be able to do it ...'

She looked at her watch.

'... twelve hours from now, so say midnight.'

Marlowe worked the times out in his head.

'If you can get us midnight, we can be on the Eurostar first thing in the morning,' he said. 'That would work perfectly.'

'Okay,' Helen replied, already waving Marlowe off. 'Leave me the blanks, and I'll do this.'

Marlowe placed the second blank onto the table beside the one Helen had been examining.

'No, I meant pass me *all* the blanks,' Helen insisted.

'You might have known my mum, Helen,' Marlowe replied slowly, the smile now fading as his voice lowered. 'But the one thing I did learn about you was never to give you payment up front.'

Helen grinned at this, as if Marlowe had just given her some kind of weird, back-handed compliment.

'My days grinding through grunt work for Emilia Wintergreen died a long time ago,' she said. 'I understand you no longer work for her, either.'

'Let's just say I took a path that left me a little high and dry,' Marlowe shrugged modestly.

'I heard. I was speaking to Marshall Kirk a little while back.'

Marlowe grimaced at this; Marshall Kirk had been his mentor in MI5. And the reason he was no longer a member of this prestigious Intelligence Agency was because he had taken the blame for something that Marshall's daughter had been accused of.

'Did he say anything nice?' he enquired politely.

'He said he owed you his life, and that his daughter owed you hers as well,' Helen chuckled. 'If you hadn't offered me all those blanks, I probably would have done this for free.'

'I pay for good work,' Marlowe threw back.

'And I appreciate it. But still, as you're giving me those, you'll have it by midnight. So come back around then, and I'll have them for you. After we take some snippy snaps first.'

And with the deal organised and set up, and then with some passport photos taken against a blank white wall in a variety of different clothes Helen had for such occasions, all with their faces emotionless and blank, Marlowe and Kate eventually made their farewells, and left the strange alleyway forgery den of Helen Bonneville.

'Are you really sure we can trust her?' Kate asked, once they were a fair distance from the location, partly because she didn't trust Helen to have the outside of the building bugged, but also because she didn't want to accuse someone Marlowe almost thought of as family, as being someone who could betray them.

Marlowe thought about the question for a long minute as they walked along the Parisian road.

'No,' he eventually replied. 'But in the grand scheme of things, we don't really have many people we can trust right now.'

Kate gave a little smile.

'Thanks,' she said.

'For what?'

'For being honest with me,' Kate shrugged, looking out across the street. 'You could easily have just said it was fine, she could be trusted, and come back later, with me none the wiser, but you didn't.'

'Some people would rather that,' Marlowe suggested.

'And I'm sure they like spending their lives in ignorance,' Kate retorted. 'Anyway, come on. If we can't do anything until midnight, we've got a day to spend in France, it seems.'

'True,' Marlowe stopped. 'You know, it's weird. I've been running forwards for so long now, I don't know what it's like to stop and wait.'

He stared up at the surrounding buildings.

'So what do you want to do? Do you want to go see a film or something? Catch a train to Disneyland Paris or Asterix World?'

'Actually,' Kate beamed at the thought, 'I've never been to the Moulin Rouge.'

'Well then, let's get that sorted!' Marlowe exclaimed. 'Let's have a day out as tourists, go to an early show of the Moulin Rouge, and then grab our new identities – before we return to

England and our possible arrest for treason against the Crown.'

'You make it sound so romantic,' Kate laughed, linking her arm into his. 'Can we stop for some lunch first, though? I'm starving.'

14

SLEEPING SOLDIERS

AFTER THE LAST TIME THEY'D SPOKEN, TRIX HADN'T EXPECTED a return visit to McKellan's Ops room, but here she was, still not returning to her apartment since landing, and feeling the jet lag encroaching onto the back of her brain as she was once more called across to the "wrong" side of the Thames.

'Good, you're here,' McKellan said, nodding from the desk he was standing beside, looking quizzically at Curtis, standing beside her. 'I didn't call for you, though.'

'Preston is in my team, so if you're calling her in for another MI6-based bollocking, you can go through me,' Curtis muttered. 'Sir.'

'And why in God's name would you think I was bollocking her?'

'Perhaps because the last time I was here, you told me to "follow bloody orders and go back to work, leaving the grown-up work to MI6," and then reminded me I'd done nothing of note here?' Trix suggested innocently.

'I was angry,' McKellan mumbled. 'I snap. I do that. If you can't deal with it, don't work in the department.'

'Again, sir, she doesn't work in your department, she works in mine,' Curtis interjected.

'And you work for me.'

'No, sir, you're my superior by Civil Service grading, and I report on some items to you when there is a mutual need, for MI5 and MI6 to work together, but that doesn't mean MI5 staff by default are yours to play with.'

McKellan went to reply, but instead breathed in slowly, as if counting to five, and then nodded at the monitors.

'I need her to identify someone,' he said. 'And it was from before she started with you, so it's technically not connected to you. Hence why I didn't invite you.'

He nodded to Hill.

'Pull it back up,' he said.

On the screen, a CCTV image appeared of a bar. In it was a line of booths, and two people were sitting in one. The man was facing away, but Trix already knew from his jacket it was Marlowe. The woman facing him was in a suit, and Trix recognised her red hair straight away, even though the CCTV image was black and white.

'Few weeks ago, Tom Marlowe met with this woman in an Irish Bar in New York,' McKellan said.

'You've been following Marlowe?' Trix wasn't surprised at this, but was impressed they'd found the bar.

'No, we were following someone else,' McKellan nodded at Hill, and the image changed to one of Marlowe and another woman.

Trisha Hawkins, the missing CEO of *Phoenix Industries,* and onetime management of *Rattlestone Security.*

'I'm guessing you recognise Miss Hawkins,' McKellan said, and for a moment Trix wondered if he was mocking her, until she realised he wasn't even thinking about her, more interested in the woman on the screen.

'Yes sir, I used to work for her. And her boss, Francine Pearce. It's what got me picked up on MI5's radar.'

'So we've been watching Miss Hawkins for a while,' McKellan replied. 'And imagine our surprise when we learn she's met with Marlowe there.'

'He was closing off an old thread,' Trix replied coldly. 'He was telling her to get out of his life.'

'Yes, well, I don't care,' McKellan shrugged. 'All I care is that we kept tabs on this pub, and then here we are, a couple of days later, and Marlowe meets this filly.'

He looked back at Trix.

'I'd like to know who she is.'

'Can I ask what this is in connection with?' Trix squared her shoulders.

'No you bloody well can't!' McKellan almost exploded. 'Don't you understand how this all works? You work for him, you work for me—'

'But sir, I didn't work for either of you when I met this woman,' Trix smiled pleasantly. 'I was suspended from MI5 and waiting for review. So, by admitting I met this woman, in, say, a hypothetical off the books operation on US soil ...'

McKellan sighed, realising he'd been played.

'Okay, fine,' he said, tapping Hill on the shoulder. 'Pull up the file.'

The screen now showed an image of a dark-haired man.

'Luis Gonzalez,' he explained. 'Asset to about a dozen different agencies. Came to MI6 a few hours ago to say he'd placed two people, one matching Marlowe's description, into the bowels of a FedEx Airbus at San Diego International, heading for Paris.'

'Why did he come to you?'

'Because he knew the US wouldn't give him anything for it,' Curtis answered for McKellan, looking at the screen. 'This was an American op, right?'

'Luis works for Garcia Lopez, but claimed he was going under the codename Steve Trevor, and he was working for a Diana Prince,' McKellan, annoyed his reveal had been stolen, spoke quickly. 'We contacted Mister Lopez, showed him this image, and he confirmed this was the same woman.'

McKellan looked back at Trix.

'Is her name Prince?' he asked. 'Because we have no knowledge of her.'

Trix shook her head.

'When I met her in New York, she called herself Sasha Bordeaux, but Marlowe said it was based on a DC Comics character. I'm guessing this is another such alibi?'

'Why?' McKellan seemed genuinely confused by the answer.

'Because Diana Prince was the secret identity of Wonder Woman, and Steve Trevor was her kissy kissy,' Hill said, before remembering her place was to operate the computer and not speak. 'Sir.'

'She's definitely CIA though,' Trix added, as if hoping this would at least count for something.

'So a CIA agent so secret nobody knows her real name, sticks Marlowe and this rogue GCHQ analyst onto a plane into Europe for no reason? I don't buy it,' McKellan snapped. 'Marlowe is a CIA asset. He has to be.'

'No, sir,' Curtis shook his head. 'I can't believe that.'

'Personally, Curtis, I couldn't give a rat's arse what you or your uptight chums at Box think,' McKellan returned to the screen. 'Why would Marlowe and this woman go to Paris, of all places, after stealing Brian Tooley's arm?'

'Sir?' Trix, unsure if she heard this correctly, spoke. But before McKellan could answer, Hill was typing on the screen.

'Tooley had an account with SecureTrade,' she said. 'And it was accessed today.'

'They found his secrets,' McKellan was nodding at Hill now. 'You can find them, right?'

'We have the time the box was opened, we can check CCTV, I reckon we can.'

'Good,' McKellan went to add something, but stopped, looking back at Trix. 'You can both piss off now.'

Reluctantly, and without protesting, Trix turned and started for the door, but not before glancing at the screen. And, now out in the corridor, she was already typing into her phone as Curtis stormed out after her, his face a mask of impotent fury.

'The nerve of that prick,' he hissed. 'If you want to raise a complaint, I can—'

'Sir,' Trix dropped her voice now, interrupting him. 'I know we haven't worked long together, but do you trust me?'

Curtis frowned.

'I wouldn't have you working for me if I didn't.'

'And do you trust Marlowe?'

Curtis went to reply, something likely insulting and joking, but stopped as he saw her expression.

'He's proved himself to me more than that shower of bastards in there,' he muttered. 'What's the problem, Preston?'

'The woman, Hill, she was sending a message,' Trix replied. 'It was codes and cyphers, because nothing's ever easy in the Intelligence Service, but I recognised them. She was activating two sleeper assets in Paris, sending them after Marlowe.'

She leant closer.

'It was a "kill on sight" order,' she hissed. 'They don't want Marlowe talking. I need to warn him.'

'Are you about to tell me you've had a secret phone line to Marlowe all along?' Curtis started pulling Trix down the corridor, away from the door.

'No, sir, but I have a message board we use, and a phrase, something that would let him know to check it.'

'But you don't know where he is,' Curtis hammered the button for the elevator, but stopped as Trix smiled.

'Yet,' she said. 'Hill gave me a place to start, and I'll bet whatever you want I can find him before she does.'

'It'll be close,' Curtis said as they entered the elevator. 'You'd better start immediately.'

KILLING TWELVE HOURS IN PARIS WAS ACTUALLY HARDER THAN you'd think, especially if you were doing your best to keep yourselves off CCTV footage and public gaze, but Marlowe and Kate had done their best to do it. After walking around Père-Lachaise cemetery for a couple of hours looking for Jim Morrison's grave, they'd then returned to Paris for eight-thirty pm, as Marlowe had organised dinner and a show at the Moulin Rouge. With the show finishing by ten, they had plenty of time to get back to Helen, and so, for the first time in ages, they sat at a table and relaxed slightly.

'He wasn't there, you know,' Kate smiled as she ate a mouthful of sweet and sour mixed vegetables, holding the fork up to express her point as she continued. 'In the grave we saw.'

'Jim Morrison's body was stolen?'

'Never there. He faked his own death,' Kate grinned. 'Think about it. So it's 1971, he's with his girlfriend, Pamela Courson, in Paris. He claims he has trouble breathing, has a bath. She finds him in it a few hours later, dead.'

'So how's this a conspiracy?'

'The night before, he's apparently seen at the Circus Club, buying heroin.'

'So it was a heroin overdose, then,' Marlowe ate a mouthful of his own food as he replied. 'Still not seeing why the body isn't there.'

'Morrison died at five in the morning, and the doctor they called in certified that it was because of heart failure,' Kate smiled. 'An autopsy was never performed on the body, even though it was buried several days after his death.'

Marlowe shook his head, already dismissing this as hearsay.

'There's more,' Kate tapped her nose with the fork. 'So, Morrison was accused of exposing himself on stage during a gig in the US. And, despite the lack of evidence, Morrison was found guilty and sentenced to jail. It was in the Mid-west, Bible Belt area, and they'd been gunning for him for a while, anyway. His lawyers appealed the decision, but Jim Morrison was going to jail. But, before this happened, he upped sticks and moved here, to Paris, where there wasn't an extradition treaty. While he was here? No prison for Jim. But in a way, Paris became a prison.'

'So he faked his death to what, create a new persona and return?'

Kate shrugged.

'Seems convenient that months after he flees the US, he suddenly "dies" in his bath,' she continued. 'There's no autopsy because French law doesn't require it, and the funeral is closed casket. Only Pamela sees the body. Pamela, by the way, who, although never being married, is quickly made Morrison's heir, in Paris, before his death, and who, a couple of years later mysteriously dies herself, her body quickly being cremated.'

'So dig up the grave, check the body?'

'Ah, but where's the story there? Where's the romance?' Kate smiled. 'The story isn't *is he dead*, but *what happened?* Did he die of heart failure at twenty-seven? It's unlikely, but possible. Could it have been a heroin overdose? Well, he was seen buying it. And there was no autopsy. Nobody knows the truth, and the misdirection allows escape.'

She looked at the stage.

'We're spooks, Marlowe. We learn the best misdirection from the best magicians.'

'You sound like it's something you'd like to try,' Marlowe observed Kate, wondering if this was some kind of message.

'We are,' Kate replied. 'We're literally getting new lives given to us at midnight. Tom Marlowe and Kate Maybury are, for all intents and purposes, dead, until we return.'

She stared at the stage.

'The show will start soon,' she said. 'You need to observe, or you get lost in the performance.'

Before Marlowe could say anything, though, a young man in a server's uniform walked over, looking nervously around before leaning close.

'Are you Mister Lister?' he asked. 'Mister David Lister?'

Marlowe felt a sliver of ice slide down his spine. Only one

person would ask that: Trix Preston. Dave Lister was the name they'd always used for contacting off books.

'I am,' he said. 'What's the message?'

'Your sister called, she gave us your description and told me to let you know your—' the server paused, unsure how to phrase this. 'Let's just say there's been a loss in your family, and you should contact her in the usual manner.'

Marlowe nodded.

'Was it in Budapest?'

The server shook his head.

'I'm sorry, but no,' he replied. 'That's all we were told.'

Marlowe considered this. The Budapest Protocol was a term created by Marlowe and Trix as a cypher for messages. As far as he knew, only one other person who knew this was a lawyer in New York. The location of the message was the cypher used, usually "Budapest," but it could be any city name, as long as there was one given.

To *not* name one was unheard of.

'Do you have a phone I can use?' he asked, rising. Kate, seeing this, looked back, but Marlowe shook his head.

'Back in a moment, enjoy the show,' he said. 'Message from Trix.'

Following the server, Marlowe walked out of the main restaurant and followed him up the stairs.

'Mister Lister needs to speak to his sister,' the server said to one man up there, and although in Marlowe's mind, the translated French rhymed, it didn't in the language the server spoke in. A woman at a desk nodded, allowing Marlowe to sit.

'Can I use the internet?' Marlowe added. 'The server said there was a death, and I'm guessing she wants me to organise some kind of funeral director.'

The woman leant back over, opening a browser window, before picking up the phone, dialling nine for an outside line.

Marlowe took the phone, dialling a number. In fact, it was his own number; he didn't know what number Trix was on right now, and she probably didn't want people to know she was in contact with him.

Using the browser, be began to quickly search for an old Reddit group. It was created for fans of *Red Dwarf*, and hadn't really been used for several years, apart from the occasional thread or spam message, removed when the moderators of the group saw them.

This was why Marlowe needed to move fast, as he needed to see a message before it was removed. And there, on the screen, was a new post.

L1sterRawx: 21:04pm

Six minutes earlier. The same time she would have called.

'Hi, it's me,' he said into the phone's mouthpiece, pretending to be on the call. 'What happened?'

Marlowe was keeping his voice light, but sombre, as if expecting to hear of the death of someone close, but while he did this on autopilot, he was reading the message, trying hard not to bolt from the chair.

Usually, it would be rubbish text, a random spam post of unconnected words, and the cypher would discover the genuine message. This time, however, the message was simple and to the point.

Two sleepers coming for you.

Get out now.

Marlowe closed the browser, faked a farewell down the phone onto his own answerphone before disconnecting, and then rose from the chair, working out his next steps.

Trix was in a hurry. She was racing the clock. She knew he was here and what he was wearing, which meant she'd tracked him, possibly even from SecureTrade.

Which meant there was a chance she saw him go to Helen.

'Shit,' he growled as he walked to the door, but the server paused him.

'Apologies for your loss,' he said. 'Is there anything we can do to help?'

'No, it's fine,' Marlowe gave a sad smile. 'It was an aunt I was never fond of.'

'Ah, well we all have those,' the server gave a wry grin, and Marlowe continued down the stairs, now on a heightened sense of alert, and his hidden SIG Sauer burning a hole in his back.

Someone had given him up.

There was no way they could know he was in Paris, unless they'd been told by SecureTrade, the people who flew them over, or Helen. Had he made a mistake going to her for help?

No. This was MI5 or even MI6 doing what they did best.

He had the dice, he'd given them a roll. Now he just had to keep with the plan.

It was nine-fifteen now, still a good few hours before his meeting with Helen.

Tough. She'll have to work harder.

Kate was already in the lobby as Marlowe came down the stairs, the concern obvious on her face.

'We've been made,' he whispered, taking her by the arm

and leading her towards the main entrance. 'We need to get out of here fast.'

Kate, to her credit, didn't even argue as the two of them walked out onto the street.

'Where now then?' she asked. 'Which direction is safe right now?'

Marlowe watched the two men walking towards him, one black and burly, the other Armenian in looks and slimmer.

'I think we've gone past that point now,' he said as, grabbing her arm once more, Marlowe started running through the streets of Paris.

15

PARIS ALLEYS

It's one thing to travel the streets of Paris during the day as a tourist; it's a completely different situation to run for your life in the middle of the night.

Marlowe had been to the local area many times over the years, but had never actively scoped the streets for any kind of foot-based chase, and so instead he relied on instinct as he zigzagged down the streets, the two attackers following close behind. Luckily for them, or, rather unluckily, the back streets of Paris were empty as the moon shone bright in the sky, as even though the lack of people didn't slow them down, it also didn't give them crowds to hide within.

Marlowe chanced a glance back at the lead assassin; the slimmer of the two, he was struggling to keep up so not as active and fit as the burlier man beside him. However, even if they could outpace their pursuers, Marlowe knew this would be a short escape, as he could see the glint of guns in their hands.

The moment they gained too much distance, the

attackers would decide the risk of losing them outweighed the attention gunshots would bring, and fire.

Suddenly, Marlowe caught sight of a nearby alleyway; it could be a dead end, and it could be the biggest mistake of his life, but it was still a lifeline. He pulled Kate towards it, hoping to lose the assassins in the smaller, maze-like streets.

But the assassins were hot on their trail, and they didn't hesitate to follow them into the alley. Marlowe knew they were in trouble if they kept running, and braced himself for the worst. Kate wasn't a field agent, she was an analyst. If these two men were trained as much as Marlowe assumed they were, it meant Marlowe and Kate were technically outnumbered and outgunned, but he refused to give up without a fight.

Deciding a proactive approach was better than a reactive one, he paused, pulling Kate to the side.

'Get behind me,' he hissed, pulling his own gun out. It felt light in his hand, and Marlowe knew with a sinking sensation it was almost out of bullets, if not empty. He'd been so caught up in the movements of the day, he hadn't considered this.

Rookie, rookie move.

He hoped he had at least two bullets, but he wouldn't use them unless he was a hundred percent sure of a kill shot. A wasted bullet could mean death. At the same time, if these were MI6 sleepers, then they were brother agents – could Marlowe really kill them? Or, rather, should he? Killing MI6 agents would definitely place him on a dozen different kill lists, even if it was proven to be self-defence. If they were Caliburn, there was an argument to be made, but even if he won the argument, he'd never be able to work in the Intelligence or Security Service again. Nobody would trust him enough to work with him.

No. He had to do his best to subdue these men without shooting to kill. Which made things even more fun.

The attackers approached, their guns raised, but held uncertainly now, unsure of what was about to happen. Marlowe guessed they weren't expecting him to stop and confront them, and therefore now reassessed what their target was currently packing, but could still feel his heart racing as he assessed the situation. He knew he had to act quickly to protect Kate and himself, but he also really wanted to know who sent them.

Deciding enough was enough, the slim man moved forward, aiming his gun at Marlowe's head, most likely planning a point-blank shot. Marlowe had been expecting this, hoping for it even, and dodged the attack, grabbing the slim man at the wrist and twisting it behind his back. With a swift kick to the back of the man's knee, Marlowe sent him tumbling to the ground.

The burlier of the two attackers was a little quicker to react now, firing his gun in Marlowe's direction. Marlowe, sensing the shot rather than seeing it, ducked, narrowly avoiding the bullet as it whizzed past his head. And, before they could fire a second shot, Marlowe was already on the move. He tackled the assassin, knocking him violently to the ground. In the process, the gun went off again, but the bullet missed Marlowe and hit a nearby car, the alarm going off with a piercing whine as the window shattered with an explosion of safety glass.

Marlowe was close now, and intended to keep the attackers too close to fire, but out of the corner of his eye, he saw the slim man clamber to his feet, aiming his gun at Marlowe, too far away to tackle—

The man dropped his gun with a yell of pain before he

could fire, however, as Kate, picking up a length of chain from beside an alleyway door, had whipped it down onto his hand, slapping the gun aside. As he grabbed at his possibly broken wrist, Kate threw the chain over to Marlowe.

'Here!' she cried as, grabbing the chain, Marlowe hooked it around his knuckles. It was about a metre in length, and with a couple of loops around his fist, Marlowe now had a pretty vicious knuckleduster, using it quickly to hammer down on the burly man's jaw, noting with a slight smile the man's eyes rolling back, already unconscious.

The slim man, still favouring his wrist pulled a blade from his hip, likely hidden within the belt of his trousers and moved towards Marlowe menacingly, but Marlowe grabbed the other end of the chain, now holding it out in front of him, taut and waiting for the slim man to make his move.

The attacker didn't disappoint; with a yell of anger he charged at Marlowe, blade raised, but Marlowe loosened the chain, and with a flip of his wrists looped around the attacker's wrist holding the blade, yanking tight again, pulling down hard as the man's momentum took him past Marlowe, pulling his hand back into the air, wrenching it behind his shoulder, the blade falling from open fingers as Marlowe quickly lessened the tightness and looped the chain again, this time around the slim man's neck, slamming himself backwards into the slim man's back, pulling down with both ends of the chain as the helpless attacker grabbed at his throat in a futile gesture.

'Who are you?' Marlowe demanded, pulling harder.

The assassin remained silent, and Marlowe wondered whether the chain was too tight to speak, but one glance back at the slim man's face gave him everything he needed to know – he could tell from the man's eyes that he was determined to carry out their mission, no matter what, and give away nothing.

In the distance, Marlowe heard approaching police sirens. Someone had reported the gunshots, most likely, and he knew they had to act fast.

The chain loosened, Marlowe stared down at the slim man.

'Did Caliburn send you?' he snapped. 'MI5? MI6? CIA? Who?'

'You're a dead man, Marlowe,' the slim man spat. 'It doesn't matter how far you run. We'll still catch you.'

Marlowe considered this, pulled his SIG Sauer out and, pleasantly surprised that it had bullets, shot both attackers in their thighs. As the two men yelled out, writhing in pain, Marlowe stepped back.

'Good luck chasing me now,' he smiled, cocking his head as the sirens gained in noise. 'The police will be here soon. They'll take you to hospital, ask loads of questions about your illegal weapons. Have fun, and see you later, chaps.'

And, with the lights at the end of the alley now reflecting the lights of the police sirens, Marlowe and Kate turned and continued down a side alley, into the network of narrow lanes that led out of the kill zone.

AFTER A FEW MINUTES, WITH THE SOUNDS OF SIRENS RECEDING and no obvious signs of pursuit, Marlowe allowed them to slow down.

'Are we safe?' Kate, still shocked by the encounter, whispered.

Marlowe nodded. And, as he caught his breath, Marlowe knew he had just narrowly escaped death.

But he also knew that the danger was far from over. He had to find out who those agents were, who'd sent them, and why they were after him and Kate.

But first, he needed to find Helen. If they followed him to the Moulin Rouge, they must have seen him with her earlier, and that placed her in immediate danger.

She's really going to hate me now, he thought miserably to himself as he waved for a taxi, giving the address of Helen Bonneville. *Not only am I early, I've brought a whole ton of shit down on her.*

TRIX HAD BEEN SCROLLING THROUGH THE PARIS CCTV cameras for a while now. She knew Marlowe had been in the Moulin Rouge, and it was a matter of minutes from the message given to the front desk to his appearance on the message board, but she wasn't able to follow in real time, as the feed was already being watched by someone else in Thames House; most likely McKellan, checking on his sleeper agent kill squad.

So, instead, Trix had been trying to find cameras that weren't on the same feed, looking for video that could help her identify any clues as to Marlowe's status, but keep her from being taken off the network.

So far, she hadn't found anything. So, instead, she'd looked from a different angle, checking to see if she could find anything on the two sleepers.

Instead, she found herself on the back end of a network conversation between two departments in Vauxhall's offices;

the first was most probably Hill, the second someone in Paris. The conversation was encrypted, and this hadn't surprised Trix, but she knew enough about MI6's cyphers that she could almost read it without working through codes.

Marlowe had escaped.

Both assets were down, but not terminated.

Trix wanted to punch the air, celebrate the moment, but she knew there'd be a witch-hunt happening right now. McKellan wouldn't take long to work out Marlowe had to have been informed. He'd learn about the message given to Marlowe, and he'd work it back.

Trix knew she'd outstayed her welcome for the moment. It was time to get out.

However, as she gathered her things, she saw the door to the main office open, and two suited men walk in.

They didn't look like agents, and she hadn't seen them with McKellan, and they screamed "security", or "Special Branch", with their in-ear pieces, looking around as they approached, walking towards her while trying to give the impression they weren't doing this.

Trix threw the last pieces she needed into her backpack and, trying to do it as nonchalantly as possible, rose from the cubicle she was currently in and walked away from them, aiming for the southern exit.

'Miss Preston?' one officer, or the guards, whatever they were, spoke now. And, hearing her name, Trix sped up.

'Miss Preston! Stop right there!' the second man was shouting now, moving to the side, attempting to flank her. Trix reached into her bag, pulling out a small can of pepper spray – if they tried to tackle her, she'd make sure they regretted it.

'Miss Preston, we've been sent by the Home Secretary,' the first man added.

And Trix mentally updated her identification; they were Special Branch. Police. Probably the close protection unit Joanna Karolides used.

'What?' Trix sighed, turning to face them. 'It's been a long day, I'm tired and still on US time.'

'We get that, but the Home Secretary has asked to see you,' the lead officer said, his hand out, indicating a side door. 'And tomorrow morning is a little late for what she wants to discuss.'

Sighing theatrically, while secretly fist-pumping once more, Trix smiled.

'Fine, come on then,' she said, following the second officer as he led her through the door. She might now be on her way to a more difficult situation, but Karolides wasn't Caliburn, or even a fan of them, and currently this meant Trix was safe.

Currently.

For how long, she had no idea.

HELEN LOOKED UP IN ANNOYANCE AS MARLOWE SLAMMED INTO the room, gun out, eyes narrowed in expectation of something else.

'You're ninety minutes early,' she said, but then stopped as she saw blood on Marlowe's jacket sleeve. 'Fall over?'

'Two MI6 assets after us,' Marlowe passed Helen a phone. On the screen were both men, gripping their legs, and in pain. 'Recognise either of them?'

Helen picked up the phone, staring at the image.

'Yeah, I met the Armenian in Vauxhall,' she said. 'He was MI6. I say "was" because they kicked him out. Dunno what for, never bothered asking. Guessing they were sent by your bosses?'

'Unsure,' Kate replied. 'We were actually worried they'd come for you.'

'They wouldn't dare,' Helen grinned. 'The two of you only walked in armed right now because I'd been watching you since the alley.'

Marlowe nodded, expecting such an answer.

'Either way, take a holiday for a few days,' he suggested. 'It might get a little hot.'

'I can take the heat,' Helen was still working on a passport as she spoke. 'I think it's *you* being burnt.'

She reached to the side without looking and grabbed two British passports from the side, throwing them over.

'Kim Philby and Anthony Burgess,' she smiled. 'Kim being for you, Miss Maybury.'

Marlowe gave a double take at the passports.

'Your super-secret "get us into the country" IDs are two of the Cambridge Five?' he exclaimed. The Cambridge Five had been a ring of spies in the United Kingdom that passed information to the Soviet Union during both the Second World War and the Cold War and were active until at least the early 1950s. In its ranks were British Diplomats Don Maclean and Guy Burgess, Intelligence Officers Harold "Kim" Philby and John Cairncross, and Art Historian Anthony Burgess, all revealed over time to be Russian double agents.

In response, Helen chuckled.

'Nobody gives a shit about the past,' she replied. 'And the IDs are solid.'

Marlowe looked uncertainly at the passports.

'I have the paperwork, they're based on real people, even if the names are unfortunate, and you're logged into the UK Border Services network servers under these new identities already – don't ask how,' she explained. 'Basically, if you don't shit the bed or bring too much badness onto you, these should be good for a while now.'

She reached across and picked up another envelope, tossing that across to Marlowe.

'Here,' she said as Marlowe picked it up, opening it. 'The blanks you paid me with came to way more than the work spent. So I bought you a present.'

Marlowe pulled out the sheets of A4 paper to see print-outs for flight tickets.

'I don't understand,' he said. 'Why buy me a ticket to Rome?'

'Because it's the first flight out of Paris tomorrow morning,' Helen leant back in her chair. 'And, from that you can connect to the flight on the next page, that gets you into Stansted by lunchtime.'

Her voice softened and lowered as she straightened.

'They know you're coming,' she said. 'They're watching for you. Anything from Paris will be taken apart with a fine toothcomb. But flights from Italy? Why the hell would they watch for that? They can't look at all the flights. And you said it was an evening issue with Karolides, right? You can get into London with time to spare.'

Marlowe moved close and gave Helen a hug.

'I owe you,' he said.

'Damn right you do,' Helen replied with a smirk. 'So when you save her, tell that smug bitch it was me that made it possible, and we're square.'

JOANNA KAROLIDES WAS AT HER DESK WHEN TRIX WAS escorted through the doors and into her Whitehall office.

'Nice,' Trix said, looking around. 'Your entire room is bigger than my gaff.'

Karolides smiled, looking up.

'Are you Caliburn?' she asked.

'No,' Trix replied calmly.

'But you worked for *Pearce Associates* and *Rattlestone*, right?'

Trix wondered whether to bluff her way out of this, but in the end decided the truth was the best answer here.

'No,' she smiled, waiting for the inevitable surprised expression.

Karolides didn't disappoint.

'No?'

'No,' Trix repeated. 'I worked for Francine Pearce because she effectively bought me out of a rather nasty debt I had. I spied for her, working in the background of a police unit she was having issues with. And, when I was found out, I was "adopted" by Charles Baker, then just an MP with Star Chamber privileges, and folded into a little MI5 experiment he was working on with Emilia Wintergreen.'

She drew a breath.

'I left *Pearce Associates* before it collapsed, and I was nothing to do with Trisha Hawkins, *Rattlestone, Phoenix Industries* or any other bloody stupid boys' club they have in Westminster.'

Karolides nodded, happy with the answer.

'I apologise,' she said.

'No need,' Trix walked to a chair in front of Karolides'

desk and slumped into it. 'I worked for bad people. It'll stick with me forever. They suspended me from Section D when I helped Tom Marlowe hide a serial killer for a detective friend, and then helped him take down Baroness Levin, when she tried to kill the US President at a Government event.'

She leant closer.

'An event including, as you already know, *you*, Ma'am.'

'Yes, yes, you saved my life and we're all very grateful,' Karolides said. 'I remember you that night. Shouting out at the gunmen, risking yourself. You're not field trained, right?'

'Correct, Ma'am.'

'So it's all self-taught?'

Trix considered this.

'Let's just say I have excellent mentors,' she smiled. 'Wintergreen, Monroe, Walsh, even Marlowe, all of these people have given me advice, and had skills I could take and adapt for myself.'

'And Brad Haynes?'

Trix laughed at this.

'Yeah, with Brad, I look at what he does and go the other direction,' she said. 'But sure, I've gained lots from being with him. Mainly paranoia, though.'

Karolides chuckled at this for a moment.

'Your boss, Curtis. Can he be trusted?'

'Yes, Ma'am.' Trix didn't even consider the question. 'He's solid MI5. And, before you ask, Marlowe can also be trusted.'

Karolides clicked her tongue against the top of her mouth for a few moments as she considered the information.

'McKellan wants me dead, doesn't he?' she eventually asked.

'I couldn't say,' Trix replied honestly. 'I barely know him. I know, however, that someone doesn't want your meeting with Senator Kyle to happen, and that our own agents were in on it.'

'Do you think my life's in danger?'

Trix looked at the two Special Branch guards, standing at the door and observing her.

'I don't know if it's McKellan, or Caliburn, or whoever, but yeah, I reckon someone has you in their sights.'

Karolides nodded, picking up a pen, and jotting down a note on a piece of paper. She folded it, passing it to the closest officer.

'Pass this to my assistant,' she said. 'Tell her it's effective immediately, so to move fast.'

The guard nodded, pocketed the note and, with a wink of reassurance at Trix, left the office.

Karolides knitted her hands together, elbows on the desk as she stared at Trix.

'I have a job for you,' she said. 'I've seconded you from MI5 for a couple of days. You good with that?'

'Will it help Marlowe?' Trix couldn't help herself.

'I somehow think Tom Marlowe doesn't need any help,' Karolides smiled. 'He seems to be a force of nature.'

'So, what do you need from me?' Trix asked.

Quietly, and leaving out nothing, Joanna Karolides told her.

16

SWANKY PARTIES

HELEN'S WORK HAD BEEN AS TOP-NOTCH AS EVER, AND Marlowe and Kate had caught their flight to Rome without any problems; not even a sideways glance in their direction as they travelled through French security, and then Italian Customs. Marlowe knew that Italy and France, being part of the European Union, would be the easier of the immigration points, but even with that, landing at Stansted Airport, they were through the biometric gates and out of the main exit within minutes of landing.

Deciding to aim for the minimum of exposure, they'd caught a shuttle coach from Stansted to Victoria in Central London, arriving around two in the afternoon. And then, after a quick journey by taxi to Kensington, they now stood across the street from the Kensington Hyatt Hotel.

'Security's already tight,' Marlowe said as he nodded towards the front entrance. There, as organisers and suppliers of the event that evening went through the doors, every box and bag was being scrupulously examined before being let in.

'I recognise that guy,' Kate said, nodding at one of the men at the door. 'He's Special Branch. And the woman by the side entrance, I think I saw her in Vauxhall once.'

'It's a speech by the Home Secretary,' Marlowe mused. 'Stands to reason it'll be filled with Special Branch and spooks. But in a way, that actually helps us.'

'How so?' Kate asked as they made their way back from the hotel, heading in the other direction, giving the impression of two tourists having a day out.

'Because their protocols won't have changed since I was kicked out,' Marlowe smiled. 'Which means I can use that to our advantage.'

He stopped, glancing around.

'We need to find a high street,' he said. 'I need a fluorescent jacket and a clipboard.'

It was close to five when Marlowe returned, on his own, to the Kensington Hyatt. He knew that even if he infiltrated the hotel now and found a place to hide for a couple of hours, there'd still be an opportunity for him to be caught in one of the many pre-event sweeps the agents would perform up to the start of the event.

Instead, what Marlowe needed to do was find a way in right now, purely to enable an easier entrance later in the day; and that was the tough part. However, knowing the red tape and bureaucracy of Whitehall, he knew exactly how to do it.

The event was primarily a black-tie event for the Royal Society of Veterans, and Marlowe couldn't help note the similarities to the event in San Francisco, wondering whether

Senator Kyle was now sneaking into this event the same way Karolides had intended to sneak into hers. However, there wasn't any information available on Kyle from the usual channels. It was like she was a ghost, disappearing the moment she was shot, and probably for the better.

It was times like this Marlowe wished he had Trix on a comms link. He could ask her the question and, within moments, have the answer.

Time to go old school, it seemed.

Marlowe didn't have a plan, as such, but he did have a small roadmap of directions he could take, hidden up there in his head. He'd been taught a long time ago while in the Royal Marines that when you were about to go into action, no matter what the mission was, you'd pick a course of action and then make damn sure you committed to it. However, although you definitely needed a plan A, you also had to plan out the briefest sketches of a plan B, and even plan C or plan D, each one covering a variety of eventualities and possible obstructions.

The movies always made the mistake of having the plans as completely different options: plan A was to go in through the front, while plan B was to utilise an asset, or parachute in from the roof, that sort of thing. However, Marlowe had found over the years that when creating alternate scenario plans, every plan should still be a variation on the central theme – as once you were on site, and the mission had begun, then everything else tended to change, anyway. In those cases, having some kind of credible tactical adaptation of the plan was always necessary.

The main reason for not having wildly different plans, however, was that on a mission, you needed to give yourself as few things to worry about as possible. Changing major parts of any plan only meant the plan was flawed in the first place, or that you had some kind of lack of faith in the original research, which meant the plan was screwed from the start.

So, with this in mind, Marlowe was effectively going with the flow, having a basic structure of what he needed to do and say, while relying on his years in MI5 and similar to be able to circumvent the set in stone guidelines of the British Security Service.

Hence the high-vis vest he was now wearing over his shirt.

The first thing he and Kate had done on finishing their perusal of the hotel was to find a nearby internet cafe and spend an hour gaining as much information as they could on the relevant staff of the hotel. Most hotels had "about us" pages for the corporate team, the people connected to the hotel who mainly dealt with company events, and who were likely therefore involved in tonight's gala, and through these links, Marlowe could create a small list of direct email addresses, each one leading to someone who was important, somehow, to the event planning. He also looked for links to the Royal Society of Veterans; this was a yearly event, so anyone who'd worked on this before was also of special interest.

This done, and now with about twenty email addresses banked, Marlowe had moved to phase two, sending everyone on the list an email, from a fake Hyatt email account he'd created on Hotmail, but spoofing with a real one, which looked like it was from a US branch of HR, asking them to consider donating to a charity page connected to abandoned dogs. Marlowe always used dogs, as many people seemed to have an affinity to the little four-legged friends, and even if they weren't interested, there was a chance they'd click on the link, anyway.

The link was broken, of course, leading to a "503 page cannot be loaded at this time" screen, with a brief text underneath explaining about planned maintenance work, leading to unplanned downtime on the server. The person clicking would close the browser, assuming it was probably overcome by so many Hyatt employees wanting to help dogs, turn off the screen and carry on with their days.

What they didn't realise was the broken link was access for a nasty little key logger to latch onto their system, noting every key they pressed after that. And for Marlowe, the other side of the coin were the emails Marlowe's Hotmail account now received from employees out of the office, and with their "automatic reply" on.

Now, Marlowe had a list of about five important people who had told him, in these automatic replies why they weren't around, and who to speak to in their absence, and Marlowe took these emails and repeated the process, gaining a few more key logs, and a more important second level of people not around.

Apparently, it was common for people to take these sorts of events off, probably because of the amount of extra work they'd have to do.

And now, with a clipboard holding papers printed with the hotel's logo and taken from the website, Marlowe walked with his high-vis jacket up to the side guard at the hotel.

'Hey,' he said with a smile, noting the woman almost disparagingly stare him up and down. 'I've been sent to sort the dinner orders.'

'What dinner orders?' the woman was young, maybe mid-twenties, and Marlowe assumed she'd either come into the

Services from the military, or University. Either way, she was still low down on the pecking order.

'Your ones,' Marlowe kept his smile up. 'You know, sandwiches while the event's on?'

He held up a hand as she went to reply.

'I know, you rarely get food, but we're the Hyatt. We do things differently.'

The guard looked a little thrown at this.

'I'll need to speak to my supervisor,' she said.

'Sure,' Marlowe nodded. 'What's their name? I'll need to get their order too.'

The guard went to press on her earpiece, and Marlowe showed the clipboard. At the top was a list of printed names.

'Melanie Haddow? Here? She's the woman your boss needs to speak to,' he said, pointing at the name. 'She's HR and employee satisfaction. And if she's not about, speak to Carrie Palmer, her assistant.'

He frowned.

'They might be off site because of all, well, this,' he waved his hand around. 'But they'll give the PO code to confirm everything.'

'Guv, it's Kelly,' the agent now known as Kelly spoke. 'I've got a guy named—'

'Chris,' Marlowe nodded. 'Chris Deakins.'

'—Chris Deakins from the hotel, asking about our dinner orders?' Kelly continued, moving the clipboard so she could see it again. 'Says the HR woman, Haddow sent him, or her assistant—'

She paused as someone spoke down the earpiece.

'They're checking,' she said to Marlowe with a slight smile. And Marlowe knew from that smile he had her. He'd made sure to be unassuming, servile, even, while offering her something for free. There was a term within a human's cognitive bias called the "primacy effect"; the tendency for a target to focus on the first thing someone says to them. You will decide within seconds on whether you like someone you meet for the first time, and that bias will stick with you throughout your relationship – even if it's a bad start and you grow to like the person, you'll always remember at one point you didn't like them.

Marlowe had been a simple man, doing his job for a higher up. And Kelly seemed to be the MI5 equivalent.

'So, you work for MI6?' Marlowe asked. 'Wow. That's cool. I could never do that.'

'It's MI5,' Kelly replied, with the tone of someone used to having to explain the difference. 'MI5 focuses on domestic intelligence, while MI6 is foreign intelligence.'

'So James Bond is MI6?'

'Well, he doesn't actually exist, but yeah,' Kelly smiled.

'Sure, yeah, that's dumb,' Marlowe gave a sheepish expression as Kelly straightened, listening to her radio.

'They can't get hold of either, but it's mental out there,' she said. 'My guv said to speak to him and he'd sort us all out.'

'Is he in the ballroom?' Marlowe looked to the door.

'Yeah,' Kelly leant closer. 'But when he does the meals, make sure I get something nice instead, yeah? He's bound to pick something bland.'

Marlowe noted this down on the clipboard.

'Who do I ask for?'

'Oliver Casey,' Kelly replied with a slight twitch of the lips, an almost snarl. Which was lucky, because she was so fixated on holding back any anger she had against the man, she didn't notice Marlowe's pale expression.

'Mister Casey?' he asked carefully. 'Mid-thirties, black spiky hair?'

'You've had the pleasure of meeting him already?'

'In passing, when I started to do this,' Marlowe forced his smile to stay on, fighting the urge to run. It was one thing to infiltrate a place filled with MI5 officers, but another completely to do so with someone who was actively gunning for him, running part of the op. 'I thought he said he was MI6?'

'He's seconded to them on a joint-ops, but he's still one of us.'

Are you sure of that, Marlowe wanted to say, but instead he gave a winning smile.

'I'll chat to him.'

He looked at the closed door.

'Would you be able to ...?' he asked optimistically. 'Otherwise, I have to go all around the building.'

'Sure,' Kelly opened the door with a key card. 'But remember, something good for dinner, okay?'

Marlowe promised such, entering the hotel and closing the door behind him. He felt bad for tricking Kelly, and if Casey was her boss tonight, Marlowe knew she'd get it in the neck, so he made a mental note to retroactively ensure she wasn't punished once he'd saved the world.

Because if he failed, it didn't really matter, anyway.

ONCE IN THE HOTEL, MARLOWE DIDN'T INTEND TO FIND CASEY or go anywhere near the ballroom; instead, he made his way into the administration department, once more holding his clipboard up as he walked along the corridor, leaning into a random office.

'Is Ken Hayes here?' he asked, looking around the room. It had three desks, with one woman on the far right looking up in confusion.

'He's off today,' she said. 'Can I help?'

'Which one's his desk?' Marlowe waved the clipboard. 'Got a work order to update his systems and his anti-virus.'

'That one,' the woman pointed. 'Anything in particular?'

'Yeah, we got hit today with a cyber-attack,' Marlowe said, watching the woman. 'You didn't click on a dog charity link today, did you?'

That the woman's face paled at the question gave Marlowe all he needed to know.

'And you didn't think it strange it took you to a site that didn't exist?' he grumbled, walking to Ken's desk as he continued. 'Bet you didn't even log it. That's the problem with these attacks, they seem so normal.'

'What has it done?' the woman literally flinched back from her desk in fear.

'Nothing, as long as you don't give your credit card details to anyone,' Marlowe said as he opened up the desktop on Ken's PC, the screen away from the now calming office worker. 'I'll get someone to check your anti-viruses, too.'

The woman still stared at the screen, her fingers refusing to touch her keyboard as, working on Ken's keyboard, Marlowe used the log-in name and password of one of the other people he'd managed to get to click the link, logging in under a management ID they'd typed later and, quickly inserting two more names onto the night's guest list – the two IDs, currently clean, that Helen had made them. This done, he gave both IDs reasons to be there; Marlowe was a donor, which gave him access to the stage, while Kate was a journalist, which had been her suggestion, meaning she could get close to the rear of the room to keep an eye out for familiar faces.

This done, he logged out, gave the worried woman a smile and a wink, said it apparently wasn't "that" bad a virus, and left the building through the front door, making sure not to be seen by anyone who might know him.

MARLOWE NEEDN'T HAVE WORRIED, BECAUSE ALTHOUGH CASEY was there, he wasn't in the ballroom at this point. In fact, as Marlowe had made his way both into and then out of the hotel, Casey had been sliding along crawlspaces between floors, even going so far as to take a few calls while doing so. Now, in a larger area behind a large vent, he moved aside one of the slats, staring down at the ballroom beneath him.

The room was large, enough for several hundred people to sit at tables comfortably, and the stage was the other end of the room, but staring through the scope he had in his hand, Casey smiled.

It was almost as if the lectern at the front of the stage was next to him.

This done, Casey unzipped the long case he had with him, pulling out the pieces of a rifle, a small tripod attached to the grip. As he started to snap these out, assembling the scope onto the top of the sniper rifle and peering down it at the stage, his phone rang.

'Casey,' he said, answering it.

He listened for a moment and smiled.

'Thanks,' he replied. 'I guessed Marlowe would be here tonight. You have the name he's under?'

Pulling the phone from his ear, he tapped a name on a notepad screen.

'It'll be good to catch up,' he said, returning to the rifle. 'I'll do it right after I kill the bitch.'

17

BLACK TIED

'ARE YOU ABSOLUTELY SURE THIS IS GOING TO WORK?'

Kate was nervous, adjusting the shoulders of her dress as the two of them walked towards the main doors of the Kensington Hyatt.

The front of the hotel was chaos; paparazzi were held to the side, snapping photos of the celebrity attendees as they walked down the red carpet, security checking them in once they walked from view, as the image of an A-Lister being denied access wasn't something the hotel, or the Royal Society of Veterans wanted splashed over the internet. Marlowe hadn't recognised anyone on the door but that didn't mean there weren't people there he knew well, or had even worked with, and so he was grateful that he'd made sure they could enter through the side entrance, the "tradesman's door," so to speak, where the less interesting guests could enter without fear of being photographed.

In answer to Kate's uncertain question, however, Marlowe turned to look at her and gave her his most winning smile.

'Haven't a clue,' he replied jovially. 'But if it doesn't, we'll be whisked off to a black site quicker than you can scream, so it's all a bit of a moot point, to be honest.'

Kate went to reply, stopped herself, and took a deep breath, following Marlowe to the door.

While Marlowe had been in the internet café, Kate had spent a couple of hours purchasing the right clothing for the event, based on his notes; Marlowe now wore black tie, but had opted for the more modern "black tie" than "black bow tie" look, mainly as it gave him a rope if needed. After the internet café, he'd also wandered around Chinatown, looking for a back-street martial-art store that could provide him with another item, something his Paris fight had reminded him of, and was now wrapped like a bracelet around his wrist.

Kate, meanwhile, wore a modest navy-blue dress with a cream handbag over her shoulder.

Neither of them were armed; it was decided there was no way Marlowe could get anything in, and if he was honest, he was berating himself for not secreting a gun earlier in the day when he'd entered before.

Walking to the door, Marlowe nodded to the Special Branch officer, watching them listlessly.

'Hi, we're on the list,' Marlowe nodded. 'Tony Burgess and Kim Philby.'

If the officer was a fan of Cold War history, he didn't reveal it, nodding at the list on the iPad he held.

'ID?' he asked.

Marlowe and Kate dutifully handed across their doctored passports, and after a cursory glance at them, the officer nodded, passing them back.

'I need to check the bag,' he said.

Kate opened it, and the officer looked inside, pulling out what looked to be a two-pronged taser.

'What is—' he started, but Kate leant across and pressed a button. '—this?' the officer finished, and Kate smiled, pressing the button again, and then clicking a middle button for good measure.

'This?' the officer's voice spoke through the speaker.

'I'm a journalist, this is my recorder,' Kate explained.

The explanation accepted, the officer placed the digital recorder back into the bag and passed it back to Kate.

'Enjoy the event,' he said morosely, probably annoyed he didn't get one of the cooler body-guarding jobs.

Marlowe and Kate thanked the officer and entered the main lobby.

'Why do you have that, anyway?' Marlowe whispered as they walked to the side of the lobby, pausing to look around.

'In case I get to record a confession,' Kate shrugged. 'You said Casey was here. If he works for McKellan, maybe we'll get something juicy.'

'Let's hope so,' Marlowe replied, looking around the lobby. 'I gave myself access to the front of the stage, but the journalists stay at the back. You good with that?'

'You mean, am I good at not being anywhere near the front of the ballroom where the inevitable assassination attempt could kill me?' Kate asked mockingly. 'You know what, Marlowe? I think I might be.'

There was a commotion by the door, and Marlowe looked over to see Joanna Karolides enter the lobby, flanked by her security and staff. Marlowe wasn't worried about Karolides seeing him; he'd never really worked with her, so he would have been surprised if she recognised him across the room, but there was one member of the entourage, a blonde woman in a gold dress, walking incredibly uncomfortably in high heels, who glared, almost in surprise at him.

'Evening, Trix,' Marlowe smiled, tipping an imaginary hat at her.

Trix carried on, turning her attention away from Marlowe, either to keep him away from the guards, or, possibly because she was now working out things were about to go south, pretty quickly, if he was around.

'So, what's the plan?' Kate asked, bringing Marlowe back to the present.

'Fractal Destiny said the revised stage eight was a UK Cabinet Minister assassinated on British soil,' he replied. 'So let's make damn sure that doesn't happen.'

THE MAIN BALLROOM TO THE HOTEL WAS ABUZZ WITH BLACK ties and military dress, with hundreds of affluent attendees already seated around round tables. Above them, and along the sides of the ballroom were banners proclaiming this as a "Royal Society of Veterans" dinner.

At the front was a stage with seating – five chairs in total – and a lectern in the centre for the speakers. Several of the speakers, ignored by the tables, were already on the stage, sitting awkwardly, probably wondering whether they'd jumped the gun by walking on too early, but no longer able to simply wander off. They were watching the ballroom's floor as Home Secretary Karolides appeared, a flash of red and sequins, backed up by her Special Branch Bodyguards, and walked to the side of the stage, shaking hands with a retired soldier, in a suit with regimental tie and beret, and his jacket dripping with medals.

'Home Secretary, I'm glad you could make it,' he smiled, shaking the hand warmly.

'My pleasure, Brigadier Sullivan,' Karolides said, looking around. 'Are we ready to go?'

'We're waiting for a last speaker to arrive,' Sullivan glanced at the main door, as if expecting the missing speaker to miraculously appear. 'You might know her. Harriet Turnbull.'

'The Minister for Defence?' Karolides wasn't happy about this. 'I was under the assumption I was the only Government Cabinet Minister here tonight.'

'I know, and you were, but as I'm sure you know, Mrs Turnbull was, before she became a serving MP, a Captain in the Grenadier Guards,' Sullivan's tone was clipped, irritated that someone would even consider criticising his decisions. 'And, unlike you, having served, she's one of the Patrons of the organisation, and as such has an open invite.'

Karolides clenched her teeth into a forced smile.

'Of course, Brigadier,' she hissed. 'I just wish we'd known, so we could coordinate things.'

'To be brutally honest, I was under the assumption you did know,' Sullivan replied tartly. 'Harriet told me a month ago she was attending. And you only decided at the last minute.'

'I thought I'd be in America,' Karolides conceded. 'Thank you for letting me know now.'

Massively irritated, as another VIP guest tapped Brigadier Sullivan on the shoulder, distracted from the Home Secretary for the moment, she took the opportunity to face Trix.

'Bloody Turnbull,' she whispered, her voice dripping with venom. 'She's trying for the party favourite role. *My* role.'

'So she's Defence,' Trix replied, confused. 'You're Home Secretary. Isn't that bigger?'

'Not for the press,' Karolides muttered. 'I'll put money

down right now she turns up in full dress uniform, all the participation medals she could carry, everything. The papers tomorrow will be full of pictures of her in all her military regalia, while I stand next to her like ...'

She looked down at herself.

'Like a sodding flamenco dancer.'

'I thought retired soldiers couldn't wear uniforms?' Trix asked, nodding over at Brigadier Sullivan. 'Because let's face it, if they could, he'd totally be wearing it right now.'

'I don't think Turnbull understands rules,' Karolides said mockingly.

Brigadier Sullivan had finished his conversation, and was now looking around, concerned.

'She should have been here by now,' he muttered. 'We start in three minutes.'

'Such a shame when people let you down,' Karolides cooed. 'Let me help.'

She glanced at Trix.

'Miss Preston, could you help find a missing Defence Secretary?' she smiled.

Trix pursed her lips.

'I don't know her,' she replied. 'Not a fan of the news, missed the recent Cabinet shakeups. What does she look like?'

Karolides glanced back at Sullivan before replying.

'I'd guess she'd be ignoring the rules and dressed like a soldier, with all her little medals glinting for the press, and surrounded by Special Branch?'

Trix grinned.

'Right. Gotcha,' she said. 'And if I don't find her?'

'Then we'll all be very sad,' Karolides replied with a straight face, ignoring Sullivan's annoyed expression.

FROM HIS SNIPER'S NEST, CASEY WATCHED PRESTON WALK AWAY from Karolides. He hadn't realised she'd been sectioned away from Curtis, and it made him wonder for the briefest of moments whether Curtis too was here, in the hotel.

With Marlowe, that made three potential problems.

Casey shuffled his position, lying prone on the floor of the service duct, a towel taken from a hotel cart as he passed by, under him. It wasn't because it was more comfortable to lie on; it was because he had no idea how dirty the floor was, and he was in an expensive suit.

Some scuff marks could be explained. Looking like he'd been crawling through ventilation shafts, even if he had been, was a harder thing to get over.

He looked down the sight once more, focusing on Karolides. It would be so easy to fire now and get out before anyone realised. But he needed to do it at the moment of maximum impact – as Karolides started her speech.

Casey turned from the scope now, examining the rifle. He wasn't happy to be doing this; it would have been far easier if Kyle had been killed, but at the same time, he knew why this had to happen. He understood the steps that needed to be followed, so that all the pieces were in the right places on the game board when the important stuff began.

Because this? All this was just theatre, to make the top brass look up and notice.

Casey smiled, looking down the scope once more.

They were going to damn well notice this.

MARLOWE AND KATE WERE WALKING ALONG ONE OF THE corridors that flanked the ballroom, and if Marlowe was honest, he didn't really know what he was looking for.

What he was definitely *not* looking for, was an MI5 operative who recognised him, but that was what he received as, from a side entrance, two double doors opened and Harriet Turnbull, the Government's latest Defence Minister walked through, flanked by Special Branch Officers. Marlowe had met Harriet a couple of times over the years, and he was too close to the door to turn away without drawing attention, and so he lowered his head slightly, hoping Harriet was too busy in her own thoughts to look at him. From her military get up, considering that wasn't usually allowed, she was obviously there to be seen and make a statement, so he hoped she would—

'Marlowe?'

The male voice, confused but at the same time almost delighted, made Marlowe groan inside as, behind Turnbull, an Indian man in a black suit looked over at him, his thick brows furrowed together. Marlowe had worked with Vic Saeed a couple of times since the older man had moved back to the UK after time abroad, and although they got on well, there was no way in hell Saeed didn't know of Marlowe's current situation.

At the name, Turnbull turned to glance at him, and Marlowe saw recognition on her face as well.

'Saeed, Ma'am,' Marlowe replied, deciding to bluff it out. 'Stage is to the left.'

'I heard you were kicked out,' Saeed asked, his face still conflicted. At this, Marlowe noted the two officers either side of the Defence Minister twitch a little, as if reaching for guns.

'It's complicated,' Marlowe replied. 'Agent Maybury and I

are here on an off-the-books basis, and my leave of absence was a good cover.'

He decided "leave of absence" was a better line than "black-listed and burnt", and hoped Saeed would run with it.

He didn't.

'I should call Box, see what—'

'There you are! You found our missing guest!' Trix exclaimed as she walked into the corridor, spying the conversation and instantly turning to Saeed. 'Alright, Vic?'

'I was, Preston,' Saeed admitted. 'Then I saw—'

'Yeah, Karolides had the idea,' Trix smiled, keeping eye contact with the Agent. 'Marlowe's at a loose end, so she threw him a bone.'

She looked at Marlowe.

'Good boy,' she mocked as she then turned to Turnbull.

'Brigadier Sullivan is ready to start, Ma'am,' she pointed back the way she'd come. 'Just that way.'

Turnbull was staring at Trix, confused.

'And you are ...?'

'She's solid, I vouch for her,' Saeed interjected here. 'She's part of Curtis's crew. And if she vouches for Marlowe here ...'

Harriet Turnbull had obviously had enough with the delays, and with a nod of her head, marched off, her protection hurrying after her.

'Swap jobs?' Saeed asked Marlowe. 'I'd rather be on MI5's shit list than work for that bitch.'

'Only for the night,' Marlowe smiled, but paused Saeed from moving, holding his arm as he went to pass.

'Keep an eye out, Vic,' Marlowe implored earnestly. 'I have a bad feeling about tonight.'

'Intel or gut?'

'Let's say a little of both.'

Saeed's lips set into a thin line.

'Appreciated,' he said as he hurried off to catch up with the Minister, and Trix looked at Marlowe.

'What the hell?' she asked, almost as a whisper. 'You're public enemy number one, and you come *here?*'

'Karolides is in trouble,' Marlowe replied, glancing at Kate. 'We found an algorithm, a neural network. Fractal Destiny. It talks of a Cabinet Minister dying here today.'

'Yeah, it'll be Karolides then,' Trix frowned. 'She had a barney with McKellan earlier. And I heard that name, Fractal Destiny while I was in the Ops room.'

'McKellan created it,' Kate added. 'He's Caliburn.'

Trix glanced at Kate now.

'You must be Kate Maybury?'

Kate nodded.

'Marlowe saved me. More than once.'

'Well, if you keep allowing him to stick you in places where you'll get into danger, it'll happen,' Trix replied. 'Look, it's about to start. Go stand at the side of the stage, do whatever you're here to do. I can vouch for you, but not for Kate here.'

'That's okay,' Kate nodded back down the corridor. 'I'm here as a journalist. I can mingle at the back.'

And, this decided, Kate gave Marlowe a brief nod, and walked away.

'You trust her?' Trix asked.

'Let's just say it's very much a case of "enemy of my enemy is my ally," rather than trust,' Marlowe replied.

Trix smiled.

'So you haven't slept with her,' she said as they walked back towards the stage. 'Because you always trust them after you sleep with them.'

KAROLIDES SAT ON THE RIGHT HAND SIDE OF THE STAGE, WHILE other board members of the society flanked her. She was smiling, while seething internally; she'd been correct, and bloody Turnbull had arrived dripping in medals, and had instantly been given the central seat, facing out to the audience from almost behind the podium.

Brigadier Sullivan smiled at her, unaware of her annoyance – or, maybe he was aware, and he just didn't care, she couldn't work it out – and then he adjusted his beret and rose, walking to the microphone, waiting for silence, as the ballroom, realising the talk was about to start, quietened down.

'Firstly, thank you for coming tonight and helping the Royal Society of Veterans,' he started, his voice booming and authoritative. 'Every pound you donate helps our veteran servicemen and women readjust to life outside of the military, be it due to injury or choice.'

The ballroom applauded this, and as Karolides glanced out into the audience, she could see amongst the guests many soldiers, in uniform, some injured, sitting at the tables.

Bloody Turnbull must be having a ball, she grumbled internally.

AS SULLIVAN SPOKE, MARLOWE SCANNED THE ROOM WITH A small sniper scope from his pocket, using the magnifier to zoom in on the more distant faces, taking in the opulent surroundings and the impressive gathering of dignitaries and guests from the relevant anonymity of the wings of the stage.

Every single person there was a potential threat, and although this was a mammoth task, he was a little relieved to see Vic Saeed, on the other side of the stage, staring out with equal intensity.

On the stage, Brigadier Sullivan was continuing his introduction.

'The Home Secretary, Joanna Karolides has been a great champion of the military since she arrived in Parliament, and we're honoured that she's agreed to attend the dinner tonight, at the last minute,' he said to a smattering of applause, and Marlowe heard the visible dig at her in the message. 'We're also honoured to have the Defence Minister, our own Harriet Turnbull here.'

At Turnbull's name, the room erupted into cheers and applause, and for a moment Marlowe felt sorry for Karolides; Turnbull obviously had home ground advantage here.

'Our other speakers include Andrew Thomas, writer of "The War at Home, what happens when you return", and Lance Corporal Thomas Martingale, who has just returned from his most recent tour in the Middle East.'

There was a smattering of applause at the names, as in turn two men raised their hands to acknowledge the crowd. Marlowe wasn't listening though, as he was too busy scanning the crowd with the scope.

At the back, standing with the press, he saw Kate, watching.

If it's going to happen, it'll be soon, he thought to himself. *The problem is, from where?*

Up in the vent, behind the cover and up in the rafters, the sniper scope sight now concentrated on Marlowe, just visible to the side, some kind of scope of his own to his eye.

'There you are, you arrogant little prick,' Casey whispered to himself. He wanted more than anything to take the shot, but that wasn't his job tonight.

And so, once more, he moved the sight back to the lectern and Brigadier Sullivan, now looking back at Karolides.

'First, I'd like the Home Secretary to say a few words,' he said, the microphone echoing through the ballroom's speakers, and Casey tightened his grip on the trigger.

Soon.

The atmosphere in the ballroom was electric as Karolides rose and walked to the lectern.

As she did so, Marlowe continued to stare around the hall, trying to work out, if he was the assassin, how would he do it—

And then he saw it.

Out of the corner of his eye, he caught sight of movement from behind a vent, some kind of air conditioning unit, high up in the rafters, at the back of the ballroom.

Eyes narrowing, he aimed the scope up at the vent, zooming in as he focused harder, and through the gaps of the cover, almost as if he wanted to be seen, Marlowe saw Casey through the crosshairs of the scope, rifle at his cheek.

I'm too late, he thought as he looked back to the lectern, his heart leaping into his throat.

Without a second thought, he sprang into action, racing

onto the stage with a singular purpose – to save the Home Secretary's life.

But as the gunshot was heard, Marlowe knew he was correct in his assessment.

He was too late.

18

CORRIDOR CONFRONTATION

WITH THE SOUND OF THE GUNSHOT STILL RINGING IN HIS EARS, Marlowe dove onto the stage, tackling Karolides to the ground just as a second bullet whizzed by. The room erupted into chaos as panic set in, and Marlowe could feel the heartbeat of the Home Secretary beneath him, her body trembling with shock at what had just happened.

The Special Branch officers, unsure who the threat truly was had decided for the moment to allow Marlowe to stay behind the lectern, and instead made their way towards the back of the ballroom, guns raised, focusing on the likely empty ventilation duct.

Marlowe looked down at Karolides, confused, as he rolled away from her.

'You should be dead,' he said, checking her for wounds. 'The bullet was fired before I could get to you.'

He looked around, noticing a crowd now at the back of the stage.

Around Harriet Turnbull.

'Ah, shit,' he muttered, rising, looking back up at the vent. 'They needed a Cabinet Minister. We gave them two.'

As he spoke, the officers finally snapped to their senses, pulling Marlowe away from Karolides.

'Not him! He saved my life!' Karolides snapped. 'Get the shooter!'

'Who was it?' Vic Saeed asked, running over.

'You have a spare?' Marlowe indicated the gun in Saeed's hand. Nodding, Saeed waved to an officer to the side, grabbing his gun and passing it over.

'It was Casey,' Marlowe said, checking the gun over. 'He's part of Caliburn. They have this kind of doomsday thing that can end the world based on a set amount of algorithm steps.'

Saeed went to speak, but then instead glanced at the crowd at the back.

'What's your plan?'

'Find him, kill him,' Marlowe replied, already rising, looking at the officer who'd donated his gun.

'I hope you have a backup piece,' he said.

And with that, Marlowe ran for the door, through the crowd.

As chaos hit and crowds ran for the exits, Marlowe forced against the crowd, heading for the stairs, taking them two at a time.

He'd seen officers checking the attendees; they knew the shot had come from the back of the ballroom, but they might not have put two and two together, and there was a chance that Oliver bloody Casey was still there, heading upwards rather than down.

After all, it's what Marlowe would have done.

ON THE MEZZANINE LEVEL, AND CURRENTLY LEFT TO HIS OWN devices, Casey clambered out of the ventilation duct, placing the metal grille back against the wall, pulling his rifle bag over his shoulder, shifting the weight so he wouldn't have it bumping against him as he ran, and started towards the emergency stairs.

His original plan had been to shoot, hide the gun and then join the search, leading the MI5 contingent as they hunted the rogue agent who'd tried to kill the Home Secretary. However, he knew without a doubt that Marlowe had seen him, somehow, through the vent. He'd had to snap a couple of them so he could aim clearly through and there had to have been enough space and light for Marlowe to see him with that bloody scope.

He'd tried to kill Marlowe with the second shot, but he'd missed; the chaos had thrown him off enough to pull to the left as he fired, and he now knew with Marlowe alive, he'd been witnessed as the killer.

It wasn't great, but to be honest, his time with MI5 – and MI6, for that matter – was effectively over from tonight, anyway. That'd always been the plan.

All he had to do now was stay alive and get out. Pulling open the door, he stopped as he saw Marlowe, moving towards the same door.

Their eyes locked, and before Marlowe could stop, Casey grabbed the handle with both hands and slammed the door into Marlowe's face, running the other way.

Marlowe held his nose, checking for blood, before he

smashed through the door and raced down the dimly lit hotel corridor, his heart pounding with every step. He couldn't let Casey slip away now.

The sound of Casey's frantic footsteps echoed off the walls, urging Marlowe to push harder. He burst through the door at the end of the corridor, to see Casey, already making ground, reaching the other end.

Casey spun around, brandishing a Glock 17, and fired a shot at Marlowe. The bullet whizzed past Marlowe's ear as he dove to the ground, rolling behind a nearby cart.

'Well, this is awkward!' Casey yelled, firing again. Marlowe raised his gun to fire, but another shot from Casey hit the barrel, snapping it from Marlowe's hand.

'Ten points!' As if enjoying this, Casey yelled out.

As he caught his breath, Marlowe quickly scanned the area for any weapons, checking his wrist to make sure the bullet hadn't caught it either. It stung like hell, but it looked like this was nothing more than the force of the impact. Either Casey was an incredible marksman and had aimed to disarm Marlowe, or Marlowe had been bloody lucky there.

He guessed it was the latter.

He did, after all, have a very good defence around the wrist. But for the moment, he wanted to keep what was around his wrist locked into place; he reckoned he might need to deflect more things before this fight was over.

His eyes locked on a set of steak knives resting on the cart next to him, and he knew it was a good option. Grabbing two of the knives, risking another barrage of shots, he leapt to his feet, throwing one at Casey to distract him as he batted it away with the gun, before charging at Casey as fast as he could.

There were no bullets, and Marlowe realised this was

because Casey's gun had jammed, his opponent now pulling out a vicious looking curved karambit blade, a small Indonesian curved knife resembling a claw, settling into a defensive pose. He was ready for Marlowe, and the two men collided in a blur of brutal motion. The blades flashed in the air as they exchanged blows, each man determined to come out on top.

Casey was faster and more agile, but Marlowe was stronger and more experienced in close knife work, mainly from his years in the Royal Marines.

Backing apart for a moment, they circled each other, looking for an opening.

'Why?' Marlowe asked.

'Because,' Casey smiled, lunging with the blade. Marlowe, instinctively reacting, fell back, rolling to the side, slashing blindly—

Still attacking, Casey moved in fast, kicking Marlowe hard in the side, sending him sprawling against the wall, the steak knife falling from his hand as he clambered quickly to his feet.

'Getting slow, old man!' Casey grinned. 'This is what happens when you lose something to believe in!'

Marlowe pulled his shirt cuff back, revealing a length of chain wrapped around his arm. In fact, it was a steel self-defence bracelet chain, wrapped around his left wrist and secured by the dragon-head clasp; something that not only deflected knives but also, when held loose, became a metre-long whip of vicious steel.

They were illegal in the UK but easy to pick up, and earlier that day, Marlowe had picked one up from Chinatown, his previous one left in New York a couple of weeks earlier.

The problem he had, though, was although it was an excellent weapon, it wasn't one he was skilled at, yet.

Still, practice makes perfect, and all of that.

Unclasping it, he now whipped the vicious chain at Casey, who was backtracking down the corridor, knocking side tables and lampshades at Marlowe in an attempt to stop him. Marlowe, in turn, batted these away, but each moment deflecting meant Casey could gain space.

However, before Casey could use this to his advantage, as they reached the double doors at the end of the corridor, ones that according to the sign beside them led to the fire exit, Casey staggered forwards as, from the stairwell behind him, Kate appeared, ramming a fire extinguisher into his back. Marlowe moved in, but as he did so Casey spun around, grabbing Kate, the knife now held to her throat, using her as a shield.

'Uh-uh. Drop it,' he hissed.

'Don't do it!' Kate struggled, the blade nicking her throat. 'Kill him!'

Marlowe paused, torn between two options.

'Drop the chain and kick it over to me,' Casey demanded.

'Not happening,' Marlowe straightened. 'Let her go and I'll drop the chain.'

Casey glanced down the side corridor, as if working out his next step.

'I don't have time for this,' he muttered, mainly to himself. Marlowe looked at Kate, to see her slowly pull the digital recorder out of her pocket, turning it on.

'At least tell us the truth about what's going on here,' she said, and Marlowe understood her plan.

She wanted it on record.

'Did McKellan send you here?' she continued.

'McKellan controls everything,' Casey replied. 'You know that.'

'Even Caliburn?'

Casey stared at Kate in shock.

'You want me to tell *him* the truth about Caliburn?' he asked. 'You want *me* to do this?'

'What's that supposed to mean?' Marlowe replied.

'It means that your partner in crime here's been lying to you as much as I have,' Casey sneered. 'Isn't that right, Miss Maybury?'

Kate glowered at Casey. This wasn't going the way she'd planned.

'Tell him who you really are,' Casey demanded. 'Tell him about Fractal Destiny.'

'He knows about it.'

'Does he?' it was an almost mocking response.

Kate paused, reluctant.

'The truth is ... I created Fractal Destiny,' she eventually explained. 'Look, I didn't know what I'd given birth to. It was supposed to be for hypothetical strategic extrapolation exercises. McKellan, he saw what the possibilities were. And, when he had it in his hands, he bastardised it.'

Marlowe stared at Kate. In a way, he'd expected something like this. It made sense, in a Frankenstein's Monster kind of way.

She'd created something terrible, and now she needed to stop it.

'So McKellan created it?'

'And Caliburn. Like-minded colleagues in Whitehall and Millbank.'

'The box? The virtual light room?' he asked.

'Created by Tooley, based on my designs. It's the only one in existence.'

'Then why lie to me?'

Kate slumped a little, still held tight by Casey.

'Because I'm ashamed of what they did to it. And scared that if they succeed ... that it's all my fault.'

Marlowe nodded.

'I get that,' he said, and Casey, seeing this, laughed.

'Now we all know the truth, I suggest—'

'How long have you worked for McKellan?' Marlowe interrupted. 'And I don't mean this recent secondment.'

'He was my sponsor into the Services,' Casey shrugged. 'Saw something in me when nobody else did—'

His story stopped, however, with a yelp of pain as Kate slammed a foot down on his, the heel digging into his shoe with a vicious twist. As he let her go in an instinctive motion, she dived back through the doors to the stairwell, leaving the two men alone again.

'And then there were two,' Casey smiled.

Marlowe flexed the chain.

'Round two, then,' he snarled, but Casey lowered the blade in his hand.

'Actually, no,' he replied, nodding behind Marlowe. 'I meant to say, "and then there were four."'

Marlowe turned to see what Casey was talking about and froze. Walking towards him were two familiar figures, two men he believed dead in a San Francisco hotel.

'Alright, Mister Marlowe,' the burlier of the two, the man Marlowe knew now was named Foster flashed a grin as he pulled his gun out. They were both dressed in the sombre clothing of the Security Service. Even the slimmer, younger one of the two, Peters, was out of his tracksuit, his own gun aimed at Marlowe.

'I killed you,' Marlowe said.

'Obviously not,' Peters mocked. 'Some super spy you are.'

Marlowe, realising he was massively outgunned here, reluctantly dropped his chain to the floor, holding up his hands in surrender. At least this explained why Sasha had found nothing in the room.

'Good man,' Casey said, but before Marlowe could reply, Peters slammed the butt of his gun into the back of Marlowe's head, sending him down to the ground.

'Bring him with us,' Casey ordered as he stared down at the now unconscious Marlowe. 'Now the fun bit starts.'

OUTSIDE THE HOTEL, THE SCENE WAS STILL ONE OF CHAOS; paramedics were running into the building as guests and attendees were still escorted out, and Trix was staring worriedly into the hotel as Karolides was being ushered into her car by her protection unit.

'What do we know about Turnbull?' Karolides asked before entering the vehicle.

'She's critical, Ma'am,' Trix replied. 'Last I heard, they were trying to keep her alive long enough to get to hospital.'

Karolides made the sign of the cross as she considered this.

'There, but for the grace of God go I,' she whispered. 'And Oliver Casey?'

Trix was about to reply when she saw the side doors open and Kate emerge into the evening madness, staring around in desperation. Her eyes caught Trix's, and the message was unspoken, but obvious.

'Where's Marlowe?' Trix shouted.

'Caliburn have him!' Kate replied, looking back into the lobby. 'It's Casey!'

Karolides looked at Trix, seeing the concern on her face.

'Well don't just stand there!' she said, spurring her protection unit into action. 'Go with Miss Preston and find him!'

With a brief nod of gratitude, Trix pointed at two officers to go with her, and ran back into the hotel with Kate.

'Is he still alive?' she asked as they ran through the milling guests.

'He was when I last saw him,' Kate said, leading them up the side stairwell. 'But Casey – he's unhinged.'

'Yeah, I'll agree with that,' Trix's mouth was set hard as they reached the next level, the officers readying their weapons as they burst through the doors—

Only to find an empty scene, a metre-long chain left on the floor.

Reaching down, she picked it up, looking around, as if hoping there was a clue somewhere close that explained what had happened.

There wasn't.

And, as Trix straightened, rising back to her feet, Kate vocalised the thought everyone had.

'They've taken him,' she said forlornly.

19

STATELY HOMES

Marlowe didn't know how long he'd been out for. After Peters – or maybe Foster, he didn't know which of them had done it – had clocked him around the skull with their gun, he'd been caught in a haze of half consciousness, remembering only moments of the journey. He vaguely recalled being dragged along the corridor by his arms, and then hefted up in a fireman's carry through a crowd, too out of it to cry out, as Foster, carrying him called for people to make way, as he had an injured guest to get out.

They hadn't left with the others, and Marlowe was pretty sure they had brought him out through the same side entrance he'd snuck into earlier that day. He hoped the agent he'd spoken to there was okay. He didn't remember gunshots, or any kind of confrontation, but he remembered regaining consciousness for a moment as he was dumped into the back of a windowless panel van, but had no clue how they got him into it in the first place.

They'd driven for a while; Marlowe couldn't be sure but he thought they'd headed out of London, maybe westwards, as he'd heard planes at one point, which meant possibly London Heathrow. Or was it an RAF base, like Northolt? He wasn't a hundred percent accurate, face down on the van's floor, a hood over his head and he'd only know once they arrived.

As it was, he didn't get a chance to look outside, as the hood blocked pretty much everything from his view once the van stopped, and two sets of hands picked him up, pulling him out of the van and onto a gravel walkway – maybe some kind of gravel driveway? He wasn't sure. The gravel crunched under his feet as he was led up steps into a house; the sound echoing as they entered a large hall. A manor house, perhaps? Did McKellan have a house like this? He was a "sir", after all. It wouldn't be that much of a stretch to assume such a place could be his.

He was half-dragged along wooden floors, his feet echoing as they scuffed along the route. It must have been less than a minute though, before he was sitting on a chair, his hands tied behind his back, the hood still on.

There was a muffled discussion, faint, maybe across the room. Someone was concerned, someone was arguing, but he couldn't make anything out. Then he heard steps approach, and the hood was pulled from his head.

He blinked to focus, the lamp lights hurting his eyes as he looked around. He'd been correct as he was in a manor house. It was an ornate, wooden-panelled room, with old, likely family paintings along the walls, green wallpaper underneath. The walls were high, so he was still on the ground floor, and the bay window was covered with a curtain; but this wasn't important as it was still night outside, and he wouldn't see anything out there.

In here, however, was a different matter.

Standing in front of him, still in his dusty tuxedo, was Oliver Casey. Beside him, but stepped slightly back from Marlowe, were two familiar men, Peters and Foster. And, like they were when he saw them in the hotel corridor, neither man seemed as dead as they had been when Marlowe fought them in his hotel room in San Francisco.

'Where am I?' he croaked.

'An estate in Buckinghamshire,' Casey smiled darkly. 'Far from anyone who gives the slightest shit about you.'

Deciding Casey was enjoying the attention a little too much, Marlowe turned his attention back to Foster and Peters.

'Thought I killed you,' he muttered.

Without replying, Foster opened his shirt. Under it was a thin Kevlar vest.

'You were supposed to think that,' he said, nodding at Peters. 'We both wore them.'

'How else do you think we cleared that room before the police or MI5 arrived?' Casey moved back into view now. 'You were supposed to run. You didn't have the data, so we needed you to go find it, like a good little bitch.'

'And the attack on Senator Kyle?'

Casey shrugged.

'An incentive,' he added. 'We didn't want you feeling, well, too comfortable about staying.'

'And did McKellan agree to that?' Marlowe glanced around the room. 'Where is he, anyway? Not like him to miss some gloating.'

'He's on his way. And yeah, he signed off on everything.'

Marlowe leant back on the chair. There was something off here, and he couldn't work out what it was. He needed to stall, find out what was really happening.

'So what now?' he asked.

'We make sure that Fractal Destiny continues,' Peters interjected here, leaning in close and sneering at Marlowe as he spoke. 'And stop busybodies like you from stopping it.'

'You're too late,' Marlowe smiled back. 'We stopped your algorithm when we saved the Home Secretary.'

There was a moment of silence, broken by laughter.

'Who said she was the target?' Casey, the perpetrator of the laugh, asked.

Marlowe stopped smiling.

'The shot wasn't for Karolides,' he said, remembering the moment on the stage. 'You were aiming at Turnbull.'

Casey slowly nodded, almost patronisingly, as if impressed with a slow student grasping something basic.

'And I was dead on target,' he replied. 'With emphasis on "dead," Marlowe.'

Marlowe looked at the ceiling, furious at himself. He should have second guessed this, from the start. Now the neural network continued, and he was helpless to stop the damned thing.

'You didn't think we had a backup?' Casey cooed sarcastically. 'We only needed a Cabinet Minister to die. We aimed you at Karolides, and you fell for it. Should have known better, being a spook. We learn the best misdirections.'

Something in the words pinged at Marlowe, and he frowned, thinking back to something, half remembered, his mind still cloudy from the concussion. *Was it Paris? Before then?*

Before he could continue, however, Casey carried on.

'We've been a step ahead of you since the start. Everywhere you went, we knew. And now with Harriet Turnbull dead, the Stock Exchange will plummet. Steps eight and nine are complete. We just need to ensure that you and your little friend don't try something else.'

'She'll carry on without me,' Marlowe replied, defiantly.

Casey looked at Foster for a moment and then checked his watch. Marlowe only caught a glimpse, but saw it was still before midnight.

He hadn't been out that long, then.

'We'll see about that,' Casey finished, nodding to Peters. 'Bring him. It's time.'

Peters pulled Marlowe to his feet, reaching into his jacket and removing a vicious-looking blade. As Marlowe flinched back, Peters chuckled, using the blade to cut the zip ties that held Marlowe's hands together.

'No funny business,' he said. 'I've got more than a blade.'

'Don't worry,' Marlowe smiled humourlessly. 'When I kill you, I'll give you fair warning. I wouldn't want you to miss the chance to film it, after all.'

As Peters paled at this, Foster pushed Marlowe hard from behind, and the three men followed Casey, already leaving the room. As they walked along the corridors, Casey slowed to let Marlowe walk alongside him, with Foster and Peters walking behind them.

'This was built during Henry the Eighth's reign,' Casey explained as he waved idly at the walls of the corridor. 'It's a veritable fortress, so don't think you can escape. The cellar had a secret room filled with gunpowder, but don't get excited, it's gone now. They reckon it's where Guy Fawkes planned his attack on Parliament.'

He pointed out of a window at the fields outside – Marlowe couldn't see anything, bar the blackness of night.

'We thought it fitting that we stayed here, considering our own attack on Parliament,' Casey continued. 'It's too dark to see, but we're surrounded by acres of woodland and open fields. There used to be a smugglers' tunnel too ...'

'Let me guess,' Marlowe interrupted. 'It's gone now as well?'

Casey stopped, staring at Marlowe, unsure if this was a joke or not.

'Of course it's bloody well gone,' he eventually snapped, and Marlowe grinned. He was getting under Casey's skin, and these were the moments when mistakes could be made. He had to gain an advantage, throw Casey off somehow.

'Casey,' he said, simply, stopping once the name was spoken.

Casey frowned, waiting a moment for Marlowe to continue before speaking.

'Well, go on then,' he snapped. 'What?'

Marlowe stretched his neck muscles as he moved his head from side to side, hearing the muscles pop as the tension was released. He wasn't about to fight, but there was a little psychological joust here, allowing Casey to think he was about to be attacked.

Marlowe waited a moment longer, allowing the tension to build before speaking.

'When I finally get out of here, I'm going to kill you for what you did to Turnbull. And Senator Kyle. And probably Lyons as well. Did you kill Scrapper Lyons? Doesn't matter. I'll kill you for all of these.'

He leant closer, lowering his voice.

'And I always keep my promises,' he hissed.

If Casey was concerned by this, he hid it well as he considered the words.

'That's fair,' he replied, nodding. 'I've done bad shit. You come get me when you're ready.'

'I'm ready now,' Marlowe growled.

'Nah, it's not time yet,' Casey smiled, and again Marlowe had that feeling that something more was going on. In the same way Marlowe was playing for time, it almost felt like Casey was doing the same thing, as they turned away from the corridor and started down some stairs, towards the basement, or probably the kitchens; Marlowe still hadn't gained his bearings yet, and his head was still aching from the pistol blow.

All of this was more misdirection, while something else was being planned.

At the end of the stairs was a small passage leading to a doorway. The door was metal and heavy-looking. Pulling out a large, iron key, Casey opened the door, allowing Foster to push Marlowe forwards.

'You stay comfortable, okay?' he said, pulling the door aside as Marlowe went through. 'Sir Walter will be here in the morning, and we'll start all over again.'

Before Marlowe could respond to this, he found himself propelled at speed by Foster, stumbling and sprawling to the floor of a small cellar room. It was completely empty, apart from a small battery operated lamp in the corner, and with no windows, the door was the only source of light.

'You have a good night's sleep,' Casey smiled.

'What, I don't even get a blanket?' Marlowe tried to bluff the arrogance back, but he wasn't fooling anyone.

Casey shook his head at the question, walking away from the door, Peters behind him. Only Foster stood in the doorway.

Marlowe climbed to his feet.

'You not going with them?' he asked.

In response, Foster nodded at the lamp.

'I'm waiting for you to turn that on,' he explained. 'Once this door is shut, you'll be blind.'

Marlowe nodded thanks, walking over to the lamp and picking it up. There was a dial on the back that turned it on and off with three levels of intensity.

'Hey,' he looked back at Foster, the lamp now on. 'Any chance of something to eat? I didn't manage anything at the hotel and it's been a while since lunch.'

'No.'

'Aw, come on,' Marlowe pleaded. 'You can't deny a man his last meal, right? We both know once McKellan arrives tomorrow, I'm dead. And it's not like you haven't killed before.'

Foster furrowed his eyebrows at this, puffing out his cheeks with frustration.

'We've got soup.'

'I love soup,' Marlowe smiled. 'What type?'

Foster glowered at Marlowe, and he shrugged.

'Hey, any soup is great,' Marlowe continued. 'Anything. Please. After all, I'm sure McKellan doesn't want me to pass out from hunger.'

Foster sighed loudly, and then left the cell, the door slamming shut behind him.

Now, with only the light of the lamp to illuminate the cell, Marlowe turned his attention back to the cellar, walking along the walls, examining the old brickwork, tapping it as he moved along.

It was old. As Casey had said, the building had been built hundreds of years ago, and this foundation didn't look to have been touched since then.

With his nail, he scratched at the mortar between the bricks, seeing it flake off with each movement. If he had a tool, something harder than a fingernail to scrape with, he'd probably remove some bricks before morning. Maybe even get into the next room, see if there was anything there.

Marlowe sat down on the floor, watching the door.

Soup would come with a spoon. He could use that.

And, with this plan of action decided, Marlowe closed his eyes.

It'd be awhile before the soup came, and once it did, he wouldn't be getting any sleep that night.

20

INTERROGATION

TRIX HADN'T GONE TO BED IN THE END – INSTEAD, SHE'D returned to Whitehall with Joanna Karolides. The mood had been sombre; the news had arrived in the car that Harriet Turnbull had died on the way to the hospital, and this had affected Karolides badly.

Trix hadn't really known the woman, but she felt guilty for this. After all, she was the one who found Turnbull and sent her to the stage. And she'd been so thrown by Marlowe's appearance she hadn't followed her.

But then what would she have done if she had? Vic Saeed was the MI5 agent watching her, and if he couldn't save her from a sniper's bullet, then Trix wouldn't have been able to do anything. Worst still, she could have taken the place of Turnbull, and she could be the one in the morgue right now.

There was going to be an autopsy, and nobody was saying anything right now publicly, but Trix knew all hell was about to break loose. They'd travelled back to Whitehall rather than Thames House, though. With Oliver Casey, an acclaimed MI5 agent now outed as the assassin, and with

Caliburn now being targeted as a terrorist organisation, Trix understood why a Cabinet Minister wouldn't want to go to a secure location surrounded by possible traitors.

Traitors. The word felt wrong, somehow. MI5 wasn't filled with traitors. But there were indeed traitors inside MI5 – or, more accurately, MI6.

They'd arrived in an undercover Whitehall car park, and Trix had exited the vehicle to see Curtis waiting for her, a concerned look on his face.

'You okay?' he asked.

Trix nodded.

'Not my first "black-tie event turns into utter shit-show bloodbath," boss,' she faked a smile. 'What are you doing here?'

Curtis nodded to the second SUV as it pulled up. Out of it, nervous and trembling, climbed Kate Maybury.

She'd come to Karolides when Marlowe had been taken, and, realising that Kate being hunted by Caliburn as well placed her squarely into the "enemy of my enemy" category, Karolides had immediately placed her under Special Branch protection, bringing her with them as they tried to work out what the hell was going on.

Trix nodded at Kate and looked back at Curtis.

'Interrogation?'

'More a quiet questioning,' he said. 'I'm London Chief. I took priority, especially with McKellan, well ...'

He looked around, to make sure nobody could hear.

'McKellan's gone AWOL,' he whispered. 'The moment Turnbull died.'

'You think he knew we were coming for him?'

Curtis shrugged.

'Why else would he run?'

Kate walked over, a Special Branch officer beside her.

'She's all yours,' he said.

'Any trouble?'

The officer shook his head.

'Unless you consider constantly badgering us for news on Marlowe, no, sir.'

As if spurred to life by the name, Kate spun to face Trix.

'Is he okay?' she asked urgently. 'Have you found him?'

Curtis nodded to a female agent.

'Take Miss Maybury in,' he said, 'We'll answer all her questions, once she answers ours.'

As Kate walked past, Curtis glanced back at Trix.

'Get some sleep,' he said.

'No sir,' Trix replied. 'I'm guessing there's an Ops room here. A laptop I can use?'

Curtis smiled faintly.

'I've set you a space up already,' he replied. 'I guessed you'd be wanting to find Marlowe.'

'Thanks, boss,' Trix said, walking past Curtis and entering the building.

Curtis looked back to the first car, and Karolides, who'd watched the whole thing.

'I'll send you a report the moment I have something, Ma'am,' he said.

'I want to be in the room with you,' Karolides folded her arms.

'With all due respect, Ma'am, let us do our job, while you do yours?' Curtis replied. 'It's late, we've lost someone, there's suspicion everywhere and possibly the end of the world by the weekend. Please?'

Without replying, Karolides stormed past Curtis.

'I'll take that as a yes, then,' he muttered to himself, before finally entering the building himself.

KATE SAT ALONE IN THE ROOM, TWO CHAIRS AND A TABLE THE only furniture. In the movies there was usually a large, two-way mirror, where people watched from the other side, but here there was simply a camera in the corner, the red light flashing.

She'd been sitting here for almost an hour now; they'd let her keep her watch, at least, and she'd watched the minutes pass with inexplicable slowness as she waited for something, anything, to happen.

Eventually, after an hour passed, the door opened, and the man Trix had been talking to entered, sitting down at the table, facing her.

'Miss Maybury? I'm Alexander Curtis. Alex to my friends,' he said.

'Was Marlowe a friend?' Kate asked.

'I like to think so.'

'Alexander Curtis,' Kate let the name roll around her tongue. 'That your real name?'

'You think I'm lying?'

Kate shrugged, leaning back on the chair.

'I'm thinking I've seen MI5 do more for less,' she replied.

Curtis watched Kate carefully for a moment, and then reached into his inside jacket pocket, removing the digital recorder Kate had been carrying at the hotel from it, and placing it between them.

'This was found on your person, I believe?'

Silently, Kate nodded.

Acknowledging this, Curtis turned on the recorder, and the recorded conversation from earlier echoed out of the tinny speaker.

'At least tell us the truth about what's going on here. Did McKellan send you here?'

'McKellan controls everything. You know that.'

'Even Caliburn?'

'You want me to tell him the truth about Caliburn? You want me to do this?'

'What's that supposed to mean?'

'It means that your partner in crime here's been lying to you as much as I have. Isn't that right, Miss Maybury? Tell him who you really are. Tell him about Fractal Destiny.'

Curtis paused the recorder here.

'For the record, that's Sir Walter McKellan, right?' He leant closer.

'Yes.'

'And you worked for him.' he stated it as a fact, not as a question.

Kate frowned at this and shifted uneasily in her seat.

'I'd like my solicitor please,' she said.

'This isn't shoplifting from Tesco, Miss Maybury – this is high treason against the Crown,' Curtis continued, his eyes locked onto hers, never wavering. 'Let's skip things like solicitors for the moment. Did you work for Sir Walter McKellan?'

Kate sighed.

'I worked at GCHQ, out west, before being brought to a satellite office in London,' she reluctantly replied. 'I only ever met him once. Look, we really need to get after Marlowe.'

'People are getting into that. I'd like to talk to you about this,' Curtis leant back now, pressing "play" on the recorder again.

'The truth is ... I created Fractal Destiny. I didn't know what I'd given birth to. It was supposed to be for hypothetical strategic extrapolation exercises. McKellan, he saw what the possibilities were. And, when he had it in his hands, he bastardised it.'

'So McKellan created it?'

'And Caliburn. Like-minded colleagues in Whitehall and Millbank.'

'The box? The virtual light room?'

'Created by Tooley, based on my designs. It's the only one in existence.'

'Then why lie to me?'

'Because I'm ashamed of what they did to it. And scared that if they succeed ... that it's all my fault.'

Curtis turned off the tape once more.

'Let's start again,' he said, straightening in the chair. 'I'm Alexander Curtis. Alex to my friends. Exactly who the hell *are you*, Miss Maybury?'

MARLOWE HADN'T KNOWN HOW LONG HAD PASSED SINCE Foster had left, but he guessed it wasn't more than ten, maybe fifteen minutes before Foster opened the cell door again, a bowl of soup now in his hand.

As Marlowe rose from his sitting position, Foster pulled a gun from his side holster, waving Marlowe back as he placed the soup on the floor.

'Eat up,' he stepped back to allow Marlowe to retrieve the bowl. 'It's all you get until morning.'

Marlowe took the bowl, spooning a mouthful before grimacing.

'It's cold,' he complained.

Foster gave a vague half-shrug at this.

'So's life,' he replied.

Marlowe took another mouthful, still unhappy with the soup. But before his jailer could leave, he spoke up.

'Why do you do it, Foster?'

Foster paused at the doorway.

'Do what?'

'Work for Caliburn. You've got to see what they're doing isn't going to end well.'

Foster grinned.

'Who said I work for Caliburn?' he asked, pointing the gun at the soup. 'Eat up. Might be the last meal you ever have.'

This ominous statement given, Foster slammed the cell door shut behind him, leaving Marlowe on his own in the cellar.

He took another mouthful. Grimaced. And, taking the bowl and drinking down the cold remains, he wrinkled his nose at his dinner as, with a yell of frustration, he threw the bowl away, allowing it to shatter against the wall.

Marlowe didn't care about the bowl if he was being honest. The shards were more valuable as a weapon, anyway. But all he wanted right now was the metal spoon.

With a little whistle, and using the bowl of the spoon as his handle, Marlowe started on the mortar, scraping away around the brickwork.

It could have been worse, he thought to himself. *They could have given me cold soup and a wooden spork.*

In a Whitehall office, Joanna Karolides stared at a monitor screen, Curtis beside her. On it was the feed from the interview room, currently holding Kate Maybury.

'So, who is she?' she asked.

Curtis shook his head, pursing his lips as he replied.

'Not sure,' he replied. 'She helped save your life, but if that tape's genuine, she's also the reason we're in this mess in the first place. If Maybury designed the neural network that gave birth to this Fractal Destiny, whatever it is—'

'Then Kate Maybury becomes very interesting to us,' Karolides interrupted, leaning closer to the screen, observing Kate.

'You can't be serious, Home Secretary,' Curtis straightened in surprise. 'Are you saying ...'

'I'm not saying anything,' Karolides moved away from the monitor now, walking across the room. 'Leave her there for the moment. Let's focus the search on Tom Marlowe now.'

'MI5 has safe houses all over the world,' Curtis argued. 'We have no idea which ones Caliburn has corrupted.'

'Then we start here, in London, and work our way out,' Karolides replied, as if it was the easiest thing in the world. 'Grab a coffee, Alex. It's going to be a long night.'

With a last nod, she turned from Curtis, walking off down the corridor.

'Only my friends call me that,' he muttered, barely a whisper, turning away himself and storming off in the other direction.

Now alone, Karolides pulled a phone and dialled a number, holding it to her ear.

'It's Joanna. Get me the Prime Minister right now,' she said, waiting, listening to the voice on the other end of the line. 'I know it's the middle of the night and he's in a COBRA meeting! Why do you think I'm calling?'

She smiled, as she listened to another round of replies down the phone.

'Tell him ... tell him I think I've found a way to win the by-election and remove Sir Walter at the same time,' she said. 'Tell him Harriet Turnbull's death wasn't in vain.'

This message now passed, Karolides disconnected the call.

Baker might be a pain in the arse, but he was an opportunist. And with the upcoming by-election polls showing a significant loss to the Conservatives, this was a very strong chance to turn everything around.

And if it didn't, she could still blame Charles Baker, oust him from power and lead the party into the *next* election.

In a secret underground room, deep within a Manor House in Buckinghamshire, there was blackness, with nothing more than a *chink chink chink* sound to show life outside.

There was a rumbling. A brick fell from the wall, shedding light from outside into the room.

Marlowe stared through the hole before looking back at the door, worrying that this had been heard. But, after a few moments there were no sounds coming from outside, so Marlowe returned to the wall, kicking at the bricks around the exposed hole with the sole of his boot. A few more tumbled into the black room, the hole growing.

Eventually, when there were enough bricks dislodged,

Marlowe peered back in, the lamp in his hand. And, as he observed the room next door, he laughed.

This was more than a way out.

This was a way to gain *payback*.

And, this revelation now fresh in his mind, Marlowe put away the sharpened spoon and started kicking a bigger hole in the wall.

IN AN UNDERGROUND ROOM IN WHITEHALL, TRIX PRESTON stared at her borrowed workstation laptop, and with a wipe of the trackpad moved it up onto an external screen in front of the surrounding people. People who included Curtis and Karolides.

Now, on the screen for all to see, was the GCHQ pass for Kate Maybury.

'Kathleen Maybury,' Trix explained. 'Thirty years old, graduated from the Cambridge MIT Institute at the top of her class, headhunted by us the same year. Probably joined Caliburn a few years later, while working in Cheltenham.'

'So she's clever?' Curtis asked.

In response, Trix shook her head.

'No, *I'm* clever,' she replied. 'Her grades, the work she's done for the Intelligence Services over the last few years – she's genius level. Tactical, practical, every type of "al" you can find.'

Karolides clicked her tongue against the top of her mouth unconsciously as she stared at the image.

'Could she have created Fractal Destiny unknowingly?' she wondered aloud.

'Probably,' Trix gave a humourless half-smile. 'Every

terrible thing ever created had its start in something innocent.'

Curtis looked at the agents at the door.

'Call her in,' he ordered.

With a nod, the agents opened a door and Kate was brought in by a Special Branch officer.

Curtis walked over to her, blocking her way.

'Okay. Let's say for the moment that we believe you,' he said, his tone flat and emotionless. 'Where would they have taken Tom Marlowe?'

Kate considered this for a long moment.

'You don't have ANPR on the van?'

Trix turned from the monitor.

'Automatic Number Plate Recognition was conveniently disconnected for a ten-mile radius during last night,' she said. 'The van could be anywhere. We don't even have CCTV on what type of van it was, or what colour.'

'We're hoping you can give us a destination,' Curtis added.

'Well, McKellan has safe houses and satellite offices littered everywhere. What data do you have?'

'Here,' Trix pulled up some uncrunched numbers onto the monitor screen. 'It's still raw, I'm afraid.'

'That's how I like it. Scoot over,' Kate moved up to the desk, and Trix, following a nod from Curtis, did so, allowing Kate to take control of the computer.

'She can't do any damage while we're watching,' Curtis replied as Trix now stood next to him. 'Let her do her thing. You said she was a genius, after all.'

Kate smiled at Trix.

'You said that? How sweet of you.'

Kate now sat at the chair, working on the computer, her

fingers flitting across the keyboard. On the main screen, snippets of CCTV footage were appearing, following what looked to be a Transit Van.

'The ANPR was turned off, but there was still footage from the building next door,' Kate explained.

'I checked that footage,' Trix frowned. 'There was nothing there.'

'Maybe your search shook something loose?' Kate suggested. 'Either way, the timestamps on the CCTV footage shows that this van left the hotel's back alley moments after I left Marlowe with Casey.'

She looked back at the others.

'I think he was taken.'

Trix went to reply, to scoff that of course he was taken, but Karolides leant forward.

'Willingly?'

'Unlikely,' Kate was typing with speed now, and on the screen, images of the van appeared. 'The van travels west down the M4 motorway, but there are roadworks that kill the cameras there, near the M25 Interchange and we lose it.'

She typed again, and new files appeared on the screen as Kate methodically worked her way through.

'But, using MI5 purchase records and work orders for buildings in the area that were signed off by McKellan, I can see ...'

She stopped typing, leaning back triumphantly on the chair.

'That there's an old manor house in Denham, about five miles north of that. I mean really old. Sixteenth century old. McKellan uses it for company retreats and training weekends.'

Trix stared suspiciously at the screen.

Kate Maybury had, in seconds, done better than she had in several hours.

There was no way she could have done that. Unless she really was a genius.

Damn. She really was a genius.

'You think he's there?' It was Curtis that spoke now.

In response, Kate shrugged.

'From what I've learned about Marlowe these last couple of days? If he is there, we'll soon know.'

Curtis stared at the screen.

'Get someone there now,' he hissed. 'Preston, go with them.'

'Me sir?' Trix was surprised at the order. 'I thought you'd rather I was here?'

Curtis looked back at Kate.

'Currently, Miss Maybury can work your station,' he said. 'I need you to meet Marlowe. Because if he is there, and he does escape, he's not going to trust a single sodding member of MI5 he meets. At least if you're there, we have a chance of bringing him in before he kills any agents.'

'And McKellan?' Karolides asked.

'He's being picked up as we speak,' Curtis growled. 'It's time we started playing offensive, and wipe those bastards off the board.'

21

DRONE RANGER

FOSTER HADN'T BEEN HAPPY ABOUT BEING THE ONE TO TAKE breakfast to Marlowe; it meant he wasn't being classed as part of the plan anymore, and this made him feel expendable, while the others got to move ahead.

Still, a job was a job, and so he reluctantly picked up a bowl of porridge, placed it on the tray and started down the stairs to the corridor. He'd not signed up to be a jailer, but that seemed to be his role now, which was stupid, considering the fact they intended to kill Marlowe within a couple of hours, but ever the trooper, he held the tray against his body with one hand while, with the other, still holding a gun – just in case Marlowe tried something annoying and heroic – he unlocked the door, pushing it in.

'Wakey wakey, eggs and bakey—'

Foster paused as he stared into the cell.

Marlowe wasn't there.

Instead of a prisoner, the cellar wall had a massive hole in the bricks on the eastern wall, leading into another darkened corridor. A pile of bricks lay on the floor in front of it.

Now suspicious, his eyes focused on the hole, Foster walked into the cellar, the door opening against the wall.

'Shit,' he muttered to himself, dropping the tray and bowl of porridge and using the now free hand to pull a radio.

'Guys, I need help down here,' he said into it. 'It looks like Marlowe's—'

Foster didn't finish the statement, as from behind him, having been hidden by the door, Marlowe emerged from the shadows, the sharp shard of a broken bowl now against Foster's neck. He was sweaty and covered in brick dust, his jacket and shirt removed, a small amount of cuts and gashes on his fingers.

'Drop it,' he hissed.

Foster complied, dropping the radio.

'I meant the gun.'

Foster smiled, dropping that too.

'It's no use,' he replied calmly. 'They'll be here shortly.'

Marlowe reached down and picked up the gun, now training it on Foster.

'Then you'd better lock us in,' he suggested.

Frowning at this, Foster reluctantly took the key from the door's other side, shut it and then locked it from the inside.

'Now what?' he asked, turning to face Marlowe. 'You're trapped.'

With a noncommittal shrug, Marlowe indicated through the makeshift hole in the wall.

'You still think that's true?' he asked. 'I mean, you know what's through there, right?'

Marlowe grabbed at Foster's wrist now, checking the watch.

'Seven am?' Marlowe nodded. 'I thought it was eight. Close enough. I'm guessing McKellan hasn't arrived yet?'

Foster didn't reply, his mouth set into a tight, thin line, and Marlowe smiled darkly.

'He was never coming, was he?' he suggested. 'You're not working for McKellan or Caliburn. You're working for Oliver Casey.'

'There's a lot of pieces in play right now, Marlowe,' Foster argued. 'Don't be a fool.'

Marlowe walked Foster over to the hole now.

'Oh, don't worry. I've got a plan,' he continued.

'Yeah?'

'Yeah. I blow the hell out of this building and go find Casey, shoot him in the face.'

They clambered through the hole, Foster in the lead, Marlowe guiding him with the barrel of the gun. Behind them, there was a thud against the door, as if someone outside was trying to break into the cell.

'They'll need something bigger than their shoulders,' Marlowe said, glancing back through the hole.

'They have bigger,' Foster muttered. 'Give up.'

'And what, accept a quick death?' Marlowe smiled. 'Come on, Foster, we both know I'm just bait. There was no need to keep me alive unless you're playing with MI5.'

'We were given our orders.'

'Even Casey?'

'Even Casey has a boss,' Foster reluctantly admitted, and then paused in horror as his eyes adjusted to the darkness of the room, and he finally saw into it. It was old, forgotten, and had several small, ancient wooden barrels pushed against the back wall, with a crude fuse leading to them.

'Is that ...' he started, unable to finish.

'Seems they didn't find all the gunpowder,' Marlowe said with a small amount of enjoyment in his voice.

Foster looked around now, realising the extent of what was about to happen.

'Give up, man. You're trapped,' he pleaded. 'There's no way out.'

Marlowe, instead, walked Foster deeper into the room.

'See where the barrels are? That's an external wall,' he explained. 'It's made different. Feels different. And once it blows, we've made a door to the outside, and I can make my own way out.'

Behind them, Marlowe could hear the noise of the cellar door being smashed against. It sounded like something large was being used as a battering ram now. Which meant time was running out.

He looked back at Foster.

'But I need a light for the fuse,' he explained. 'And I know you smoke, as you stank of cigarettes in my hotel room.'

He gave a sniff.

'Yup, smells like you had one recently,' he smiled. 'Lighter or matches?'

Foster reluctantly passed Marlowe a matchbook.

'Thanks,' Marlowe said, looking at the book. It had the logo of *Champions*, the bar in San Francisco. Which made sense, as Foster had been there.

But there was something about the matchbook ...

'You're gonna kill us,' Foster's eyes were wide now as he stared in terror at Marlowe.

'Probably,' Marlowe replied as he lit the book, allowing the matches to burst into flame before tossing them onto the makeshift fuse, which ignited.

'You said you were wearing a Kevlar vest when I shot you in the hotel room,' Marlowe looked at Foster. 'You wearing one now?'

Foster's eyes were still glued to the moving fuse.

'Sure. Why—'

He didn't finish; Marlowe raised the gun, shooting Foster three times in the chest at close range, the force of the impact and the pain knocking the jailer out.

'That's gonna leave a mark,' Marlowe mused as, while the fuse moved towards the barrels at the wall, he pulled Foster to the other side of the room, pulling off Foster's Kevlar vest as he did so. Stretching it out, and allowing Foster to slump to the floor, he used the vest's front and back to make a barrier between him and Foster, still out for the count, and the wall, crouching as low as he could behind the burlier man. He faced Foster away, shielding his torso, back of head and as much of his lower body as he could with the vest. There was a chance Foster would gain leg injuries, but considering what Foster had put Marlowe through, he wasn't that worried about the poor man's feelings.

The fuse hit the barrels. There was a God-almighty explosion. Rubble hit the vest, but it barely grazed Marlowe, with only a couple of burns on his arms for his troubles, mainly from damage gained through the head hole in the vest.

Foster, meanwhile, seemed undamaged. Marlowe was ambivalent to this, however, as rising and seeing daylight appearing as the smoke dispersed, Marlowe laughed aloud when he saw a new hole in the wall leading to outside.

In the other room, gunshots could be heard – the other agents, hearing the explosion, had given up on ramming the door and were most likely trying to shoot the lock out.

Not good.

Quickly, Marlowe rummaged through Foster's pockets, pulling out a spare ammunition clip, before picking up the vest and his tuxedo shirt and jacket in one hand, his gun still in the other, as he clambered out of the hole, heading for freedom.

As Marlowe ran, he threw the Kevlar vest on. It was battered to hell by the explosion and his close quarters attack on Foster, but it was still defence against whatever happened next. He knew there were more enemy fighters, and he knew they had guns. Any advantage he had was good.

The morning was misty and cold as Marlowe ran across the manor house gardens, aiming for the trees, the sound of the house was coming to life behind him. Pulling his shirt and jacket on over the vest, Marlowe quickly did the shirt up, tucking it into his trousers. There was a slight idea in his mind that he needed to look his best, that if the guards found him, they'd think twice if he was neat and tidy, but there was also the need to keep warm against the cold, and a shirt and jacket helped against the whipping branches of the brambles he now ran through.

Back at the house, the agents must have got through the door, or else they'd gone around the house the long way, as Marlowe could hear faint gunshots. However, he didn't hear or feel the whipping of bullets past his ears, and he guessed he must already be out of range. Now at the tree line, he hit the forest at a run, not allowing caution to slow him down, stumbling down banks, barely breaking a stride, as in the distance he heard more gunshots. They sounded closer though, and he wondered if a second, closer group had arrived, and were firing blindly into the trees.

Pausing for a moment, his back against a tree, he spun,

firing twice into the woods. There was return fire, and the tree Marlowe was hiding behind was pockmarked by bullets.

Shit. Within range.

He fired back, being careful to keep a tally of his bullets, making cover as he ran for safer ground – but then groaned as his stolen gun clicked on an empty chamber. He'd hoped for a couple more.

Ejecting the clip and replacing it with the new one, Marlowe continued deep into the woods, bullets echoing around him. One bullet whistled past his ear, and the sudden flinch to the side sent him off balance, and he stumbled on a hill bank's tree root, tumbling through the trees and bushes.

It wasn't a long fall, but it threw him into deep cover. And, as he lay there, regaining his senses, realising he'd lost the gun in the tumble, he heard the sounds of men running towards him—

And then running past.

They can't see me, Marlowe realised to himself, rising to his feet and waiting for a moment to run. He could have stayed there, but all it took was someone with a thermal camera, and he was screwed.

Ahead, one agent who'd been chasing him paused, looking around.

'Cut back!' he yelled. 'He slipped past us!'

But he was too slow, as, on the other side of the woods, Marlowe ran out of the tree line and into a clearing. Without thinking, working purely on instinct, he cut across a brook, looking for cover.

He paused, however, as he heard a high-pitched buzzing noise approaching. Looking behind as he ran, Marlowe groaned inwardly – a drone was swooping down at him.

Diving to the floor as the drone swooped above him,

missing him by inches, Marlowe clambered back to his feet, leaping down the bank into a shallow river, running for his life as he heard the drone swing around again—

Meanwhile, the agents were through the woods also by now, following Marlowe's path—

Marlowe got across a second clearing before the drone could reach him, diving to the floor again as the drone came down once more, picking up a stone and hurling it at his pursuer. He missed, but then he hadn't really expected to strike true from the angle he was throwing from. He cursed softly as he dove into deeper woodland – if he'd kept the gun, this would have been an easy fix. The drone wasn't armed, but while it followed him, the other pursuers had real-time intel on where he was.

The drone, now rising back up, circled as desperately, Marlowe lowered his head, pumping the adrenaline into his hurting limbs, feeling the lactic acid in his calves and thighs building, his muscles screaming at the effort.

Still running at speed through the woods, Marlowe suddenly stopped and stumbled onto the tarmac of a road, the appearance of the flat surface surprising him and giving him hope, but this was quickly removed as he heard an engine approaching and, turning to the right, he faced a black van as it drove towards him, slumping in tired resignation as it pulled beside him.

The side door opened.

'For God's sake, get in!' Trix yelled at him, looking up at the woods.

Grateful, Marlowe leapt through the door, closing it behind him as the van drove off.

Moments later, the agents hit the road, looking around.

But Marlowe was gone.

'How did you find me?' Marlow wheezed as Trix leant over him, checking him for wounds. 'Get off. I'm fine.'

'Kate found you,' Trix replied. 'There's more to her than you know. There's a recording—'

'I was there when it was made,' Marlowe said, closing his eyes. 'Fractal Destiny. It was created by her, wasn't it?'

'Looks like it, buckaroo,' Trix smiled. 'You really do pick them, you know.'

She placed a lump of metal in Marlowe's hand.

'Your weird sex whip thing,' she said, patting it closed. 'Thought you'd want it back.'

Marlowe chuckled weakly, holding the chain tight.

'And McKellan?'

Trix looked at her watch.

'I think he's being picked up right around now,' she said.

Sir Walter McKellan wasn't in the best of moods – his op was being taken from him, he'd had messages informing him he was in trouble, that Caliburn was in trouble, and it was all bloody Karolides's doing.

His phone, resting on the passenger seat beeped as his car drove along the Kensington street. He glanced down at it, grimacing as he saw the message.

It's over. They're coming for you.

He didn't have time to form a reply, however, as within

seconds of the message appearing, he was suddenly surrounded by police cars and vans, bringing him to a stop.

Looking around, he counted armed response units, Special Branch, a couple of MI5 officers, the whole nine yards.

Slowly, his hands up, McKellan emerged from the driver's seat.

'This is all a bit overkill, isn't it?' he asked, good-natured, as the police rushed in to cuff him.

22

MISDIRECTION

MARLOWE HADN'T GONE TO THE HOSPITAL TO HAVE HIS BURNS treated, instead returning to Whitehall with Trix and the MI5 agents she'd travelled to the manor house with. He was glad to know his internal compass hadn't been too screwed, and that he was found to the northwest of London, the direction he'd assumed while under the hood.

Trix had also updated him on the journey on what else had happened, and had been in contact with Saeed's second unit, who'd gone into the manor house through the front while Marlowe had been running, and taken down the remaining rogue agents, including Foster, with curious ease.

Of Peters and Casey, there'd been no sign.

Eventually, after around an hour of driving into London, mainly through the early rush hour traffic, the van pulled up in an underground car park in Whitehall, and Marlowe clambered out, still in his dusty and torn tuxedo.

'You really should change out of that,' Trix smiled as she watched him stretch, groaning as his shoulders clicked loudly. 'You look like you're homeless.'

Marlowe ignored the jibe, as Joanna Karolides was now walking towards them.

'Mister Marlowe, it seems I owe you my life,' she said, shaking Marlowe's hand.

Marlowe smiled.

'Actually, it wasn't just me,' he replied. 'I had help from Helen Bonneville, in Paris. She was the one who got me close enough to save you.'

Karolides's mouth thinned at the name, and Marlowe realised Helen hadn't been overestimating the hatred the two women seemed to have.

'I'm just sorry I didn't save Harriet Turnbull,' Marlowe continued, the smile dropping. 'I hear that you have Sir Walter McKellan in custody?'

Karolides nodded.

'He's being questioned right now.'

'I'd like to speak to him, if that's possible?'

There was a moment of silence.

'Are you looking to talk, or execute?' Karolides eventually asked. 'We'd like him alive for the moment.'

'Honestly, I'd love to do either,' Marlowe replied truthfully. 'But I wanted to speak to him, because there's something not right with this picture, and I can't work it out yet.'

Karolides frowned at this, as they walked back into the building.

'Not right?' she asked. 'How so?'

Marlowe shrugged.

'A feeling, nothing more, Ma'am.'

Karolides accepted this.

'Of course,' she smiled. 'Your gut feelings kept me alive, so I'd be a fool to ignore them. I'll sort the conversation for you. Oh, and Miss Maybury was asking to your wellbeing.'

'Oh, he totally wants to speak to her, too,' Trix grinned.

Marlowe glared at Trix, who smiled winningly back at him.

'We can arrange both,' Karolides tried to hide her own smile, and Marlowe couldn't help but grin as well. Bloody Trix was infectious. 'Miss Maybury is currently preparing for her briefing, so she'll be a little longer.'

'Briefing?'

Karolides paused, looking at Trix.

'I assumed she told you?'

'About Kate being part of Fractal Destiny?' Marlowe's smile faded. 'Yeah, I knew that when we faced off Casey. It's one of the reasons I want to talk to McKellan.'

'Well, as you said, she was involved in the creation, so in a few minutes she's going to show the Security Service her device,' Karolides explained. 'Explain how stages in Fractal Destiny worked, and how we can stop the remaining stages happening.'

'How you can use them on other countries, you mean?'

The conversation was definitely becoming frostier.

'For a man still burnt from MI5, you wield a lot of arrogance right now, Mister Marlowe,' Karolides said icily. 'Remember you're still wanted for questioning in relation to the attack on Senator Kyle.'

'We have proof from Kyle herself that he wasn't part of it,' Trix interjected. 'Ma'am.'

Karolides stared at Marlowe for a long second before nodding.

'What the Intelligence Service do with the data once they have it is nothing to do with me, I'm afraid,' she smiled, the warmth avoiding her eyes. 'So if you want to speak to Miss Maybury, I suggest you do it soon.'

With a look to Trix to follow, Karolides walked off.

With an irritated click of her tongue, Trix looked back at Marlowe.

'You good?'

'Not sure. Something seems off. And I'm not sure about Kate anymore.'

Trix patted Marlowe on the arm.

'Everything's fine, Marlowe,' she said. 'We saved the world, the bad guys lost, the good guys won.'

'Did they?' Marlowe asked, but it was nothing more than a whisper to himself, as Trix had already run off after Karolides.

Marlowe was about to walk after them, but stopped as Curtis turned the corner, walking towards him.

'You've got some nerve being here,' Curtis spoke, echoing the line he'd given Marlowe when they first spoke in San Francisco. 'But damn if I'm not glad you're alive and well.'

'Thanks,' Marlowe gave a small smile in return. 'Everything seems to be "all go" here right now.'

'Caliburn is being dismantled,' Curtis shrugged. 'It's like the fall of the Berlin Wall, but instead of bricks and concrete, it's whiny little Civil Servants complaining it's nothing more than a think tank and we're fascist bastards for removing their right to hang out in Gentlemen's Clubs.'

'They could be right,' Marlowe murmured. 'I'm thinking Caliburn is a patsy here.'

'And McKellan?'

Marlowe shook his head.

'I want to ask him that exact question, because I'm not sure,' he replied. 'I want to ask him why he did all this.'

Curtis checked his watch.

'I'll allow you five minutes, but we'll be taking him to a

new location in an hour, so I'd say your goodbyes now,' he said, with the slightest hint of gloating in his tone. 'You might not see him again.'

Marlowe understood the gloating. McKellan had been a pain in Curtis's side, and also higher up the security services ladder. With McKellan out, unless they parachuted someone else into the role, Curtis was likely to make a case for transferring into the MI6 position, even if he was a recent addition to the London office and currently MI5 based.

Marlowe, meanwhile, was still burnt. Professionally, as well as currently.

'Right then,' Curtis looked at his watch again. 'Five minutes, third door on the left once you get through security, and I'll do that for you right now.'

AS MARLOWE WALKED INTO THE SMALL INTERROGATION ROOM, he found Sir Walter McKellan sitting at the table, leaning back, calm.

'Well, you look like shit,' he said, giving Marlowe a visual once over, noticing the scorch marks and brick scuffs.

'Yeah, sorry about that,' Marlowe closed the door. 'Had to blow a hole in the side of one of your stately homes.'

If this surprised McKellan, he didn't show it.

'We do what we need to do,' he said cryptically.

Marlowe brushed his jacket down, sitting opposite McKellan.

'Should you even be here, Marlowe?' McKellan asked. 'Last I heard, you were persona non grata.'

'Yeah, well, they gave me a day pass,' Marlowe replied.

McKellan sniffed.

'MI5. Place has gone to the dogs,' he muttered.

Marlowe leant forward, lowering his voice.

'Why did you do it?' he asked.

'Do what?'

'Use Fractal Destiny to destabilise your country?'

McKellan laughed.

'Is that what she said?' he wheezed. 'That we were using the algorithm? That's rich.'

'Why?' Marlowe felt that sick sensation in his stomach again. The "off" ness he'd felt earlier was returning.

'Because it doesn't work,' McKellan replied ruefully. 'The universe is too random a beast to guarantee that a pre-set amount of stages of any plan can do anything, let alone take down something the size of Britain.'

He glowered across the table at Marlowe.

'If you hadn't got in the way in San Francisco, we would have gained the hidden data from Lyons and nipped all this in the bud,' he muttered. 'But you did, and he gave it to you instead.'

'I was under the assumption he was taking it from you,' Marlowe shifted in his chair, trying to pinpoint what it was that concerned him here. 'And for the record, there was no hidden data given to me.'

'Then how did you find the box in Paris?'

'Tooley's arm. The sat nav in Foster's car took us to where they buried him.'

McKellan nodded at this, looking away.

'Of course,' he muttered. 'Nice touch.'

'What is?'

McKellan stared at Marlowe, as if weighing him up, and then nodded to himself, his shoulders slumping slightly as he made some kind of silent agreement.

'Look, Marlowe, we've met professionally about what, four or five times over the years?'

Marlowe nodded.

'About that, sir,' he said. 'Including the time you were on the council that confirmed the order to burn me.'

'We both know why we had to do that. Don't be pissed at me because you wanted to be a white knight,' McKellan growled in response. 'I know you have no reason to trust me, but know this. I don't know anyone called Foster, and we only found Tooley when we followed the same sat nav as you did, in the car you left outside a San Francisco Motel.'

There. That was the feeling. The helter-skelter "something's not right" he'd been waiting for. Swallowing it back down, Marlowe straightened.

'What are you saying?'

'Me? Nothing until my solicitor arrives,' McKellan leant back in his chair now. 'But I think *you* need to have a conversation with Kate Maybury.'

He gave it a moment to fully sink in before continuing.

'I mean, if she created Fractal Destiny, and if she knew it didn't work, then why has she been leading you on this chase?'

Marlowe rose from the chair, forcing himself not to grab the back of it. The room was spinning, but at the same time, all the feelings Marlowe had been having, all the "off" moments, were coming together. Finally, Marlowe was understanding what was going on.

And he really didn't like it.

Leaving McKellan in the room, Marlowe stormed out of the door and started down the corridors, hunting his prey.

He found her one level up, walking out of the break room, tapping on her phone. She wasn't in the black journalist suit she'd been wearing the previous night. At some point she'd changed into her normal clothes – which meant that at some point since he last saw her, she, or someone sent by her, had gone to the Kensington hotel they'd holed up in to gather their items.

Including a virtual black box McKellan claimed didn't work.

Marlowe, seeing her, paused and waited.

She looked up, seeing him – and her face lit up.

'Marlowe!' she exclaimed, running over and hugging him. 'You smell. We'll find you some new clothes.'

'Can we talk?' Marlowe asked as he led her into a side room.

Following, Kate frowned as Marlowe closed the door behind them.

'What's up?'

Marlowe shook his head, hoping he was wrong here.

'Something's not right,' he replied uncertainly. 'I can't put my finger on it.'

'You're just tired,' Kate smiled. 'It's been a long couple of days. It's all over now, you can return to your life. They might even reinstate you after this.'

'Just like you're returning to yours?' Marlowe watched Kate as he spoke. 'The Home Secretary told me. You're meeting with Karolides and all the bigwigs of MI5 and MI6 later.'

'It's just a briefing upstairs.'

'Yeah, but when they see what you can do, they'll snap you up. I might never see you again.'

Kate paused, glancing at Marlowe for a few lengthy seconds.

'Then tell me not to go.'

Marlowe and Kate stared at each other for a long, meaningful moment.

'Don't go,' Marlowe eventually replied.

'Too slow,' Kate said sadly. 'Look, it's being held upstairs, it's not like I'm leaving the country or anything. Anyway, you should see the doctor about the burns on your arms. Come on, I'll take you there.'

She turned to walk out, but then paused. As Marlowe watched the back of her head, she spoke without looking back.

'You haven't been debriefed yet,' she said.

'No.'

'You haven't mentioned the burns on your arms.'

'The ones from the explosion? No.'

Kate's shoulders slumped.

'Ah.'

She turned around, a silenced pistol now in her hand.

'How long have you known?' she asked.

Marlowe shrugged.

'I suspected a little when you were grabbed by Casey, when you oh so conveniently had a recorder on you as he named you as the creator,' he said. 'And there was your line about misdirection, the same line Casey used when he had me at the stately home. And then there was the matchbook Foster had, the same one I saw you playing with back at the hotel in San Francisco.'

He shook his head.

'I should have known earlier,' he replied. 'But we never had a chance to stop, to work out what was happening next.

And then Trix said it was you that found me. Which was convenient for you, and showed you, to MI5, to be an expert and an ally.'

He shook his head, his lips thinning.

'But for you to do in seconds what Trix hadn't been able to do in hours? It didn't ring true. But then I suppose it's easy to do when you know where to look, isn't it?'

Kate didn't reply.

'So,' Marlowe continued, stepping away from Kate, backing across the room. 'Every step of the way, you've led me by the nose. My own journey, with each step guided by you. Even Casey, when he casually told me that the cellar I was in was next to a onetime gunpowder haul. Constantly moving me on. Never letting me catch my breath so I could look into the obvious flaws more. Why?'

Kate continued to watch him dispassionately ... but then sighed, the tension leaving her body.

'Because we needed an innocent man to convince everyone,' she said. 'And you, the burnt spy who had such a hard-on for doing good, who desperately wanted Mummy and Daddy at MI5 to love you again, return you to their bosom ... you were too good to be true. At the start, I actually wondered if you were playing us, if you'd been turned by the CIA.'

'Why?' Marlowe shook his head, his expression one of conflict. 'Why do all of this?'

Kate looked away as she spoke.

'Money, of course. A lot of it. Enough to buy my own country.'

'But Fractal Destiny doesn't work!'

Kate looked back at Marlowe now, and a smile had returned to her lips.

'It was never supposed to,' she replied.

And with that, the last puzzle piece, the last erroneous slice of information slotted into place.

'The briefing,' he breathed.

'Exactly,' Kate moved over to the door, blocking Marlowe's way. 'Once I turn the projector on upstairs, we'll hit the server like a hammer. We'll syphon off every piece of important data from MI5, MI6, any agency connected to the Government.'

'But that'll include—'

'Oh, I know,' Kate held up her free hand to stop him. 'Identities of agents in the field, details of current missions, all of their little blackmail files ... Our buyers will pay us billions.'

'People will die.'

'Oh boo-hoo,' Kate mimicked wiping her eyes.

'How much was Scrapper Lyons part of this?' Marlowe looked around the room now, searching for something he could use as a weapon.

'Oh, he didn't know. He was innocent, like you,' Kate replied. 'I drip fed him and Tooley just enough to gain their trust. And then I sent Foster and Peters – that's track-suit guy to you – to bury Tooley so he couldn't be found until *we* found him. I had Ford pressure Senator Kyle, so you'd be brought in to work on her side, knowing you had a background with everyone else, and Casey pressure Curtis to keep you away, knowing it'd make Trix Preston push back harder.'

'You thought of everything.'

Kate smiled, taking a bow.

'And more,' she said. 'I made sure that I was in the same bar as you, so that when Lyons found me, I was too close to MI5 for him to speak to me. He believed Caliburn were the bad guys, you see. He'd been with them for so long, but it only took me an hour to convince him they were the next Unabomber.'

'You really are as clever as you said,' Marlowe snarled. 'And an utter sociopath.'

'Why thank you,' Kate took this as a compliment. 'I worked Lyons so well, the moment he entered the lobby, he saw enemies everywhere. The only option was Tom Marlowe, a dear old friend from the Commandos. That way, I could be seen to be as clueless as you, while keeping all the cogs turning.'

'You set us up.'

'From the start.'

'You had me on the run.'

'Oh, I did far more than that, Thomas. I gave you a treason charge, a murder site, and a clue. A hotel that Casey set up with drug dealers next door to distract the police, and a lorry driver just waiting to give us a lift. A bag with passport blanks, in a city where you knew a family friend forger. A Minister for you to save and befriend, another as sacrifice for you to wring your hands over in pseudo-Catholic guilt, while I manage to not only tape Casey's confession, but implicate myself as the genius behind the device, thus becoming invaluable to the Government, so close to a do-or-die series of by-elections.'

'You didn't control Helen.'

'Christ, Marlowe. I had to let you do some things,' Kate sighed. 'You had to believe you were in control, after all.'

'And then you locked me away and blew me up.'

'Oh, we didn't know you'd escape, we needed you to be found when I sent the cavalry to your rescue. You were actually supposed to be dead, by the way,' Kate cocked the pistol.

'And come on. Caliburn had to become the scapegoats – and to be fair, you blew yourself up.'

Marlowe took this, nodding.

'So what now?'

Kate pondered the question, tapping her chin as she thought.

Eventually, she looked back at Marlowe, the gun rising to point directly at him.

'Now? Sir Walter McKellan takes the blame, I go live on an island under a fake name and you?'

Without warning, she fired twice into Marlowe's chest at point blank range.

Grabbing his chest, his eyes rolling back, Marlowe fell to the floor, as Kate stared coldly down at him.

'You die,' she said.

And, turning, she left the room and Marlowe, shutting the door behind her.

As she entered the corridor, locking the door, she heard movement from around the corner and tensed, reaching for her gun once more. However, around the corner walked Peters and Casey. They both wore suits and earpieces, mimicking Special Branch officers. Casey, however, had the black canvas bag she'd brought from Paris over his shoulder.

With a nod, he passed it over to Kate.

'Any trouble?' she asked.

Casey shook his head.

'They red flagged my clearance, but the back doors in the system still work,' he smiled. 'And these new IDs work a treat.'

'Come on then, the Government's waiting,' Kate started down the corridor. 'What about Foster?'

Casey shook his head.

'He won't be talking,' he replied.

'You sure?'

Casey raised an eyebrow.

'Shame,' Kate sighed. 'I liked Foster.'

'What about Marlowe?' Casey asked.

'Finished,' Kate replied.

'Good,' Casey smiled. 'I hated that prick.'

23

MAGIC BOX

WHATEVER KATE HAD BEEN EXPECTING AS SHE ENTERED through the upstairs briefing room door, the appearance of MI5's London Chief Curtis wasn't one of them.

There were four people in total in the room, Curtis, Karolides, and two strangers, a male and a female. And, as she stood in the doorway, she tried to quickly work out how to salvage the situation; Oliver Casey was outside under a new identity, and as far as Kate knew – and had planned – Karolides had never seen his face, but the moment Curtis saw him, the game would be over.

'Mister Curtis,' she said, walking into the room, Peters following her. 'I hope this isn't another MI5 interrogation. I was under the belief I was showing Fractal Destiny to the Home Secretary.'

She glanced to the door, to see it being pushed closed; Casey hadn't entered. He'd heard the name mentioned and wisely stepped back. Which solved one problem, but now meant that there was only Peters backing her up in the room, and he was a loose cannon at the best of times.

The room was basically a boardroom, a long table in the middle. Karolides, sitting at the head of the table stood up now, smiling at Kate.

'Miss Maybury,' she said by introduction. 'I know you've already met Alexander Curtis, Section Chief of MI5's London office.'

'Alex to his friends,' Kate replied mockingly, looking at the other two people in the room. 'I don't know these two.'

'Of course,' Karolides nodded, waving to the first, a middle-aged man in a pinstripe suit. 'This is Peter Fraser, the new Minister for Defence.'

'Turnbull died last night,' Curtis added, and from the look on his face, this did not impress him. 'But the Prime Minister decided there needed to be a smooth transition, so Mister Fraser here, who was Harriet Turnbull's deputy, has been brought into the Cabinet.'

'Harriet died because of your ... well, whatever it was, so I wanted to be here to see it,' Fraser finished.

Karolides let him end his comment, and then waved her hand at a woman, in her late forties, glasses on her forehead as she read notes on the table in front of her.

'And this is Miss Walters, Chief Crypto Analyst for ... well, for one of our more secretive organisations,' she smiled. 'She'll be examining your device.'

'Okay,' Kate nodded. 'Sure. Why not?'

There was a pause.

'You have the device?' Karolides prompted, and Kate paled.

Casey had the bag.

Casey who was still outside.

'I left it, Ma'am,' Peters, improvising quickly said, walking to the door. 'Outside. In case it was ... you know.'

'A bomb?' Fraser almost sounded mocking. 'Christ, man. You had one job. Bring it in.'

Peters walked to the door, grabbing the bag from the still hiding Casey. Passing it to Kate, he stepped to the side of the table as she pulled the black projector out of the bag, glancing back at him.

'If you could help me?'

Peters grabbed one of the four stands, directed by Kate on where to put it, as, one by one, all four stands were placed around the room. As he did this, Kate set up the box in the middle of the table, aiming it towards her willing audience.

After a moment, Peters stepped back, the stands now prepared. Kate plugged the box into the power socket under the table and stepped back, rubbing her hands together nervously.

Fraser leant closer, peering at the box.

'It's rather small,' he complained.

'Well, you know the adage,' Kate smiled weakly. 'It's not the size, it's what you can do with it.'

'Well then,' Fraser sat back. 'Whenever you're ready, Miss Maybury, show us what you can do with it.'

Leaning over the table, Kate switched the box on.

After a moment, the box's speaker emitted words.

'Caliburn holocrom active. Satellite Wi-Fi active. Accessing cloud drive.'

Karolides looked nervously at the technician, Walters, who had pulled her glasses down now, staring at the box, her eyes wide.

'Cloud drive protected,' the box continued. *'Enter password, using the prefix "keyword" on entry.'*

'Do you know the password?' Fraser asked.

'Of course,' Kate replied, her tone almost offended at the

accusation as she turned to face the box. 'Keyword. Helen of Troy.'

As the people around the table watched in surprise, the box began to glow while the stands hummed with power. And, after a moment, the same three-dimensional holographic line-art wireframe that Kate had last seen in a Paris hotel now covered the room.

However, this time it was different, more bare, as Kate had used another password to start it. And as the streams of data lined the holographic walls, Kate smiled slightly.

Everything was working perfectly.

After a second, the data stopped, and the speakers burst into life; a snap of white noise, followed by words.

'Preset activation protocols instigated. Helen of Troy active.'

Fraser stood now, looking around the virtual room, completely buying the same lie that Marlowe had two days earlier, that this was more than some pretty light show misdirection.

'Impressive,' he said. 'And what's it doing now?'

Kate lowered her tone, making it more matter-of-fact as she replied.

'Right now, it's just searching for relevant data to match its surroundings,' she said. 'Following the protocol.'

SEVERAL FLOORS ABOVE, IN AN EMPTY AND ABANDONED SERVER room filled with flashing lights and banks of drives, a single screen lit up. On it, and at unnatural speed, numbers flashed across it, as code was forced into the network.

A single phrase flashed up.

INCORRECT PASSCODE.

And then, as if the plug was pulled, the screen fritzed, as if some kind of glitch had passed through.

More numbers then flashed across the screen. And then, words appeared.

PASSWORD OVERRIDE
FILE "HELENOFTROY" UPLOADED
DOWNLOADING CORE DATA - 0.02%

And, slowly, screen by screen, the server room woke up.

IN A SIDE ROOM SEVERAL FLOORS BELOW THIS, MARLOWE LAY on the floor of a locked room. He hadn't moved from the position he fell in after Kate pumped two bullets into his chest.

But then, with a wheeze, he opened his eyes, clutching at his chest.

Slowly, and in great pain, he staggered to his feet. Leaning against a table, he opened his shirt and pulled off Foster's Kevlar vest. In it, the bullets were still embedded.

Rubbing his injured chest, Marlowe took in some deep breaths.

Stupid, stupid man.

He'd walked into the room to confront Kate, but had woefully underestimated her. He thought she'd be confrontational, but he'd not seen her with a gun before. He hadn't expected that swerve.

Lucky, lucky man.

Marlowe didn't have a watch on, and he didn't know how long had passed since the force of the bullets striking him had knocked him out. He even felt a little sorry for Foster now. Slowly, and with great pain, he walked to the door, trying it.

It was locked.

Of course, he thought to himself as he looked for something to break the lock with, picking up a flat head screwdriver from a wall shelf.

Life is never that simple.

UPSTAIRS IN THE BOARDROOM, KATE WAS CAREFULLY WATCHING Fraser stare up at the holographic wireframe, as Curtis and Walters sat with Karolides, completely caught within the lie.

Good, she thought. *The longer you believe, the longer I have to download.*

'So as you can see,' she said, waving at the visual room, 'it takes each step and extrapolates the erroneous data from it.'

In fact, it wasn't doing anything of the sort. However, none of the others in the room, even Walters, the so-called expert, could contradict her on this.

'Really? That's impressive,' Fraser said, looking over at Walters. 'That's impressive, right?'

'Yes it is,' Walters said, but her face was unsure. Kate knew with a sinking sensation that at any minute this would be the weak link, as Walters could ask for proof of something Kate wouldn't be able to deliver.

She glanced at Peters, rubbing at her wrist. It was a small, unperceptive gesture, but one that meant a lot to him.

Prepare for action.

And, as Peters slowly moved towards his gun, keeping his actions relaxed, Kate walked away from him, drawing the eyes to her.

'So, who wants to see something cool?' she asked.

TRIX HAD HEARD NOTHING FROM MARLOWE FOR A WHILE NOW, and with Kate in her briefing with Karolides and Curtis, she was a little lost as to what she should do right now. So much so that her curiosity had got the better of her, and she'd found herself walking up to the upper levels.

The door passes were above her grade, but that had never stopped her before, and she'd cloned Wintergreen's details months earlier, for just this sort of situation. She'd argued the case to herself that it would only be used in an emergency, and this was just that.

She didn't trust Kate Maybury.

Trix was good. Very good. Self-taught from an early age, while working for Francine Pearce, she'd been given access to a ton of high level and rather awful shit, computer wise, and had spent the time wisely learning everything she could. She could find back doors where there weren't even walls, and she could hack pretty much anything, given the time.

And that was the problem, the little thing in the back of her mind that irritated her. She took the time, but she could hack. Kate Maybury, however, hadn't taken the time. And, watching the lines of code appearing as she typed, she knew something was wrong. There was no way the code she was typing could have done the things she claimed to be done. She couldn't hack the systems faster than Trix, she was sure of it. And if that was the case, the information she found had to be fake.

But it wasn't fake, as they found Marlowe.

Because they were supposed to find Marlowe.

Marlowe, who, after looking for Kate and expressing his own suspicions, was now missing.

Trix didn't know what was going on, but she knew for a fact that there was something wrong with Kate Maybury. And whether or not it'd cost Trix her job, she had to do something about it.

There was a Special Branch officer outside the door as Trix walked up, facing the other way.

'Hey, have they started?' she asked. 'I need to—'

She stopped as the man turned to face her, and she recognised Oliver Casey standing in front of her.

'Ah, shit,' she said. 'Hi Casey, how's it going?'

'Hello, Preston,' Casey replied, pulling his gun out and aiming it at her. 'I think it's going rather better for me than it is for you right now.'

MARLOWE STAGGERED INTO THE OPS ROOM, STILL ONLY wearing his shredded dress shirt, half done up as he did so.

'Where's Kate?' he demanded, looking around. 'Curtis? Trix? Karolides? Where are any of them?'

One technician looked up at him in horror: this bruised, burnt and bloodied creature of the night.

'Upstairs, meeting room five,' she said, her eyes wide. 'But it's already started. I don't know where Trix Preston is—'

'Find her!' Marlowe shouted, grabbing a hoodie from a

hook on the wall. 'And turn off all power in that room! Is this yours? Can I borrow it? Thanks.'

He pulled it over his head, looking around the Ops room.

'Armoury?' he asked again, tugging the hoodie down.

'It's next door,' the technician replied. 'But why...'

'Because I need to shoot some bad guys,' Marlowe said, already on his way to the door. 'Turn off the power!'

SEVERAL FLOORS ABOVE, KATE WAS ABOUT TO CONTINUE WHEN the door behind her opened. As she turned in confusion, Trix Preston walked into the room, hands in the air.

'Preston?' Both Karolides and Curtis spoke as one. But a second later, Casey walked into the room, his pistol out, and now aimed at the others around the table.

And, as he did so, Peters pulled his own weapon out, providing cover.

'Hi guys,' Trix smiled awkwardly. 'Hey, guess what! I found the guy who tried to kill you, Home Secretary!'

Curtis went to stand, but a wave from Casey stopped him.

'What the hell are you doing here?' Kate spat at Casey. 'We're not done yet!'

'No choice,' Casey shrugged. 'Preston recognised me. I don't know whether she's alone or part of a larger group. We need to pick things up.'

'You're a traitorous little shit, Oliver,' Curtis muttered, and as he sat, his hand moved to the side of the table.

'You'd better not be pulling a taped gun from under there,' Casey waved the gun at him. 'Hands where I can see them.'

Curtis paused, looked at Karolides and then rose, pulling

a gaffer-taped gun from under the desk, bringing it up to aim at Casey—

Blam.

Peters, to the side, fired his gun and, grabbing at his chest, Curtis fell to the floor, the gun clattering across the room.

'He was mine to kill!' Casey snapped at the younger man.

'So go headshot him!' Peters argued back. 'And you're welcome, by the way, for me saving your life.'

Fraser, still sitting in his chair, looked around in horror.

'What's going on?' he asked, his voice nothing more than a whisper.

'Do we need them?' Casey asked Kate, who shook her head.

'Just Karolides.'

'Good,' Casey replied, firing twice.

Both Walters and Fraser went down, bullet holes in their foreheads, as Karolides started to scream.

'Time to go,' Casey said, turning his gun onto Karolides now. 'Uh-uh. Stay down and shut up.'

Kate walked over to the box, checking it.

'We're only on eighty percent download,' she said irritably. 'We need more time.'

'We don't have more time,' Casey replied, pointing at Trix. 'We don't know who she told, and they would have heard the gunshots. We need to leave now.'

'Then we kill all the witnesses,' Peters suggested.

Kate shook her head.

'No, we need a hostage,' she replied.

Peters walked over to Karolides, pulling her to her feet as Kate stared at Trix.

'You've cost me a lot of money, you bitch,' she hissed.

Trix glowered back at Kate, ignoring Casey to her side.

'You won't get away with this,' she said. 'Marlowe will—'

'Marlowe's dead!' Kate laughed. 'I shot him and left him in a broom cupboard!'

As Trix's eyes widened in horror, Casey started tapping on the side of the box.

'Eighty-one percent,' he looked up. 'It's enough, Kate. Pull the plug.'

Kate looked as if she wanted to argue this, but then gave a loud, angry sigh.

'Fine,' she said, turning to the black box. 'Keyword. Ride the horse.'

'Trojan Horse of Troy activated,' the voice spoke through the speakers.

This done, Kate grabbed the projector, placing it in her canvas bag.

'Let's get out of here,' she said. 'Grab the Home Secretary. She's our ride out.'

'And her?' Peters looked at Trix.

'Oh, she's not important at all,' Kate glared at Trix now.

'Kill her.'

24

HELEN OF TROY

As Peters smiled, raising his gun, the lights suddenly changed to red, and they could hear a siren in the background. He looked questioningly at Kate, still walking out of the room.

'The virus has taken hold,' she said. 'Get on with it—'

'Come on!' Casey screamed out. 'We need to go!'

He stopped as a bullet smashed into the door. Stepping back, Kate allowed Casey to look through.

'Can't see who it is, but they're taking cover down the end of the hall!' he cried out. 'Someone with a hoodie!'

Peters took his eye off Trix for a split second, and this was all she needed to dive under the boardroom table, as he fired in a futile gesture after her, moving to the door as, grabbing the gun Curtis had gone to use moments earlier she fired blind back at him, nicking his leg with a shot, and moving out into the open.

Whoever walked into the room next had better be a friendly, she thought to herself. *Because they're going to die if they're not.*

In his gained hoodie, Marlowe cautiously approached the door down the red-lit corridor, his borrowed Glock 17 tightly gripped in his hand. The blaring siren made it difficult to hear anything, but he knew he had to act fast if he was going to catch Kate, and whoever she had with her.

There was a movement, a shadow that passed, and Marlowe paused in surprise. It was a male shadow, and it was moving too quickly back and forth to be that of a calm man.

'The virus has taken hold,' a woman's voice said, and Marlowe immediately recognised Kate. 'Get on with it—'

'Come on!' Another voice, a man's one screamed out. 'We need to go!'

Marlowe knew that voice too. In fact, after missing Casey that morning, he'd guessed he'd show up soon. *Casey was just beyond that door.*

And, as the shadow moved again, the shoulder of Casey emerging, Marlowe fired.

The bullet hit the door, but missed him by inches, and Casey glanced back out into the corridor, firing back as he did so. Marlowe heard him shouting in the room, but he was firing back at that point, the words drowned out by the gun.

Casey peered out again, firing twice – Marlowe ducked into another doorway, but the door was locked, and the wall didn't give him much cover. Instead, he dropped to the floor, as the two men exchanged shots, as Casey ran down the corridor, slamming the fire door open as Peters, dressed in a suit, leant out of the door, providing cover. He looked in pain, and his leg was bleeding as the sound of gunfire echoed off the walls. Marlowe aimed and fired, hoping to hit Casey, but he was too quick, dodging and ducking with ease.

Marlowe charged forward, determined to take Casey down once and for all, but as he got closer, he saw Kate and Peters emerge from the room. He saw the fear in Kate's eyes as he closed in, but he wasn't able to take the shot, instead diving to the side as Casey, now through the door, used it as a shield as he shot at Marlowe, while the others ran through it.

Marlowe stood there, chest heaving, gun still in hand, as he watched Kate disappear into the stairwell. He wanted to scream, to shout, but as he was about to chase after them, he heard another familiar voice, Trix's voice.

'We need a medic!'

AFTER SHOUTING OUT, TRIX TURNED TO LOOK AT CURTIS.

He was pale, but still breathing.

'We'll get you help,' she said, moving out from under the table and calling out again. 'Someone help us! We need a hospital now!'

The footsteps came closer as whoever was coming to their aid moved towards the door, firing down the corridor still, and Trix held the gun up instinctively, dropping it as a wave of relief came over her, as Marlowe emerged into the room, gun in hand.

'You okay?' he asked. 'You injured?'

'No, but they shot Curtis, chest wound.'

'Anyone else?'

'The new Defence Secretary and some spook technician, both dead. Headshots from Casey.'

Marlowe turned to move towards the door.

'It's all a con, isn't it?' he asked, scanning the corridor.

Trix had clambered up, and pulled across the laptop Walters had been working on.

'How did you work out she was a traitor?' she asked as she logged into the system.

'Well, she tried to kill me, so I'm pretty positive,' Marlowe replied as three MI5 agents, one holding a medic's bag, ran into the room. 'It's Curtis. He's down. Gunshot to the chest.'

As the agent with the medic's bag pushed aside the chairs so she could get closer to the now groaning Curtis, Trix swore, hammering on the keys.

'We've been hacked! Systems are crashing!' she shouted in frustration as with a popping sound, the lights in the room, and in the corridor winked out. After a moment, the emergency lights flicked on, bathing the room in a green light. Marlowe ran for the fire exit, but found it barred to him.

'Trix? A little help?'

'I'm locked out of the network right now, and the entire building's closed to us,' Trix grumbled as she stared at the screen. 'She knew what she was doing. The moment she planted the virus command, the whole place was locked down moments after she got out.'

'Before she shot me, she said she was here for information,' Marlowe looked back at Trix. 'Did they get into the network?'

'She won't be able to get into the network!' One of the other MI5 agents muttered. 'We're the Government, for God's sake!'

Marlowe almost laughed at this, remembering a line Kate had said, back in Paris.

'It's a level five crypto-masher. It goes through network passcodes like a knife through butter. It could hack the NSA's servers in five minutes if you so wanted to.'

'She's already done it,' he replied. 'She told me the device could hack you in minutes. She's had enough of those.'

'Nothing's that good,' the agent protested.

'Kate's that good,' Trix muttered, typing. 'And they were saying they had eighty percent when they left.'

As she said this, she straightened and then screamed.

'And we let her work on a sodding terminal, when she was "hunting for you," Marlowe,' she shook her head, typing again. 'What else did she do while she was there?'

As she typed, photos of Peters and Casey appeared on the screen.

'Shit. While she played the part of the helpful spy, she inserted two Special Branch profiles. These two officers.'

Marlowe leant closer, looking.

'Casey and Peters.'

Trix had already moved on, pulling up lists of numbers.

'She hacked the server,' she confirmed. 'We've had an eighty-five percent download, interrupted before it finished.'

'Did she get any complete files?'

Trix moved away from the keyboard, her hand to her mouth as the lists of stolen files scrolled up the screen.

'Details of our agents, where they are, identities, their families, current active missions ... she could sell this to our enemies for billions,' she said, turning to Marlowe. 'If this data gets out? We're screwed. Syria? Russia? North Korea? They'd own us.'

Marlowe slammed his fist against the wall.

'Get these bloody doors open!' he shouted. 'They have to be on site still!'

'That exit leads straight to the car park,' Curtis, currently being patched up, whispered. 'They could have been out before the close down. And they have Karolides with them for currency.'

'Cameras are down. We're blind,' Trix looked around the room, as if hoping something could fix this. 'They could have gone anywhere.'

'No, Kate's had this planned to the second,' Marlowe walked to the door. 'She's going somewhere specific.'

'Marlowe,' Curtis groaned. 'You need to stop her. Take whatever you need.'

'That's going to be a little difficult, Alex,' Marlowe replied. 'What with being burnt—'

'Temporary reinstatement, Solstice-Marshall-Gamma,' Curtis grimaced as the medic agent pulled his shirt open. 'Get that bitch.'

Marlowe nodded, looking around.

'We need to work out where she's going,' he said. 'She'll have a plan. She's been working to one since the beginning.'

'That's great for her, but we don't know where they're going!' Trix exclaimed.

Marlowe looked back at Trix, and his face was death.

'I know someone who will,' he said.

VIC SAEED, IN SHIRT AND TIE, INTERCEPTED MARLOWE AS HE ran down the main staircase, the elevators currently locked down.

'You're injured,' Marlowe nodded at a red graze along Saeed's shirt arm.

'Graze,' Saeed looked at it, as if realising it was there. 'Actually gained by a gung-ho Special Branch officer.'

'Get it checked,' Trix said, and Saeed laughed.

'Yes, Mum,' he replied.

'Foster,' Marlowe said. 'He was picked up when you found me, right? Where is he?'

'Someone got to him before you,' Saeed shook his head. 'We just found him in a holding cell, slumped against a wall. Someone head-shotted him.'

'Casey head-shotted Walters and Fraser,' Trix replied. 'I think it's his thing.'

'Where's McKellan?' Marlowe spun around, gaining his bearings.

'Now wait a moment,' Saeed shook his head. 'You can't go running around the building! You're a fugitive—'

'Curtis gave him a temporary reinstatement, Solstice-Marshall-Gamma,' Trix replied. 'Curtis and McKellan are off the table, so Marlowe needed access.'

Saeed's eyes widened.

'Shit,' he said. 'You know this isn't Box, right? Not many MI5 here this morning, and you're definitely senior to me, so you might be in charge of the whole bloody department right now!'

'Great, I hate the light scheme, can someone change it?' Marlowe asked politely. 'And, while we're at it, *where the bloody hell is McKellan?*'

THE LIGHTS WERE GREEN NOW, HAVING CHANGED FROM THE RED lights of a few minutes earlier, and the siren had finally stopped blaring, as Sir Walter McKellan sat in the interrogation room, still sipping at his tea.

There was a commotion outside, and the door opened, Marlowe entering the room, Trix behind him. An armed officer, who'd been nervously standing guard at the door, glanced at them.

'Marlowe's been reinstated,' Trix explained. 'Stand down.'

As the guard, glad for anyone to take command, stepped back, McKellan chuckled.

'Marlowe,' he sipped at his tea. 'You found a way to get your traitorous arse back in the Service. How wonderful! And Curtis's woman can become your woman again, I suppose?'

Marlowe stormed across the room and swatted the cup out of McKellan's hand, the older man flinching as Marlowe, his expression that of cold fury, leant closer.

'Where is she, Walter?'

'Something bad happen?' McKellan tutted. 'Well, don't say I didn't warn you ...'

'She's got the Home Secretary,' Trix pleaded.

However, at this, McKellan simply laughed, as if his was the best news he'd heard all day.

'Joanna? Oh, that is delightful!' he exclaimed joyously. 'I hope they send you a postcard—'

'Dammit, McKellan!' Marlowe slammed his fist onto the table. 'Where is she?'

There was a moment of silence.

'I told you, I had no knowledge of who she was,' McKellan growled, his voice soft and dark. 'I told you Caliburn was nothing more than a think tank of like-minded people, like the ERG or a dozen other Government WhatsApp groups. But you didn't believe me. You didn't listen to me. And you aimed Karolides at me, who basically stripped me of all power to stop your little friend, as she single-handedly took apart the whole Intelligence Service.'

He smiled.

'I told you Fractal Destiny was a lot of old cobblers, but

you didn't believe me,' he said. 'I can't tell you where she's gone, as I don't know her—'

'But you knew Oliver Casey,' Trix spoke now. 'You even took him from Curtis's team and placed him on yours.'

'What about it? He's the son of an old friend. He asked for the transfer, saying Curtis wasn't as good as Harris was, and he needed to get out.'

'Casey killed Harriet Turnbull,' Marlowe replied. 'He also killed the new Defence Secretary, an analyst from MI5, and just tried to kill Alexander Curtis. And if I'm right, he did this all with clearance given to him by you, clearance he probably used to get Kate into the system.'

McKellan straightened in his chair. Marlowe knew he had little love for Curtis, but he did so love the management structure. That Casey could even consider shooting his previous boss was an anathema to him.

'This is on you,' Marlowe added. 'So help us here or I'll have you sent to the darkest black-ops site in the UK to rot away. And believe me, currently, I can do that.'

McKellan narrowed his eyes, as if watching Marlowe for a "tell," and, seeing none, he sighed.

'I don't know where she'd go, but I know where Casey would,' he said. 'He's used a small airstrip a few times, off-books operations. They'll be heading there, and they'll be off before you even realise they've left.'

Marlowe nodded. He'd expected similar. He'd done the same before himself.

'Where exactly is this airstrip?'

McKellan leant back, smiling.

'You want something? I want something,' he mouth-shrugged. 'Immunity for whatever the Government intends to throw at me.'

'We can't give you that!' Trix exclaimed.

'That's my proposal,' McKellan replied calmly. 'I suggest you go speak to Karolides – oh, you can't, can you?'

Marlowe looked at Trix, who shrugged, walking over to the armed officer.

'Can I?' she asked politely, while removing his gun from his holster. 'I think mine's out of bullets.'

She walked back over to McKellan, loading a bullet into the chamber.

'Here's my counter proposal,' she said as she calmly fired the gun into Sir Walter McKellan's foot.

Screaming in pain as the gunshot echoed around the room, McKellan jerked back from Trix, stumbling onto the floor, his patent leather shoe destroyed and leaking bright red blood.

'Are you insane?' he cried out.

'Let's call it "stressed induced trauma", as that'll sound well with a jury,' Trix said, priming the gun for a second shot, the *ka-chick* echoing around the room. 'So, while you delay us, I'll keep firing at body parts.'

She leant in close.

'Or do you want to give us the name of that airstrip?' she asked again.

McKellan told them.

25

THE STREETS OF LONDON

WITH HALF A SQUARE MILE APPARENTLY SUFFERING WITH communication issues, the lockdown stopping people leaving and a data virus killing all mobile phone activity in Whitehall, Marlowe had no idea what was going on out there.

All he knew, was that the only way Kate and the others could have got out was through the underground car park, and it was here he ran down to, Trix and Saeed following.

It was a bloodbath.

Medics were moving from Special Branch officer to officer, checking their wounds, and there were at least three jackets placed over the faces of dead bodies.

'What happened?' Marlowe asked as he walked through the triages. One of the medics looked up at him.

'They came out of nowhere,' she said. 'Took out the guards, grabbed the SUV and drove out before the barriers went up.'

She waved a hand at three bollards that had risen in the car park entrance, effectively blocking any car from following.

'You need that looked at?' the medic asked Saeed, who shook his head.

Marlowe, however, nodded.

'Let her fix it,' he said. 'I need you at full efficiency, not bleeding out everywhere.'

'It's just a bloody flesh wound,' Saeed said, pulling off his shirt and revealing the gash on his shoulder. The medic pulled a handheld UV-C lamp out, running it over his arm.

'What's that for?' Saeed pulled it away, but the medic forced it back onto the wound.

'Surface sterilisation,' Trix replied for the medic. 'A UV-C LED has a wavelength of 265 nm, and can inactivate more than 99.9% of viruses and bacteria.'

'Well, all I want is someone to staple it together,' Saeed slapped the wand aside as Marlowe watched him. 'If I want UV light, I'll go to a rave. Wipe it, patch it.'

'Showing your age now,' Marlowe said as he looked around the car park. 'It's a twenty-minute drive to Northolt airstrip. This time of day, we can double that. Kate's had a ten-minute advantage. We need to get through traffic.'

'In case you haven't noticed, we can't get a car out,' Trix pointed at the bollards. 'They did a pretty good job of screwing us.'

Marlowe smiled.

'I know how we can catch them,' he said, and Trix groaned as she saw what Marlowe was looking at.

A police motorcycle.

'No,' she said simply, but Marlowe was already running over to it, grabbing two jackets off a coat hanger to the side. They were black textile jackets, the latest ones for police motorcyclists to wear under their fluorescent jackets, and thanks to his friendship with Morten De'Geer, a motorcyclist in the City of London Police who both Marlowe and Trix had worked with, he knew these were designed with a hidden Tech-Air vest – a literal personal "air bag" - behind the lining.

'Great through traffic, and we can get past the bollards on it,' he replied, passing Trix the smaller of the two while he threw the second one on, a hint of excitement in his voice. It was snug, but he didn't need to zip it up, just wear it to keep his upper body safe if needed. 'Come on.'

'What about directions?' Trix reluctantly climbed onto the bike behind Marlowe, pulling on the slightly oversized black textile jacket as he revved it.

'Use your smartphone.'

'Yes, because trying to punch directions into a phone while hanging onto a speeding motorcycle is obviously sane.'

'Then class my idea as "stress induced trauma",' Marlowe smiled as Trix looked around.

'Do we even get helmets?' she asked, and a special branch officer ran over with two small scooter helmets.

'Sorry, first thing I found,' she said apologetically as Trix rammed the green scooter helmet onto her head.

'If I die, I'm going to bloody well haunt you,' she grumbled at Marlowe, as he gunned the motorcycle out of the car park.

'If you die, it's pretty much a given I'll be joining you,' he said as the motorcycle started weaving off down Whitehall.

A COUPLE OF MILES NORTH-WEST OF MARLOWE, A BLACK SUV drove north towards the A40, amid heavy traffic, its horn blaring, and lights flashing.

Inside the SUV, as Peters drove, and Casey watched

nervously out of the back window in case anyone was likely to follow with his gun pressed into Karolides's side, in the front passenger seat Kate examined the box.

'It's enough,' she muttered, placing it back into the bag. 'We didn't get it all, but we can sell this to the highest bidder.'

Karolides, sitting on the back seat, her hands cable-tied together, glowered at Kate.

'I'll see you rot in the darkest, most forgotten prison for this, you bastards,' she hissed. 'What you've done, the people you've killed ...'

'Sounds lovely. But let's take a rain check on that,' Kate replied. 'You're not still pissed we stopped your little meeting with Senator Kyle, are you?'

She tutted, shaking her head.

'We should be thanking you, really,' she smiled. 'If you hadn't decided to have backchannel talks with Washington, we'd never have had Marlowe arrive in San Francisco. When he turned up at the hotel, working for Senator Kyle? It was a gift.'

She looked out of the window.

'If Marlowe hadn't arrived, I'd have had to work somehow with Curtis,' she said. 'And he's a pain in the arse. Probably because of the stick he has up it. No, Tom Marlowe, black-listed and burnt, and oh so desperate to get back into MI5's good books ... We'd won before Ford even shot Kyle.'

'Was she supposed to die?' Karolides asked.

'Oh, God, yes,' Kate smiled. 'I wanted Caliburn to be treated like a terrorist group. I wanted everyone in the States hunting them down. All those lovely guns, all aimed at Marlowe. Only then could I be the abducted whistle-blower that saved everyone.'

She smiled, leaning closer.

'There's another terrorist group in the Intelligence Services, by the way,' she said. 'You just haven't found it yet.'

This said, she turned back to the window, watching the Edgware Road pass by.

'One you're part of?' Karolides asked.

Kate considered the question, glancing at Casey and Peters before replying.

'One we were all a part of,' she said. 'Before we realised we could make millions. Billions, even. Now, I think they might be a little pissed at us.'

'You think?' Casey chuckled. 'They'll be more pissed that they missed this opportunity.'

Kate didn't reply immediately, instead staring out at the Edgware Road as it passed by.

'The one thing I'm not going to miss? All this traffic,' she said. 'I'll be living on an island with no extradition, with my private army, and rolling in money.'

'You're not the only one getting the money,' Casey looked over the passenger seat at her. 'I've given up everything for this.'

'You'll have enough to buy a brand new life,' Kate replied calmly. 'Both of you.'

'As long as I don't end up like Foster,' Peters muttered. 'He didn't deserve that. And there'll be a receipt for that one day.'

'I'm sure there will be,' Casey looked over at the driver. 'But as it wasn't me who shot him, I think you can stop with the histrionics and just get us to the sodding airfield.'

THE JOURNEY FROM WHITEHALL TO PARK LANE HADN'T BEEN too hard, partly because Marlowe had learnt quickly which switch on the handlebars set the sirens and lights on, and once they started making a lot of noise, the other vehicles immediately got out of the way.

They'd cut down the Mall, turning right at Constitution Hill, and had been making good time, but the moment they hit the Wellington Arch, the large roundabout that linked Park Lane, Piccadilly and Knightsbridge, they realised this was about to go bad really quickly.

The only good thing was that Kate would have been caught in this too; however, they would be mostly past this by now – and from the looks of things, the traffic had snarled up because of a recent accident, maybe even since they'd passed.

As they pulled to a stop beside Hyde Park's Queen Elizabeth's Gate, Trix started swiping through the maps app currently open on her phone screen.

'There's got to be a shortcut!' Marlowe protested as he looked around. The drivers nearby were staring curiously at the two people on the police bike, and Marlowe didn't want to stay in the same place for too long.

'There's not,' Trix replied, showing Marlowe the map. 'It's a straight run up the Edgware Road to the A40 from here.'

Marlowe scrolled the map to the side, looking up at Park Lane for a moment.

'We'll catch them at the Westway,' he said, tapping the map before passing it back to Trix. 'We'll go via Shepherds Bush.'

'How?' Trix looked back at the map. 'There's no road that gets us there quicker, and Park Lane is rammed—'

Trix didn't finish the comment, instead punctuating the line with a scream as Marlowe gunned the engine, and the bike swerved into Hyde Park at speed.

As people dove to the side to get out of the way, Marlowe

steered the bike fast and furious down the Serpentine Road, a wide pavement and tarmac lane that doubled as a two-lane road at rush hour, and went northwest through the park. This was also filled with cars, all trying to avoid the Park Lane snarl up, and Marlowe made up for this by mounting the pavement, sirens blaring as the bike headed westwards.

Marlowe looked to his left, and the Serpentine Lake, with a slight smile on his lips.

'I used to go running here,' he said as he swerved to avoid a woman with a dog. 'It's a really nice mile-long circuit.'

'You're gonna die here,' Trix grunted – although Marlowe seemed to enjoy the excursion, it was a white-knuckle ride for Trix, holding on tight, for dear life.

'Hold on,' Marlowe suddenly said, and before Trix could reply that she was already holding on, he de-clutched the pedal, feathering the bike's back wheel brake as he skidded to the left, now shooting southwards across the Serpentine Bridge.

'You're going the wrong way!' Trix cried out, but Marlowe, his eyes on the road in front, shook his head as he screeched the bike to the right the moment they returned to dry land.

'I'm cutting across Kensington Gardens,' he said as he gunned the engine, the bike now speeding along a narrow pedestrian walkway.

'There're no roads!' Trix glanced at the app for the briefest of moments before shutting her eyes. 'We're going to die.'

'We don't need roads,' Marlowe replied as he pulled onto the grass to the left of the Physical Energy Statue, now speeding along the park's well-kept lawn, rows of trees on either side. At the Round Pond, he turned northwest again, trees whipping past on either side as they rode towards Black

Lion Gate across open grass. It was unlocked, and Marlowe sped through, ignoring the traffic on either side as he pulled left onto the Bayswater Road.

'See?' he smiled. 'Shortcut.'

From here the traffic was lighter, and Marlowe could weave through the vehicles as many moved to the side, his sirens and lights still blaring. And, in quick succession, the Bayswater Road turned into Notting Hill Gate, and then into Holland Park Avenue as they hit the Holland Park Roundabout, heading north up the A320.

The lights of Shepherd's Bush's *Westfield shopping centre* were to the left, the shops only now preparing for opening, but Marlowe wasn't focusing on that. In half a mile, the dual carriageway they were currently on connected with the A40 at the Westway, the best and pretty much only route to Northolt Airstrip, to the side of RAF Northolt, and a road he'd only been on a few hours earlier.

'What if we're ahead of them?' Trix shouted.

'Then we'll have time to arrange a trap,' Marlowe replied, shouting over the wind as he gunned the engine, the bike now close to a hundred miles an hour on the straight road. 'But let's be honest, we're not that lucky. There's every chance they're already past us.'

He smiled.

'But we'll be quicker,' he said as the bike pulled off onto the slip road, heading up to the Westway roundabout.

The Westway portion of the A40 was a two and a half mile stretch of elevated road, created as a six-lane motorway, although it'd been downgraded from such a term a while back. It was still several storeys high, though, and as Marlowe and Trix rode through the westwards traffic, Trix couldn't help watching the roofs of the West London buildings to the side of the road, literally under them as they passed along.

'There,' Marlowe said as he swerved into the slower lane, undertaking a coach. 'Black SUV, swerving through the traffic more than us, in front of the money van.'

'Great,' Trix shuffled back a little on the pillion. 'Now we have them, do you have a plan?'

Marlowe grinned.

'I was thinking of winging it,' he admitted, turning off the sirens finally.

THE JOURNEY HAD BEEN SLOW AND ARDUOUS, BUT NOW THE CAR was on the A40, and the traffic was opening up; in the morning, the traffic moving into London was busy, while people leaving the city were far fewer. It was mainly local traffic, and they never moved into the fast lane.

Peters, checking his mirrors before overtaking another car, looked into his rear-view mirror.

'Ah, shit,' he said, watching cars pull to the side as a police motorcycle gained on them. 'You're not gonna bloody believe this.'

Kate glanced back and mouthed an expletive. Karolides, following her gaze, smiled.

'Was this in your well-thought-out plan?' she asked sweetly.

'Bloody Marlowe,' Kate growled. 'I should have checked the body.'

Casey was already pulling out his gun, turning to lean out of the window.

'Are you insane?' Peters glanced at him in horror. 'You can't start shooting people on a motorway!'

'In the grand scheme of what we've done so far, this isn't really that bad,' Casey shrugged. 'He's on a bike. We're in an SUV. No matter how you game this, he doesn't win.'

He looked behind; the bike was gaining on them, using a security van as some kind of shield.

'Arm up, people!' Casey cried as he lowered his window. 'We got company!'

26

PILE UP

Marlowe had turned off the siren as they'd gained on them, as he'd realised early on that alerting them to the bike's presence was just an opportunity for Kate, or more likely Casey, to shoot them.

There had been a van in the middle lane; one of those contracted armoured trucks that did security deposits around the city, and Marlowe had pulled in behind it.

'Are you sure you want to use a truck as a shield?' Trix had asked.

'They're safer in there than we are here,' Marlowe replied. 'It's an armoured cash truck. I did some research on them a while back. Anti-bandit ballistic tested glass and composite steel armour, which goes through B2 to B6 ballistic level.'

'I'm guessing all those long words mean it's bulletproof?'

Marlowe grinned.

'Ready?' he asked as they pulled out to the side of the truck, now undertaking it, keeping the truck between them and the SUV. However, there was a crash of noise as in the

SUV, Casey now fired through the back window, clearing the glass as he shot at the bike.

Marlowe swerved hard to keep out of the fire, allowing the truck to take the brunt.

The passenger in the truck looked at Marlowe through his window, probably trying to understand why two such people would be on a police motorcycle, but luckily for Marlowe, the driver had decided to get involved, refusing to back down.

Which was also a problem, as Marlowe now had to slow down and go back around the truck from the other angle.

'They're shooting at us!' Trix exclaimed.

'So do something about it!' Marlowe shouted back as more bullets flew past, Casey realising Marlowe's plan and aiming accordingly. The rest of the westward traffic had wisely dropped back, and Marlowe worried the truck would drop back to be with them soon. 'Shoot back!'

Trix went to shout at Marlowe, and he knew she was going to make some snarky comment about not having something to shoot back with, suddenly rummaged in her jacket, pulling out the Glock 17 she'd taken from the Special Branch officer.

'I have a gun!' she yelled excitedly.

'I bloody know!' Marlowe snapped. 'So shoot them already!'

He pulled to the side, and Trix raised the gun, firing.

The bike immediately swerved to the left violently, with Marlowe screaming obscenities.

'Don't fire the gun beside my bloody ear!' he shouted. 'Are you trying to kill us?'

'I'm a hacker! I don't do guns!'

Marlowe sighed.

'You're doing great,' he lied. 'But next time, not by the ear, okay?'

As Casey angled himself to try another shot, Peters was screaming over the driver's seat at him.

'You didn't need to shoot the bloody window out!'

'It's easier to control my aim!' Casey snapped back. 'Shut up and keep driving!'

Karolides was watching this carefully; Peters struggling with the driving, Casey firing out the back, Kate glued to the window, watching for Marlowe to appear again—

This was her opportunity.

With her hands still secured by ties, she wasn't able to do much, but they had allowed her to have her hands tied in the front, mainly for ease of dragging forwards, so with a rising motion, she was able to loop the hands, via the cable ties, over the seat in front of her, the cables biting into Peter's face as she pulled back, his head caught by this makeshift garrotte, currently unable to move lower for the moment.

'Get off, you crazy bitch!' he screamed as the plastic bit into his cheeks. 'You'll kill us all!'

Kate, seeing Karolides's actions, leapt to Peter's defence; currently blinded by Karolides's hands, he was struggling to steer, the car slowing as he instinctively slowed. She pulled at the hands, but Karolides was fighting for her very life, a woman possessed, and eventually Kate pulled out a blade, slicing the cable ties, and in the process both Karolides's hand and Peters' cheek, but freeing him as, the cable ties no longer gaining her purchase, Karolides fell back in her seat.

'You sodding cut me!' Peters whined, wiping his bleeding cheek.

'Just drive,' Kate snarled, glaring at Karolides. 'We can dump you out right now, bitch, a bullet between your eyes—'

She stopped as a shadow crossed her peripheral vision; Marlowe had decided to pull up next to the car.

'Kate! Give up!' he cried.

Casey, who'd been distracted by both Karolides and the sound of what looked to be an approaching police helicopter during their incredibly well-planned out and misdirection'd escape, pulled his gun from the back window to now fire through the side window.

'I have had enough of you—' he started, but wasn't able to continue as Trix, seeing the movement, blindly fired the gun first at the SUV, shattering the window. The bullet had gone wild, but the damage was instantaneous, as Casey screamed in pain from the glass striking his face. And Peters, still shaken from the recent attack on his own life, now ducking as the gun struck the roof of the SUV, the car swerving violently because of this.

And Joanna Karolides took this moment to lunge to her side, grabbing at Casey's gun.

They struggled, Casey screaming at her to stop while Kate leant back over the passenger seat, slashing wildly with her knife—

Casey's gun went off.

The bullet, fired wildly out of the window, struck Marlowe a glancing blow on the shoulder.

'Hold on—' Marlowe started as he realised he'd lost control of the bike, but the two words were all he said before it skidded over, Marlowe and Trix falling from it, tumbling onto the road.

In the SUV, and still struggling over the gun, Karolides glanced out of the back window, seeing Marlowe's bike go down. However, as if deciding to step up now they'd seen the SUV shoot and possibly kill the riders of a police motorcycle, the armoured cash truck, which had left the chase to Marlowe, now sped up, slamming into the back of the SUV. The sudden impact set Casey's gun off again in the SUV, and Peters, a gaping hole appearing in his temple from the close range shot, slumped forward, dead, onto the wheel.

The armoured car came again for the SUV as Kate grabbed at the wheel, trying to push the dead Peters back – the second impact, this time catching the now slowly turning SUV actually flipped it, the armoured truck carrying on into the centre barricade with a vicious sounding *crump*, while the SUV rolled along the A40, eventually crashing to a halt fifty feet from where Marlowe and Trix had landed.

And for a moment, on the Westway, there was only carnage and silence.

MARLOWE'S EARS WERE RINGING AS HE PULLED OFF HIS HELMET, wincing as his left shoulder screamed at the action. He angled his head down to look at it; even through the textile jacket, the gunshot wound was bleeding through, but looked like a flesh wound more than an impact one, his arms and legs covered in grazes.

I'll get it fixed later, he thought to himself as, woozily, he gathered his wits and clambered, wobbling, to his feet, pulling off the jacket, noting the remains of the Tech-air vest within, which probably saved his life.

Shit. Trix.

Looking around, he saw Trix sprawled on the road; the cars had stopped a while back, the sight of a motorcycle and car gunfight being a little too bold for their tastes, so there was no chance of her being hit by one of them, but people were walking towards them, phones out, filming the scene.

Trix groaned, and Marlowe's heart almost skipped a beat at the sound.

Thank God. She's alive. Probably saved by the vest too. I owe De'Geer a pint.

He didn't have time to check on her, though. From the looks of things, as his bike had gone over, the guys in the security van, probably pissed at the SUV, had rammed them, going into the barrier, but rolling the SUV onto its top. And so, his shoulder still bleeding but usable, Marlowe shouted at the onlookers to call ambulances, and then staggered towards the SUV, unsure what he'd find.

What he found, climbing out, bleeding from a nasty wound to his forehead, was Casey. Crawling to his feet, his gun lost, Casey stood, wavering, wiping the blood from where it dripped into his right eye.

'Why won't you just die?' he asked, and it sounded more like a plea of desperation than anything else. Marlowe didn't have any weapons on him, everything had fallen away when he fell off the bike—

No. That wasn't quite right.

Marlowe smiled at Casey, taking his time as he allowed the chain, returned earlier by Trix, and back around his wrist to drop, gripping the end of his sharp, metallic whip.

'It's not my time,' he said as he started walking towards Casey, while trying to look into the car. It was on its roof, and

Marlowe couldn't see whether Karolides or Kate were still alive in there.

Casey nodded at the reply, reaching into his jacket and pulling out the same curved karambit blade he'd used the previous night in the hotel.

'If you're using that piece of trash again, it makes sense to use this,' he smiled, spitting out blood as he hefted it in his hand. 'After all, it beat you last time.'

'Really? I seem to recall last time you had two goons take me out,' Marlowe glanced through the car window, seeing the now-dead Peters. 'And that's the second of the two in there. Neither will help you now, considering you took out Foster in the cell.'

Casey shook his head.

'Wasn't me,' he replied. 'I actually liked the guy. Knew he wouldn't squeal.'

He waved the blade back at the car.

'Peters though? He was a bitch. I'm glad he's dead.'

The preamble finished, and with the sound of helicopters above them, Marlowe and Casey stood on the now-abandoned motorway. The sky was cloudy, casting a dreary pall over the desolate scene.

'You can't have the data.'

'Come get it.'

Marlowe shifted his length of steel chain, its links dull and lifeless in the muted light. In contrast, Casey's blade's glimmering edge seemed to be the only thing to shine in the bleak surroundings. The two assassins circled each other warily, their movements slow and hesitant. Marlowe's body was battered and bruised, the result of the impact from the crash. Casey was in no better shape, his movements laboured and unsteady, and he kept wiping the blood from his eye.

'You should get that seen to,' Marlowe said with mock concern. Without warning, Casey lunged forward, his blade flashing. Marlowe was quick to react, whipping his chain around to deflect the blow.

As Casey went to redirect his next slash, Marlowe's chain struck Casey's arms and chest in rapid succession and with heavy force, as he whipped the chain hard, back and forth across Casey's face, drawing more blood, but the two of them tired quickly; their movements became slower, their blows less powerful as the injuries took their toll. With Marlowe's shoulder and Casey's forehead both losing blood, Marlowe knew he couldn't carry on doing this, as swinging down hard, the chain struck Casey's blade with a dull clang, sending sparks flying in all directions.

In a final, desperate move, Casey darted forward, slashing wildly, but Marlowe had been almost hoping for this, and moved to the side, grabbing the end of his chain with his free hand and looping it over his opponent's head as the momentum took him forward, the chain links now coiling tightly around Casey's neck. With a sudden, violent twist, Marlowe pulled the chain tight, cutting off Casey's air supply, in a move similar to how he'd taken down the Paris assassin.

'Casey, I want to remind you of something,' Marlowe said as he pulled tighter. Casey struggled for a few moments, his eyes bulging with terror, the blade dropping from his hands as he clawed at the chain. 'Back in the house, I told you I'd kill you for what you did to Turnbull, and Senator Kyle, and Scrapper Lyons. Do you remember?'

He let go of the chain, allowing Casey to collapse to the ground in a breathless heap, crouching down in front of him.

Marlowe picked up the curved blade, staring at it for a moment.

'I keep my promises,' he said. 'You traitorous bastard.'

He rammed the knife home, as Casey, wide-eyed, the knife jutting out of his chest, fell back on to the tarmac road, his eyes now staring lifelessly at the grey clouds above.

Marlowe stood over his fallen foe, his chest heaving with exhaustion, taking a moment to regroup his thoughts before turning back to the SUV—

Only to find that facing him, the black holdall with Fractal Destiny inside, now slung over her shoulder, and Karolides, held tight with a gun to her head, was Kate Maybury.

'I could be wrong, Marlowe,' Kate shook her head sadly, 'but I'm convinced I shot you.'

The sirens and helicopters could be heard louder in the distance now, as Marlowe raised his hands to show they were empty.

'Let her go, Kate. It's over,' he said. 'We can make a deal. We'll tell them Casey made you do it.'

At this, however, Kate's eyes widened in surprise.

'Hold on,' she shook her head in mild disbelief. 'You're still trying to *help* me? Jesus, Thomas. You really do have some kind of white-knight syndrome, don't you?'

Marlowe cracked a slight smile at this.

'I'm just trying to save the Home Secretary,' he replied.

Kate shook her head sadly.

'This isn't going to end well, Marlowe,' she whispered, her voice barely registering above the sounds of the helicopters above them. 'Not for any of us.'

She started to laugh; the sound bordering on hysterical.

'You know the worst part?' she spat. 'Bloody Walter McKellan will gain his freedom. The story will be all about how the rogue agent tried to blow up London, and he helped stop it. They'll probably give him a medal.'

'Don't do this,' Marlowe shook his head.

'Then tell me not to go.'

Marlowe stared at Kate for a long moment, resisting the urge to look up at the helicopter before looking back.

'Don't go.'

Kate laughed, a bitter, mocking staccato bark as she took the gun she'd aimed at Karolides, and now turned it onto Marlowe.

'Too slow,' she stated sadly. 'I'm sorry, Marlowe. But you did this to yourself—'

There was a gunshot, and Marlowe winced, expecting to have been shot, but as he opened his eyes, he saw Kate's eyes widen, a fresh wound in her throat spurting blood. As she grasped desperately at it, dropping the gun and gurgling weakly, sinking to the floor, Marlowe looked behind him.

There, prone on the tarmac of the road, and with her purloined Special Branch gun back in her hand, using the ground to steady her aim, was Trix.

'Is she dead?' she asked, her voice trembling.

Karolides went to speak, but Marlowe shook his head.

'I think you nicked the throat,' he said. 'I'm sure it's okay.'

'Good,' Trix said, passing out onto the road.

Marlowe now ran over to Karolides.

'Are you okay, Ma'am?' he asked.

'I'm okay, battered and bruised, but I think I'm doing better than you are,' Karolides said, kicking Kate's very dead body. 'Why lie to the girl?'

'She's not an agent, she's never killed,' Marlowe replied. 'I'd rather she was in a better place when she learnt what she did.'

Karolides nodded at this, looking around at the devastation.

'You saved us a lot of trouble today,' she said sadly. 'I'm just sorry that the cost was so high.'

She turned back to Marlowe.

'The only damned issue I have is bloody McKellan,' she muttered. 'I was trying to get him removed from his role in MI6, as the man's a bloody misogynistic dinosaur, but his solicitors will make sure now he won't be removed. They're probably spinning a story right now on how he single-handedly tried to stop Casey and Miss Maybury. And of course, with both of them dead, we can't contradict his story.'

'And me?' Marlowe couldn't help himself. 'It's always good to have friends in high places, especially when I'm trying to get back into the Service.'

'Marlowe, you're the man who saved the Government. More than once, I'll add,' Karolides smiled. 'Great patriotic news a few days before an upcoming by-election. Always good for the polls, you know.'

Marlowe's face darkened.

'I didn't save you so I could be used like that,' he replied, noting the now approaching police vehicles.

At this, Karolides laughed.

'And yet, here you are,' she said. 'Welcome to politics, Mister Marlowe.'

EPILOGUE

After he'd been arrested, then un-arrested, and eventually brought back to Box for debriefing, Marlowe had spent the next few weeks keeping to himself mainly.

It was the start of May by now, and the by-elections Karolides mentioned had come and gone, and strangely, although they'd used the events to great patriotic fervour, Karolides had actually kept Marlowe out of the spotlight. Even without him, however, the Conservative Party had done markedly better than expected, primarily because of the "action-styled new party" they now marketed themselves as.

After all, with a reality TV obsessed world, who didn't like a Government who had assassinations and car chases?

Marlowe had paid little attention to it if he was being honest. By-elections weren't the same as a General Election, and were mainly based around council positions rather than Parliament ones, although he had noted with some amusement that in Bethnal Green and Bow, an old friend of his uncle's, Johnny Lucas, had changed from being an East End villain to being a Labour MP. He made a point of having a chat about this with his Uncle Alex at some point. But for now, he returned to his dilapidated "fixer-upper" church in West London, and had spent the last two or three weeks continuing to recondition the crypt into his "secret" apartment. It was a place he could hide in, and escape from quickly, his life showing him on more than one occasion that this was something he definitely needed, while waiting for MI5 to call.

And here, he knew he had an intriguing problem. He'd originally been burnt by Alexander Curtis, very much by reluctant mutual decision, the same London Chief who had reinstated him several weeks later. And Curtis was now off on sick leave himself, because of the almost-fatal chest wound he'd received in Whitehall.

Marlowe didn't envy Curtis. He'd had his share of bullet wounds, and he knew it was a long journey to get back to fighting fit from. But when Curtis came back, there was every chance that he would be given awards and promotions and treated like the hero he was going to be painted as, while Marlowe sat at the side, doing nothing. That was if Marlowe was still allowed to stay in MI5. He was aware it was a battlefield promotion, of sorts, with no long process of vetting and scrutiny, just a man, believing he was dying, doing what he thought was best. And there was every chance that once somebody took a good hard look at this, Marlowe would be removed once more, an administrative oversight.

And so it was by the Serpentine Lake in Hyde Park, that only a few weeks earlier he had sped past on a motorcycle, that Marlowe sat on a bench waiting for his MI5 contact.

He hadn't expected it to be Emilia Wintergreen.

Looking like Helen Mirren, if Helen Mirren was a serial-killing assassin, which to some people was basically Helen

Mirren, Wintergreen was harsh, slim and unfortunately for Marlowe this day, not in a good mood.

She sat down beside him, staring out across the lake.

'Thomas,' she said.

There was a long pause, as if Wintergreen didn't know what to say next. Marlowe made it easier for her.

'So am I in or out?' he asked.

Wintergreen shifted uneasily on the bench.

'Here we have a bit of a problem,' she said. 'I'm sure you know that when Curtis reinstated you, your seniority in the organisation meant that you were above people like Vikram Saeed, which meant you were effectively the leading agent.'

'I *was* aware of that,' Marlowe replied, unsure where this was going.

'And then, within five minutes of being reinstated and given this position, you entered a room and shot the director of MI6 in the foot.'

Wintergreen turned and smiled at Marlowe.

'Yes, I know it was Trix. But I also know that you're going to claim it was you, to keep her out of any shit, so let's just get to that.'

'We thought he was a spy.'

'Yes, I get that, I saw the notes. And to be perfectly honest, most people would see that too ... if they were a bloody idiot.'

'Oh, come on,' Marlowe stopped Wintergreen from continuing, waving his hand. 'You can't throw that on me.'

'What can't I throw? You willingly followed an enemy combatant? You had a traitor to the nation, leading you by the nose, convincing you that everybody that you knew was against you?'

Wintergreen shook her head in disgust.

'And you believed them. Your mother is spinning in her grave right now.'

'Emilia, don't—'

'McKellan has been a mainstay of MI6 for decades. You think Caliburn is some sort of Masonic order for spies? For God's sake, it's a research caucus! Nothing more!'

Wintergreen looked as if she wanted to rise and pace, but kept herself under control, instead simply looking like a coiled spring ready to explode.

'I'm a member of Caliburn, Tom. Your mum was a member of Caliburn. It's been around for decades. Technically, if you wanted, *you* could have been a member of Caliburn.'

She paused.

'Although I think that membership's probably out the window right now.'

Marlowe sighed.

'Okay. I accept that I shot McKellan in the foot.'

'And then you stole a police motorcycle,' Wintergreen gave Marlowe a humourless smile as she carried on. 'Proceeded to then destroy the well-kept grass of the very park we're sitting in right now, *with* the motorcycle, drove on to the Westway and created a six-lane car accident. We had the whole place closed for hours. Do you know how much grief that lands on our doorsteps?'

Marlowe flushed angrily at this.

'I think you're forgetting the parts where I saved the Home Secretary and the nation,' he muttered.

Wintergreen smiled at this.

'Oh believe me, that's the only reason you're not in prison.'

'I think there's a lot of reasons I'm not in prison, Emilia,'

Marlowe laughed. 'You don't mind me calling you Emilia, do you? I mean, "Wintergreen" sounds so formal when it sounds like I'm not working for you anymore.'

Marlowe went to rise.

'And if you're honestly going to give me some bullshit about *torn up grass* being the reason I'm back on a shit list? Come on! That's utter—'

Wintergreen's hand on his elbow paused him from rising. As he stopped and looked at her, she stared at him for a moment, before shrugging.

'They videoed you, Tom,' she said. 'The public. On the Westway. They filmed you fighting Casey. And, when he was down, able to be restrained, and unarmed, you rammed a blade into his chest and walked off.'

'I was in the middle of saving the entire Security Service at the time,' Marlowe snapped, but deep down he was berating himself. He'd seen the people getting out of their cars and filming, when the bike had gone over. He'd simply forgotten about them. 'I haven't seen any footage on the news.'

'No, that's because we're very good at removing things like that, but it was a ball-ache, Tom. I don't even have them, and they were aching. And it made you stand out again, and not in a good way.'

Marlowe deflated, slumping back onto the bench.

'Great,' he muttered. 'So I'm in, but already with one foot out the door.'

'Don't worry, you have a chance to redeem yourself,' Wintergreen smiled. 'We have a problem, and weirdly and annoyingly for me, it's something that *you* are uniquely positioned to look into.'

Marlowe groaned.

'No,' he said.

'You don't know what I'm about to ask.'

'It's a bloody favour, isn't it?' Marlowe shook his head. 'I was brought back in. Now I'm kicked back out, but "oh, before you go, could you just do me this small thing before you piss off out of Thames House" and all that?'

Wintergreen ignored the mockery.

'You finished?' she eventually asked. 'Good. Now, maybe I can ask my question?'

Marlowe gave a vague hand wave of allowance.

'What have you ever heard about a secret society known as the Orchid?' she asked.

Marlowe paused.

'Orchid as in the flower?'

'How many other types of orchids do you know?'

Marlowe went to reply that flowers weren't really his thing, but after a moment, a memory came flooding back.

'Your scar looks like a flower,'

'It is a flower, but it's not a scar.'

'Kate had a tattoo on her shoulder,' he said slowly. 'It was small, less than an inch. It was a flower – what they call a black-light tattoo. The UV ones. They only show up under nightclub lights.'

'Did this flower look like an orchid?'

'Well, I'm not a flower expert, and I'd say it was pretty crude. But yeah.'

'You'll be happy to know that you're not incorrect here,' Wintergreen replied. 'Kate Maybury was a member of Orchid, and we believe it was Orchid that tried to do this. I mean, she was making money for herself, but there was an element of anarchy being created by Orchid in the process.'

Marlowe considered this.

'Orchid's global isn't it?'

'Why would you think that?' Wintergreen asked with the kind of smile that gave the impression she knew what the answer already was; she just wanted Marlowe to say it.

'Ford,' Marlowe replied. 'The agent, Senator Kyle's one – who decided he wanted to try to kill her. I never understood why he would do such a thing, as from what I could find out, Caliburn wasn't really a US agency thing, it was more UK-based.'

He looked around the park as he worked through the hypothesis.

'And Secret Service agents are quite hard to bribe unless they're part of something global,' he added.

Wintergreen nodded.

'We spoke to our American friends,' she replied. 'Senator Kyle thanks you, by the way. She's aware that you and Miss Preston saved her life, apparently for the second time. It's good to see you like saving Americans.'

Marlowe smiled.

'I get a lot more thanks from them than when I do it for British people,' he stated.

'We asked our American friends to check Ford's body with a UV light, and when they did, they found under his armpit a small UV tattoo of an orchid.'

'Let me guess. You found the same thing on Casey, Foster and the annoying tracksuit guy.'

'Yes,' Wintergreen replied. 'All of them had little orchid symbols. From what we can work out, it's the way to show your loyalty.'

'But surely putting a secret tattoo on your body isn't a great way to show that you're a loyal member of an ultra secret society?' Marlowe frowned at this. 'All we'd have to do is have UV scanners in every room.'

'True, but these weren't in obvious places most of the time," Wintergreen argued. 'Foster's was behind his knee. Peters was under his scrotum.'

'Ouch.'

'As long as they have it somewhere, that's all that seems to matter to them,' Wintergreen continued. 'We've been tracking Orchid for a while. And we think Kate Maybury was the first wave of a coordinated attack. We think there are still people out there, people who in every way are trying to take us down, while working alongside us—'

'Vic Saeed,' Marlowe said instantly. 'He's Orchid.'

'That's a hell of an accusation to make, considering you didn't even know who they were a minute ago,' Wintergreen replied.

Marlowe, however, shook his head.

'He was Turnbull's agent,' he explained. 'He failed to save her – but he wasn't even checking on her, instead was instantly around for Karolides. They knew Turnbull was the sacrifice.'

He weighed his next words, aware he was damning a possibly innocent spy.

'But then later on, when everything was going crazy, he found us and told us that Foster was found dead. We assumed it was Casey, but he said it wasn't him.'

'And you believed him?'

'He had no reason to lie,' Marlowe shrugged. 'It would have been just as easy for Saeed to go in and put a bullet into the man's head. And he'd been shot in the arm at some point, so I forced him to have a medic look at it. She used the UV light on his arm to sanitise it, and he pushed her away. Just demanded she stapled it. I think if you actually put a UV light somewhere around the wound, you might find a little UV tattoo.'

'He didn't want anybody seeing that before he could get out of there,' Wintergreen nodded, understanding now. 'It's a plausible theory and Saeed is on our list. Maybe we'll let that ferment a little. See what he does.'

She paused.

'So, this is how it's going to go, Marlowe,' she said. 'Officially, and in the records, you have been placed back into the Security Service. Publicly. You haven't, because once you took on the role Curtis gave you, you did enough things to have you removed again.'

She pointed at the grass on the other side of the bridge.

'Destroying this park is the official reason, as well as the videos of you and Casey,' she said. 'And this goes for Trixibelle Preston, too. She's still on suspension, as Curtis was her guardian, so to speak, keeping her away from any trouble that she'd be going through the next few months.'

'Trouble connected to me?'

'Trouble is always connected to you,' Wintergreen made the comment sound like a compliment, although Marlowe was pretty convinced it wasn't meant to be. 'So I'd like you, as far as anybody else is concerned, to be placed under review for the next two months. Still travelling, still researching, boring little gopher jobs that keep you in and out of the building. You're going to be a liaison with our American friends because Senator Kyle likes you.'

Marlowe understood now where this was going.

'And in the meantime, me and Trix will hunt down Orchids and remove them?'

'Well, let's just go with hunting, to start with,' Wintergreen said. 'We don't know what their plan is. We don't know if this was the start of an ongoing campaign, or just an opportunistic moment by Kate Maybury to make her own money.'

She puffed out her cheeks.

'What we *do* know is that Orchid almost took down both MI5 and MI6, and cause global, inter-agency distrust and confusion with barely any problems.'

She reached into her jacket pocket and passed Marlowe a flash drive.

'You'll be given a medium-sized budget, slush funds, so to speak, but you will have to provide receipts for anything you use,' she explained. 'Details on here. You'll have your own oversight, as technically you're off the books, and you'll create your own team.'

Marlowe raised his eyebrows at this.

'Can I use anyone?'

'I've already contacted Marshall Kirk and told him he should expect a call from you,' Wintergreen pre-empted Marlowe's next line. 'I'm expecting you'll probably also go and find your drunk friend in America, Brad Haynes. And I would probably assume that Sasha Bordeaux, or whatever name she's going to use this week, will be looking out for you as well. She seems to know about more leaks going on than we do.'

Marlowe wasn't sure, but he almost believed Wintergreen crossed herself.

Is she worried about Bordeaux, or working with Americans in general, he wondered as Wintergreen straightened on the bench.

'In the meantime, Sir McKellan will be returning to look after MI6, and I will replace Curtis at MI5,' she continued.

'McKellan is aware of what you'll be doing, and he has agreed not to try to kill you during this planning.'

Marlowe grimaced.

'He's really that pissed at me?'

'No, he's more pissed at himself, to be perfectly honest.' And, for the first time that meeting, Emilia Wintergreen gave out a warm laugh. 'He didn't see it coming. He's always branded himself as the "great tactician" and he was caught with his pants down. For that alone, I thank you.'

She leant forward on the bench, staring across the water.

'This isn't going to be easy, Marlowe,' she whispered. 'They've made the first move and we need to counterattack. But we can't be *seen* to be doing it, because the moment Orchid understands that we're looking for them, they'll go. They'll disappear. The only way it'll work is if they think you're rogue.'

'Which means they'll think they can come after me with no blowback,' Marlowe mused.

'This isn't going to be a straightforward route,' Wintergreen agreed. 'Is there anything I can do for you in the meantime?'

Marlowe nodded.

'I'm not burnt anymore, am I?'

'Not as such, but you're not as "allowed into the room" as you used to be,' Wintergreen smiled. 'But I know what you're angling towards. The bounty on your head has been removed, if that's what you're asking, and the whole mess with the murder at Heston Services—'

'The self-defence killing.'

'Whatever, they're no longer looking at you.'

'I'd like you to do something else,' he said, passing an

envelope. 'There's a man named Karl we've worked with before—'

'His name's not Karl, but I know who you mean,' Wintergreen nodded. 'This related to the LA gig you did for him? We heard he'd reached out.'

Deciding he didn't want to know how they knew, Marlowe nodded.

'The mission was a lie, and was personal to him,' he said. 'Left a nasty taste. Everything's in the envelope. I'd appreciate it if you'd have a look, see if there's anything we can do for the poor bastard I threatened.'

Emilia Wintergreen gave a curt nod, pocketing the envelope.

Marlowe nodded thanks, leaning forwards to match Wintergreen, and lowering his voice.

'Are you recording this?' he asked softly.

'Why would I—'

'You keep speaking across the water, where someone with a directional mic could easily pick it up,' Marlowe looked directly at Wintergreen, his hand up to muffle his voice. 'I don't care if you are, but I don't want this next bit on record.'

Wintergreen said nothing, but Marlowe noticed the tiniest of finger waves across the water.

'We're not being recorded,' she replied. 'My word.'

Marlowe straightened up.

'My estranged father, the one that hates me, well, his company is called *Arachnis*. After the orchid. You knew Mum better than anyone. Is he connected?'

Wintergreen didn't reply, but Marlowe could see by her expression she hadn't either considered or expected this line of questioning.

'I never met your father, but I'll look into it,' she eventually finished. 'Good luck, Marlowe. I won't see you officially until it's all done. But know we'll be monitoring you ... and you'll still be getting judged by us every step of the way.'

'I wouldn't have it any other way, boss,' Marlowe smiled. 'I'll fix this problem.'

And with that, Marlowe rose from the bench, shook Wintergreen's hand and walked away from the Serpentine Lake, his mind buzzing with questions.

If Orchid were as secret as they believed it to be, how did people like Kate, Casey, Ford, even Peters get in? What was the audition process for such an organisation? And was his father involved in some way?

Marlowe hoped not. The last thing he needed was to have to deal with his dad one last time.

And so, pulling his jacket collar up, Tom Marlowe walked off towards Hyde Park Corner, looking for a train to catch home, a large pizza to order in, and a new mission to begin.

Tom Marlowe will return in his next thriller

COUNTER ATTACK

Order Now at Amazon:

Mybook.to/counterattack

Released October 2023

Gain up-to-the-moment information on the release by signing up to the Jack Gatland VIP Reader's Club!

Join at www.subscribepage.com/jackgatland

ACKNOWLEDGEMENTS

When you write a series of books, you find that there are a ton of people out there who help you, sometimes without even realising, and so I wanted to say thanks.

There are people I need to thank, and they know who they are, including my brother Chris Lee, who I truly believe could make a fortune as a post-retirement copy editor, if not a solid writing career of his own, Jacqueline Beard MBE, who has copyedited all my books since the very beginning, and editor Sian Phillips, all of whom have made my books way better than they have every right to be.

Also, I couldn't have done this without my growing army of ARC and beta readers, who not only show me where I falter, but also raise awareness of me in the social media world, ensuring that other people learn of my books.

But mainly, I tip my hat and thank you. *The reader.* Who once took a chance on an unknown author in a pile of Kindle books, thought you'd give them a go, and who has carried on this far with them, as well as the spin off books I now release.

I write these books for you. And with luck, I'll keep on writing them for a very long time.

Jack Gatland / Tony Lee,
London, April 2023

ABOUT THE AUTHOR

Jack Gatland is the pen name of *#1 New York Times Bestselling Author* Tony Lee, who has been writing in all media for thirty-five years, including comics, graphic novels, middle grade books, audio drama, TV and film for *DC Comics, Marvel, BBC, ITV, Random House, Penguin USA, Hachette* and a ton of other publishers and broadcasters.

These have included licenses such as ***Doctor Who, Spider Man, X-Men, Star Trek, Battlestar Galactica, MacGyver,*** BBC's ***Doctors, Wallace and Gromit*** and ***Shrek***, as well as work created with musicians such as ***Ozzy Osbourne, Joe Satriani, Beartooth*** and ***Megadeth.***

As Tony, he's toured the world talking to reluctant readers with his 'Change The Channel' school tours, and lectures on screenwriting and comic scripting for *Raindance* in London.

As Jack, he's written several book series now - a police procedural featuring *DI Declan Walsh and the officers of the Temple Inn Crime Unit*, a spinoff featuring "cop for criminals" *Ellie Reckless and her team,* and a second espionage spinoff series featuring burnt MI5 agent *Tom Marlowe*, an action adventure series featuring conman-turned-treasure hunter *Damian Lucas*, and a standalone novel set in a New York boardroom.

An introvert West Londoner by heart, he lives with his wife Tracy and dog Fosco, just outside London.

Feel free to follow Jack on all his social media by clicking on the links below. Over time these can be places where we can engage, discuss Declan, Ellie, Tom and others, and put the world to rights.

www.jackgatland.com
www.hoodemanmedia.com

Visit my Reader's Group Page
(Mainly for fans to discuss my books):
https://www.facebook.com/groups/jackgatland

Subscribe to my Readers List:
www.subscribepage.com/jackgatland

www.facebook.com/jackgatlandbooks
www.twitter.com/jackgatlandbook
ww.instagram.com/jackgatland

Want more books by Jack Gatland?

Turn the page...

MEDIA

PAINT
THE
DEAD

Printed in Great Britain
by Amazon

25442373R00202